# ALAN GOLD

# HIS HEAD ON A PLATTER

*Artemisia Gentileschi's*

REVENGE AGAINST MEN

First published by Romaunce Books in 2023
Suite 2, Top Floor, 7 Dyer Street, Cirencester, Gloucestershire, GL7 2PF



A catalogue record for this book is available from the British Library

## HIS HEAD ON A PLATTER

Paperback ISBN 978-1-7391857-6-3

Cover design and content by Ray Lipscombe

Printed and bound in Great Britain
Romaunce Books™ is a registered trademark

# ALAN GOLD

# HIS HEAD ON A PLATTER

*Artemisia Gentileschi's*

REVENGE AGAINST MEN

# Contents

# THE BOOK OF MY LIFE

Written by the hand of Artemisia Gentileschi

London, England.

# FEBRUARY, ANNO DOMINI 1641

**Anger** does not even begin to define the feelings coursing through my veins, causing me to lose the composure that defines the lady I am, nor delineates a limitless woman such as me. I am a woman who has achieved great success in a profoundly troubled life. To read of my life and accomplishments will be like listening to a performance of the buffoons and charlatans of the Commedia dell'Arte. But now that I am writing the story of my life, I am reliving events long buried because of the pain they caused me. Pain so powerful, so tortured, that I pray no other woman ever experiences it.

As I come to write this, the story of my life, I am 48 years of age. A matron. But I am unlike other matrons of my age. I do not sit by a fire, my shoulders wrapped in blankets, legs swathed in rugs, comforted by children and grandchildren who attend to my every need. No, I am robust, vigorous and forceful. How could I not be, having lived through the events which formed my life? And it is this very strength, this force, that gives me the vigour to paint twelve hours each day, and to write, without fear or favour, this account of my life.

I am angry! By God in heaven, I'm angry. And I have every right to be. My life was shattered before it had properly begun; I was a young virgin, but I was raped. He promised to give me a ring, to become my loving husband, but after a year of excuses and lies, I found that he was already married. He was brought to trial, and it was I who was tortured to ensure I was telling the truth.

Is there any wonder why I'm angry? For thirty years, I have buried the pain, the humiliation, the degradation. As an artist I have risen higher than any woman before me and my art is recognized as the greatest there is. And now, in the cold of a London winter, I am hot with indignation as I write about what happened all those years ago in Rome.

For mine has been a life which denies labelling; and no matter how those who seek to explain me might try to capture my essence and understand my mind, they will only ever draw crude outlines, imprecise features and transparent assumptions

What will it take to define me? Unless it is I who writes of my life, then how will anybody in the future know what I've accomplished? And who will believe what has been done to me? To paint a portrait which reveals who I truly am will require the genius of a Leonardo, a Caravaggio, a Michaelangelo….even a Raphael. Now all dead. Beloved men, painters of genius, gone.

Only a master of the type of art of which I am preeminent can create an image of me that will enable you, the viewer, to see me clearly, precisely, accurately. As defined and truthful, as angry and vengeful, as the women I portrayed in my paintings. My Judith, my Susanna, my Jael, my Lucretia…and oh, my Mary Magdalene!

I am a woman whose achievements have been realized through a veil of tears, pain and anguish. I was a child robbed of my innocence by a rapist, and then tortured with thumbscrews by the judge at my rapist's trial until my painter's hands were crippled and bled. Yes, it needs repeating that it was I who was tortured while my rapist looked on and smiled at my pain! They tortured me to ensure I was telling the truth.

Despite my trial and tribulation, I am a woman who has mastered her art and craft. I have risen in the ranks of the great painters of Italy and France, Germany and

Holland, Spain and England, so that I am now recognized and revered. My name is whispered in the same reverential breath as geniuses who went before me. Even I whisper their names in veneration of their prodigious virtuosity.... Leonardo, Caravaggio, Michaelangelo, and even the divine Raphael. The master painters whose skills enabled me to become mistress my own craft. And just as their work will soon be forgotten and ignored, so I am certain that my work, my painting, will soon become obscure and forgotten.

Which is why I am writing this, the story of my life. In order that in a dozen generations, when Caravaggio's and Raphael's names are no longer mentioned, people may come to read of me, and understand better my paintings, if they still exist.

When I was younger, I was commissioned by kings and princes, dukes and duchesses, Cardinals, and Bishops to paint pictures for them. Even King Charles of England commissioned me to come here, to his cold and drear country, to paint for him. Yet how can I remain in this country, for the forces of war are gathering; not from beyond the borders, but within England herself, dividing brother from brother, son from father. A civil war, as between the great families of Italy. Here, in this austere nation, the war is between those who support the King as the hand of God and Almighty Ruler of the land, and those who oppose him in support of the people in their Parliament.

I shall take my talents elsewhere. Perhaps I'll stay in France and paint for Anne of Austria, Queen of France in the court of King Louis XIII. She is a Hapsburg and perhaps she will appreciate another woman, a Catholic, as her Court Painter. Or shall I go straight back to Italy, my home, the nation which spat me out?

Wherever I go, I am opposed by men. I fear it. I know it. Mine is an occupation dominated by men. And they are jealous of my success because I am the only woman, other than whores and courtesans, since the downfall of Eve, to earn sufficient from my craft. I am dependent on no man, and am able to live a comfortable life, with all I need to survive. But when I die, my possessions, like my paintings, will turn to dust.

But not this, the story of my life. My paintings are the story of my fury, set within the story of my life. But as we begin life as dust and become dust in death, my paintings will fade and turn to dust, but the print of my book will last for all eternity. As one copy decays, another will be printed. Then, I will be remembered.

As I sit in my studio, dawn rises over the Thames River, the morning light is yielding and gentle, and a half-finished canvas lies before me, partly completed in the vibrant colours of the image I'm painting; yet my canvas looks back at me, achingly incomplete, waiting for my mind to instruct my hands, my eye to see beyond the unformed so that the ghostly outlines remind me of what the future will look like. But soon my canvas will become complete and then I shall pray to the heavens and the Divine Almighty and His Angels, because all it will take to make the character I'm painting move and talk, is the breath of God. Pygmalion accomplished the act of breathing life into his statue of Galatea, thanks to the intervention of the goddess Venus. So perhaps, one day, Almighty God with breathe into my paintings and they will come to life. But until then, I must rely upon my own artistry, and the perspective of my dear friend Galileo, about whom I'll write later in this book.

But I am still consumed by anger. So if the word *anger* will not adequately communicate to you, reader of this story of my life, the extent of my emotions, then perhaps *rage* defines how I feel, sitting here, alone in the bewitching hours of the dawn, waiting for inspiration to descend, breathing in the perfumes of the paints and the acrid assertion of the solvents which are the tools of my trade? Is *rage* not good enough for you?

Rage sees me throwing a wine bottle at the wall, overturning tables, opening my casement window and throwing out my paintings or burning them. It's said that Sandro Botticelli did this many years ago when, in a fit of religious zeal, he threw his paintings onto Girolamo Savonarola's bonfire of the vanities. Or will rage see me destroying my canvas with a knife in an uncontrolled outburst which will cause some doctor to confine me to the madhouse. But then, I'm no madman, like Caravaggio, my loving and wonderful tutor. When he was in a rage, it was murderous. My desire to harm those who wronged me evaporated years ago; all I want now is to tell the story of my life in this book.

Rage is relentless but it is fury which tends towards physically damaging those who have done me so much harm, acts which will see me taken to prison, or dragged before the Inquisition or, once more, forced to appear before a judge in some Court of Law and be tortured with thumbscrews so that my hands, my painter's hands, are crippled and deformed. And if I can't paint, what is the value of my life? How can it be measured? In the children I create? The wealth I accumulate? In the houses

I have purchased from my income as a painter, or jewels and other baubles which are temporary adornments?

These can be the mark of success for others, but not for us painters. We measure our success in life by the works we create, by the acclaim of our fellow artists, and by the wealth of the patrons who commission our art. So I can never allow rage or fury to become physical manifestations of my emotions, or I will be hauled before a court of law, and that could be the end of me.

Therefore I will constrain myself to paroxysms of indignation, which will be visible for all to see in the faces of the women I paint; women like Susanna and Judith, Salome and Catherine, Jael and Esther.

Through my paintings, people today and in the future will know the full extent of the harm I suffered after I was raped, and still suffer to this day. Because for a woman, any woman, and especially an artist, rape is but a physical act of violence by a man against a woman; and although the damage to her body is quickly repaired, the damage to her mind, her sense of worth, her possession of her very own being, is often a casualty which cannot be mended or restored.

Many women who have been raped are silent victims, so ashamed of the insult to their bodies that they remain hushed for the rest of their lives, quietly going mad inside the confines of their minds. After all, rape is not a crime in Italy. But deflowering a virgin is a crime – a crime of value. Of money. Not, of course, a crime against the victim of the rape, for she is merely a woman; it is a crime against the victim's father, because the value of his virgin daughter as a marriageable asset is sorely diminished. So the crime against me was accounted as one of money, of value, and not because I was forced to defend myself against two men — two — armed only with my wit, my words, and a painter's knife.

But all who see my paintings will know of the indignation I have suffered. Through my paintings, through the agony on the faces of the women who take revenge against men, people who see my paintings will know of my abandonment by the man who raped me, even though he swore he loved me and would become my husband. Through the faces of the women I paint, people will learn of my raging sense of injustice as the court tortured me as a victim, a witness, to ensure that I was telling the truth about the defilement of my body. They tortured my hands with rope and iron yet I still maintained my innocence and the veracity of my testimony. When the judge demanded, under torture, to know whether I was telling the truth about being raped, or whether I'd seduced the man who had my body, I screamed in agony, "It's true...it's true....it's true...." And they heard me, and they believed me. But I was so badly hurt in proving my innocence. It was a long and agonising time before I could pick up a paintbrush without wincing in pain.

So those who view my paintings will know of the way that I was judged and abandoned by society because my father dared to demand justice. And you, my reader of these my words, will learn of my hurt as my work as a painter was diminished and ridiculed because of my sex, as though being a woman was still an affliction of half of the entire world born under the curse of Eve. It was only after I left Rome, the city of my downfall, that I began to climb the steep and rocky hill towards acceptance, and approbation.

You may wonder why am I committing my life to these words, when for the entirety of my existence, images have been my vocabulary, and shades and shadows the nouns and verbs of my language?

Simply because I have no way of knowing that my paintings will still hang on the walls of houses and palaces when I am gone. How can I be sure that they will not be removed and supplanted by some later work by a painter not yet born; taken down and put into a room in some turret, gathering dust and forgotten. And the only ones who will see my work will be the Dukes and Duchesses and their guests, yet I want the whole of Italy and England, France and Germany, Spain and Russia, to see my life through my work.

Which is why I am writing this story of my life. My paintings are my conversation with my viewer today. My book will be my conversation with readers perhaps yet unborn. There is a silent dialogue between a man or woman standing before one of my paintings, and the characters who are performing on the canvas, but that's an intimate conversation. Perhaps they're seeking out meaning in the appearance, the faces of the people, their actions, and their intentions from the movements of their bodies….but nothing I paint tells the viewer the details of the assaults which befell me. They see the anguish, but not the reason the artist painted in that way.

So how can I inform the viewer of one of my works of the true depth of the horrors which have formed me both as woman and as painter? How can I be certain that they leave my painting with the message I intended? How can they know my story, when all they see is the Israelite Judith cutting off the head of the Assyrian

General Holofernes, or Jael killing Sisera, or Cleopatra killing herself with an asp, or Susanna being lecherously viewed by the Elders?

And so I have decided to write this, the story of my life, in the hope that you, some bibliophile tomorrow or at some time in the future, will read about poor Artemisia Gentileschi, painter, mother, daughter, wife, and survivor. I was victim of a rapist when I was a virgin, one who caused me to be tortured by the laws of the land and to live the rest of my life fighting against pain and injustice.

So the question now for me, as an artist unused to the canvas of a page, unaccustomed to a quill in my hand and ink as my paint, is where to begin my story. Do I start with my birth and early life, when my father, Orazio was one of the most famous and accomplished painters in Rome, or do I begin after my troubles in the beautiful city of Florence in Tuscany? Do I begin from the time I suckled at the bosom of my beloved mother, Prudentia, whom I miss so much, even to this day; she died shortly after we had celebrated Christmas when I was but 12 years of age, so I had a number of years of unbridled happiness and innocence with her before her death, learning the ineffable mysteries of life as the daughter of a man who spoke with his hands and breathed life into a flat dull canvas with just a few deft brushstrokes.

Had she lived, would my life have been different? Perhaps. No, it would have been different to an absolute certainty, for my mother would never, ever have allowed me, as an unmarried woman, still innocent of men, to be put into a position where I was alone with those men who forced my innocence from me.

Should I begin when I was a student to my father, crushing the tablets of paints and mixing them with solvents until the exact colour he demanded for his subject was ready and available to him?

My mother may have allowed me to do that, but when my father and his students, against the injunctions of the Church, painted nude men and women, she would have insisted – as a supporter of my budding talent as a painter - that I remain in the studio to observe how to reproduce the contours and outlines that define the human form. Sadly, in the year after she died, my father banned me from looking at nudes, which was an absurdity as I'd been surrounded by naked bodies all my life, my father and mother were never reticent when it came to bathing in the loggia where water was brought by our servants, and since childhood, my brothers and I had plunged naked into tributaries of Rome's River Tiber, and when we went to visit Florence, into the Arno on hot summer days.

No, Mother would never have allowed me to be in a position to be assaulted by these evil men. There were two, my rapist and another, who was little more than his lapdog, who was there just for the thrill of the moment, was a party to the crime against me. He assaulted me as he attempted to rape me yet he was never put on trial; but I'm pacing ahead, as I still don't know where to begin.

So shall I start there, with the story of my defilement, my deflowering? No, for what happened to me could have happened to any young woman left alone with a man who had already planned to kill his wife, raped other women, was guilty of incest with his sister, and God Almighty knows how many other crimes against nature he committed. So to begin at that moment in my life would certainly capture your immediate attention, like a sudden swathe of brilliant blue sky visible within an iridescent cloud of white and grey. But that would not put me, or my life into context. You would see me as little more than a hapless waif, a casualty of life's circumstances.

As a painter, I never begin with carefully created images in my mind. No, I begin imagining a painting as a cataract of emotions, a cascade of thoughts and feelings that grow and swell and engorge in my mind until they are ready to burst out onto the canvas as an indistinct orgy of colour and uncertain shapes and passions.

But that would lead to little more than aggressive blemishes, ill-formed miasmas of colour and anger. To make my passions into a painting, I have to put humanity into my emotions; I have to stop and contemplate the infinity of the glories of this world; I have to imagine a Jesus or a Mary, a Luke or a Judith and how my emotions could be portrayed through the story of their actions. Then I see their faces clearly in my mind, and I begin to sketch with a charcoal; but only the outlines of their bodies, only the torments of their movements. And once it's done, once their bodies and positions have been defined in thin black outline, then I create them as living, breathing human beings, painting their bodies and arms and legs, hands and feet, gowns and drapes. But not their faces. No their faces come later, for while their bodies determine what they do, it is their faces which tell my viewers what they are thinking, what torment or ecstasy, doubt or certainty, is coursing around their minds.

That, dear reader of the future, is how I scribe my thoughts and fears onto my canvas. But that's not how I will write this, my life story. No, for unlike a painting which is defined from the very beginning as a work which can be changed in an instant – a smile can immediately become a frown by the simple downwards inflection of a brush – words, once written in ink, are permanent, immutable, undying.

Words are not my medium. The brush and paint are my pen and ink, a canvas my paper. Yet this, the story of my life, will be written forever in words and not as an image. For only with words can my meaning be unequivocal, not open to interpretation as one might search for meaning in a painting.

So here is the testament of my life, my art, my suffering, but mainly, my triumph.

Retired and desperately seeking a reason to get out of bed in the morning, David Cabot decided that this morning, he would explore the Sydney suburbs of St. Ives, Pymble and Gordon. Yesterday, he'd explored Lane Cove, Chatswood and Roseville. Jackie, his wife, failed to understand his determination to map out and explore suburbs which were so heavily urbanised, crowded with traffic, and replete with shops and offices, restaurants and workshops. If it was her decision, she'd wander through the parks and woodlands surrounding Sydney, breathing in air scented by gum trees, pines and frangipani.

But since they'd moved from Kalgoorlie in Western Australia, where he had worked for much of his life as a geologist, he was now applying the same structure to his retirement as he'd applied to his search for traces of minerals inside the rocks and gigantic lodes beneath the ground.

Jackie had hoped that in this new city, busy, crowded and noisy, he'd be able to use his retirement to explore his love of art, but it seemed that the habits of a lifetime were still part of his make-up. He was applying the same mapping techniques of exploring his new home environment he'd applied over the other side of the continent. Only now he was on foot, whereas when he'd been a geologist, he'd used the company's aircraft or Land Rovers, full of sophisticated equipment to do ground surveying of vast tracks of seemingly empty land. His equipment enabled him to discover hidden mineral deposits deeply buried, and then he'd follow up where the roads became impassable to do his digging by riding camels into regions known only to Aborigines.

And as a geologist, taking shares in the companies for which he was working, he'd made a small fortune over a lifetime; enough to enable him to retire at 59, buy a 4-bedroom apartment in North Sydney, overlooking the Opera House and the Harbour Bridge, and live a life of indulgence.

Which had been the case for the first four months. They'd dined almost every day in the plethora of restaurants in Sydney, visited the Opera House four nights a week to see live performances, swam in many beaches, gone fishing in Pittwater, and joined Bridge and other clubs.

But for a man who had worked 15 hour days, six days a week, in the field and in the office, even a crowded retirement schedule wasn't enough. He'd always loved art, ever since he was a boy, and had a wide amateur knowledge. His particular love was the Italian Renaissance and the later Baroque period, and he'd always harboured a hope that if he made enough money, one day he'd be able to buy and own a small masterpiece. Not that it was a realistic hope, but it was always there in the back of his mind.

David had heard about a small specialist art gallery in St. Ives, one of the northern suburbs of Sydney; so he took a train to Gordon Station, and walked the hills and valleys, past mansions and parks, until he reached Mona Vale Road where the gallery was situated.

It was a small gallery, seemingly squeezed between a supermarket and a fruiterer. He wasn't impressed as he stood outside and looked in through the window. Three paintings on easels were on display to passers-by. One was a large stylized picture of the Sydney Opera House, the white sails covered in slices of oranges, apples, pineapples and mangoes. Another painting was of an old Aboriginal man, staring into the infinity of his red landscape; it was obvious, just looking at the bone structure, the facial features, and especially the blood-red terrain, that the artist had never ventured out of his city-centre atelier, and his understanding of his subject was based entirely on pictures he'd seen. He probably hadn't met an Aborigine in his life.

The third picture was of a bowl of fruit, about as boring a picture as any he'd ever seen. David stood on the pavement, and regretted his wasted journey. It was a suburban gallery where Mrs. Vapid and Mr. Pedestrian who lived around the corner exhibited their works, in the hope that one day they could rival Lucian Freud and maybe even Andy Warhol. They were the types who set up easels and canvasses and sat for hours, trying to capture the extravagance of a sunset, producing the sort of art travellers purchased in a tourist shop.

He was about to go into a shopping centre and buy himself a cup of coffee, when he entered the gallery.

Inside, he smelled the familiar scent of paintings, the same fragrance that filled the air in galleries in Rome and London, New York and Paris. He breathed in the atmosphere, and looked around the walls. Nothing attracted him.

The woman sitting behind a desk, partly hidden by her computer screen, looked at David, and knew, instantly, that he was a looker, and not a buyer. But she knew she had to go through the motions.

"Good morning," she said, brightly, "were you looking for anything in particular."

She'd offered him just too wide an opening, too good an opportunity. He replied, "Anything but these," he said. And then immediately regretted it. It was boorish snobbery of the worst kind, the sort of remark he should have kept to himself.

But for some reason, she burst out laughing, and said, "Dear Lord, I know what you mean. My boss makes me put these up because they're his taste but personally, I can't stand them."

Now David laughed. He walked over to the woman, who stood, and shook his hand.

"Lucy Carpenter."

"David Cabot. Look, I'm both a voyeur and a serious buyer. I go from gallery to gallery hoping to find something I like.....not to match the colour of my carpet or the new curtains, but because it's a work of genius."

"Oh, believe me, I know what you mean. I worked in some amazing galleries in London before my husband's job relocated us here, so I can honestly say that I recognize great painting when I see it. But now I have to convince myself and our customers that these pictures are works of art."

He looked around the gallery, and shook his head in sadness.

"But don't give up hope," she said. "Before he opened this gallery, the owner collected dozens and dozens of paintings, which he used to sell to other galleries. Most of them aren't worth the canvas on which they're painted, but some of them are really interesting. We've got some 19th and early 20th century stuff in the back. And even some which look older. Would you like to have a look?"

She took him into a back storage room, which had frames and canvasses stacked four and five deep against the wall. There must have been upwards of 100 paintings. Just looking at the first painting in the each of the rows, showed him that here was real artistic talent.

"Why the hell aren't these on display?" he asked.

Lucy shrugged her shoulders. "My boss, the owner, doesn't think that the passing trade would be interested. Only somebody with some knowledge of paintings, and there aren't that many in this area."

David stepped further into the room, and asked, "May I?"

Lucy assured him that he was free to look at any painting he wanted. She excused herself and went back to the front of the gallery.

David looked at several, which didn't impress him. They were typical heavy Victorian portrayals of smoking factory chimneys, or ships at harbour. Some were obviously French in origin and some 20th century Italian. They were vastly more impressive than the pap on the walls of the gallery, but nothing which met his specific criteria.

Until, buried deeply in the fourth row he was examining, was a picture which immediately captured his interest. He struggled to free the frame from the ones in front and behind, but lifted it up and carried it to another side of the room. There, he propped it on a high bar stool and rested it at chest level against a wall.

He looked and looked, closer and at a distance. Then he walked very close to the painting, and examined the faces carefully.

It was an old painting, in the style of the Italian old masters. But of course, it couldn't be. Why would a suburban humdrum gallery in Australia have an Italian old master?

And old masters paintings were often copied, quite deliberately, by their students. In 17th century Italy, there were no photocopiers, and so artists like Raphael and Michaelangelo created a work, and then told their students to copy it so that it could be distributed to people throughout the art-loving world. Even Leonardo's most famous work, the Mona Lisa, was hanging in at least a dozen galleries, the famous and original in the Louvre in Paris, and a truly brilliant copy by his students, in the Prado in Madrid.

So in all likelihood, this was a student's copy of a master's work. But he didn't recognize the original. And the more he looked at the painting, the more excited he became.

It was a lifesize painting of a mother and child, typical of the sorts of subject which had captured the imaginations of Renaissance and Baroque artists. But it was the mother's face, her breast, and the face of the infant which took David's breath away.

The mother was looking out of the picture to the viewer's left side, her eyes closed, her face a mask of pain; not excruciating pain, but more one of the pain of disappointment a mother feels when her child does something wrong. Her left breast, exposed to the viewer because the baby had just suckled it, was streaming with blood where the infant had bitten into the flesh.

Both of these were unusual portrayals of a common subject. But what astounded David, and caused him to look again and again, was the head of the baby who had just finished suckling at his mother's breast. It was the face of a mature child, almost an adult. The full head of black hair was parted, and he had black sideburns growing level with the bottom of his earlobe.

But his full head of hair was only one of the disturbing images captured in his face. It was his adult look, his cruel and uncaring stare, his total lack of concern that he'd injured his mother.

This was the sort of face one would expect in Oscar Wilde's Picture of Dorian Gray, Breugel's devils, Van Eyck's Last Judgement, and Bosch's Garden of Earthly Delights. This was not a Madonna and Child, but a Mother who had given Birth to a Demon.

David recoiled at the horror of the subject, but was falling in love with the quality of the painting. Yes, it must be by a student, but even so, whether or not it had value, it was just the sort of painting he loved to acquire and this would be a wonderful addition to the collection he had displayed on the walls in his new home.

He carried the painting into the front of the gallery, and Lucy stood and saw what he'd selected.

"Oh, yes, I know that painting. Do you *really* want to buy that? I find it a bit repellent. I know I shouldn't say these things, but....ugh!"

"What do you know about it?" asked David.

"Nothing. The boss picked it up in some garage sale. It's obviously European, but we have no idea how it got to Australia."

Lucy walked closer to the picture, and David could see how she felt repulsed. "Look, I don't want to be critical, and obviously I want to sell it to you, but look at the kid's face, for heaven's sake. It's so badly painted. No baby has hair like that, or those sideburns, or such a grown up expression. I really don't think that the artist was much good. The painting of the mother's ok, but not the kid. Sorry, but it's pretty amateurish."

"Do you really think so? Look at the mother," said David. "That's an expression of deep regret, bordering on incomprehension. She's saying, *'I love you and I've given you life; I've nurtured you; you've suckled at my breast; and now you repay my love and tenderness by tearing at my body, stripping my flesh. I'm so disappointed in you.'* Sorry, but I think it's marvellous. Can you tell me anything else about it?"

She went to her desk, opened the drawer and pulled out a notebook. Flipping through the pages, she looked from book to painting and then back to the book again.

"Here it is," she said, and then began to read out the notes. "*Purchased October 1972. Garage sale. Home of Jan van de Klerk (retired airline pilot). Subject woman and baby. Blood on breast. Price $67.*" That's all it says. Obviously, nobody knows the painter or the provenance. I think my boss tried to sell it to people a couple of years ago, but nobody wanted it because of the blood and the expression on the mother's face. And also they were probably repelled by the look of the boy. He's really scary. It's not what anyone wants to hang over their fireplace. So he just put it in the back of the gallery, and no doubt it'll be flogged off as a job lot at an auction."

David nodded. "How much do you think he'll want for it?"

Lucy shrugged her shoulders. "No idea. Probably a couple of hundred dollars. I could ask and then negotiate a price with you."

"And I've come here by train and on foot. Can you

deliver it?" he asked.

She shook her head in amazement, and said, "Sure. But you're certain that you want this in your home?"

He laughed. And then he gave her his details.

It took David's wife a month to come to terms with the picture. At first, she'd refused to hang it in any area where it might be seen by guests, or even herself as she walked through the house. So they'd agreed upon hanging it in his study.

And as the days and weeks and months went by, and he sent photographs he'd taken of the painting to museums and galleries in France and Italy, Britain and Spain, the letters of response came in. The British said that it looked like a picture painted by a student of a Baroque artist, but without a close examination of the original, they couldn't comment further. The Italians responded by saying that it seemed to be a copy of a late Renaissance artist, but not one which appeared in any of their catalogues. And he had no response whatsoever from the French or the Spanish.

It was then that he decided to take the picture and journey with it to Britain. When he told his wife, she reacted badly.

"But that's going to cost us thousands and thousands

of dollars. And for all you know, this could be a student's amateur work. You could be laughed out of London. What is it with you and this painting, David?" she demanded.

He sighed. Her logic was unimpeachable. "It's the expression in her face. She's so disappointed in what her son is doing to her. Biting the breast that feeds you. Biting the woman who gives you life, who suckles you. What greater act of bastardry, of treachery, could there be than an infant, biting a mother's breast?"

"But he's not a child. Look at him! He's like a young adult. A teenager. It's ugly and monstrous. For all you know, darling, it could be a joke, some artist's folly. David, I really think you're wasting your time and money going to England to get this assessed."

"But all I have left is time and money," he said. "Come with me. We could make it a holiday." But she declined and said she wouldn't participate in a fool's errand.

A month and a half later, the portrait arrived with David in the United Kingdom, carefully protected by tissue paper and strong bubble wrap in-between clothes in his large suitcase. Ensconced in the hotel, he'd removed it, placed it safely in the hotel's locked wardrobe, and purchased a large portfolio carrier. Now David Cabot walked through the streets of London, ending up in Exhibition Road. His destination was the Victoria and Albert Museum. He had an appointment with the museum's Curator of Renaissance Art, Dr. Linda Gorman.

Fifteen minutes after entering the building, he was shown into his meeting in Gorman's office. It was a large office, and on the walls were pictures whose provenance he knew were lesser known but still marvellous painters of the Italian, French and English Renaissance.

She came out into the reception area, and shook his hand warmly. "How lovely to meet you. How was your trip from Australia?" she asked.

He assured her that he'd recovered from jet lag as far as he knew, but to excuse him if he fell asleep during their meeting.

Sitting down, she said, "Well, I've seen the photos you sent me, which is why I was happy to meet you. I know I was fairly non-committal, but until I'm able to examine the original painting, any comment I make will be purely speculative. But I do think that it's certainly interesting enough for you to have taken the chance of coming over to see us. Now, can I see the painting."

David stood, and opened the portfolio, taking out the painting, and placing it on a draftsman's drawing board.

Linda carefully placed clean glass weights on the four corners to hold it down.

Just looking at it, she said, "Oh my goodness. Oh my! Oh, look at this."

Then she went to her desk and took out two surgical masks, handing one to David. "If we're going to examine this picture in minute detail, then we have to wear these."

Together and masked up, they bent over the painting, Linda using a strong magnifying glass with a brilliant light, on a moveable arm which was attached to a stand. She held the glass over the head of the boy, and examined the brush strokes, the colours, the features of the face. She kept making noises, like "Good God" and "My word."

Silently, she moved the glass to look at the face of the mother. Her soliloquies continued as "Heavens" or "Ah!" or "Oh!" and she continued to examine the painting in the most intricate and minute detail, centimetre by centimetre.

When she'd finished with the faces, she turned to David, and said, "Very very interesting. Seriously interesting."

"Do you think......?

She didn't let him finish the question. "....much much too early to say. It's interesting...no, exciting. But the last thing I want to do is to say something which will raise your hopes and then have them dashed after a thorough forensic and scientific examination proves our assumptions wrong. Right now, all I can tell you, from my examination of the brush techniques and the style, is that this is either late Renaissance or early Baroque. It's probably Italian. It could be the work of a master, or the work of a body of students under a master's guidance. I'm not leaning one way or another."

David nodded. "Ok. No pressure. But who painted it?"

Linda laughed. "It could have been Strozzi, because the woman reminds me of the maidens in his Allegory of Arts. Or it could be Cortona; his Alliance of Jacob and Laban has a woman and baby which is not dissimilar. But frankly I doubt either of them, and most other artists of the period. But of course, it could even be a late Tintoretto, painted just before he died. There's something in this picture which reminds me of Tintoretto's Muse with Lute.

"But in truth, there's a name which is shouting out to me, but I dare not even consider telling you unless I do more research."

"Please! Even if you're wrong and later tests prove that it wasn't by him, give me a name so that I can look it up."

Linda looked at him and was moved by his eagerness. "Ok. But please don't take this as gospel, because it'll need serious scholarship. But I'm leaning towards….no… I'm not going to say.  Not now. In a short while. Just give me some time."

Impatiently, he waited while Linda covered the entire canvas with the magnifying glass, inspecting the way the artist had painted folds of cloth, fingers, her dress, the colour of her hair. Then, after another hour, she asked him for help in turning the painting over, and she spent time examining the weave of the canvas and the sides and corners of the painting.

Restoring it, so that the painting was again visible, she turned off the magnifying glass's light, and looked at the painting for another five, perhaps ten minutes. Only then, remembering that David had been totally silent for the better part of an hour and more, did she say, "Thank you for your patience. Let's sit down, shall we."

They sat, David coming close to bursting with excitement and anticipation, looked at her.

"I want to put you out of your misery, but we need to examine flecks of paint and do spectrographic and X-ray analyses of the canvas to determine whether it was overpainted, whether there's another painting beneath it, as well as its age. We need to do serious scientific work on this painting before we can properly authenticate it and determine its creator, its provenance, its history and its place in the pantheon of art and artists," she said.

He asked, "So you're not just dismissing it as the work of a student."

"I can only give you an educated gut reaction. But I'd say not. It's just too damn good. There's a degree of genius in the artist's use of colour, the expressions that have been created for the mother and the infant. And then, of course, there's the extraordinary face, hair and manner of the infant. And let's never forget that his teeth have ripped the skin of his mother's breast," she said.

"Which leads you to believe...." he asked.

".....that this painting is an allegory. Usually, they're Biblical or Romano/Greek. Nymphs and Gods and that sort of thing. But this painting screams of telling a story. A story of pain and suffering. A narrative of profound disappointment, hurt and even betrayal. And there's an artist from those times which fits that bill. Have you ever heard of a father and daughter painting duo who were famous as great artists after Italian Renaissance, and at the beginning of the Baroque? His name was Orazio Gentileschi and his daughter was Artemisia Gentileschi. Have you heard of them?"

"I think so. I don't know. No, actually, I don't think I've heard of them, but I might be wrong."

"More and more people are getting to know them, especially Artemisia, and in the future, I predict that Artemisia is going to become much more famous. She'll eclipse her father, and probably become as famous as the greats of her day. And by greats, I'm talking about Caravaggio, Michaelangelo and painters as great as they.

"Not only was she one of the most brilliant painters of the period, but her life story is so exceptional, that in the future my guess is that she'll become one of the great feminist icons. The writer Germaine Greer wrote a book about women artists, and Artemisia was one of her subjects."

"So you think that this could be by this woman, Artemisia," asked David.

"No! I didn't say that. It has a Gentileschi style about it. It could be the father, Orazio, or the daughter herself, or one of their students. She became very famous in her day, although since her death, and for over three hundred years, she's been virtually forgotten. But it's not just technique and style which leads me to think that possibly...just possibly....and I stress, it's only possible.... that this might be a missing Artemisia."

"Not the father, what's his name?"

"Orazio. Yes, it could be by him. He was Artemisia's initial tutor; but then so was Caravaggio. But it's the subject matter which makes me think that this could be a genuine Artemisia."

"Why? What is it about what she painted?"

"The face of the infant. It's far too mature, too old, for a baby sucking milk. And the wounds on her breast. Teeth? Biting the breast that feeds him. To understand, you have to know that Artemisia was raped by a painter named Tassi. Her father took him to court, and instead of him suffering, it was she, Artemisia, who was tortured to prove that she was telling the truth. But eventually Tassi was found guilty. And from then on, Artemisia's paintings were angry, defiant, showing the strength of women railing against the vicissitudes of life and the unfeeling callousness of men. One of her paintings is particularly vicious. It's called Judith Severing The Head of Holofernes; there are several iterations of the painting made by her over the years, but one of the best is in the Museo e Real Bosco di Capodimonte in Naples. It's one of the most extraordinary paintings of the Baroque.... well, any age really. And if my gut is right, then this painting dates from around that period, possibly a dozen or so years after, and could very well have been painted by her."

"Would that make it valuable?" asked David, quickly adding, "not that its commercial value, its price, is particularly important."

"Yes, it would become very valuable if it was a genuine Artemisia. But more important than money, it would add to the body of her work, and fill in gaps in her life story about which we had no idea. But I will say one thing. If we authenticate it and we certify that it's a genuine Artemisia, then this Museum would be in the front row of museums to offer to buy the picture from you."

"Is it that good?" asked David.

"Yes, my friend, it's really that good," Dr. Linda Gorman told him.

Leaving the painting with her for examination, David walked back into the centre of London, realising that he had two options. The first was to wait the couple of weeks during which Dr. Gorman said it would take to assemble the Artemisia experts from London, Edinburgh, Paris, Florence and Rome who would gather in the Victoria and Albert Museum to examine the painting, as well as the scientific analyses which by then would have been produced as reports.

The second option was to leave the painting with the experts, return to Australia and await the results in a phone call from Linda Gorman.

And as he awoke in the Hotel Astoria opposite Hyde Park on the morning after his visit to the Museum he realised that he had a further option. He could travel to Rome and Milan and Florence and investigate everything he could about this mysterious painter in preparation for the good…or bad…news.

If he did that, then should the painting be authenticated, he could appear before the media in Britain, and probably other countries, and sound much more intelligent and knowledgeable than he'd been when Linda had first mentioned that there was a chance that Artemisia was possibly the painter.

It had been too early in Australia to phone home when he had returned from dinner after his day in the Museum. There was a nine hour time difference between London and Sydney. So when he'd rationalised his options in his mind, he reached over to pick up his cell phone and dialled his Sydney home. It was 10.00 in the evening when he heard his wife, Jackie's voice. After the pleasantries, and assuring her that he was eating and sleeping properly, he explained what had happened yesterday.

But before he could explain the choices in front of him, his wife asked him to explain more about the potential painters of his artwork. And that confirmed that he needed to travel to Europe to find out more than what the books said about Orazio and Artemisia Gentileschi. Because after a few moments of explanation, his wife began to ask him questions he just couldn't answer – how old was Artemisia when she painted this portrait of a mother and baby; why the baby was so old; where was she born; where had she lived; what else had she painted; where were her paintings to be found; how much were her paintings worth? The cascade of questions defined his lack of knowledge and his need to find out everything he could. And not the least of her questions was the one which had been on his mind as he walked away from the Victoria and Albert Museum – how did a priceless and lost Artemisia Gentileschi painting come to be in a suburban art gallery thousands and thousands of miles away from Italy?

He'd packed for Autumn in England, months before Swinburne's season of snows and sins. He'd expected to be able to avoid the coldness of Winter and so had only packed a couple of woollen jumpers to wear underneath his suit's jacket in order to keep him warm as he walked around London's streets in the evening.

His clothes were suitable for an American Fall or a Sydney Winter where the days were still warm, but the nights required a second or third layer. What he hadn't anticipated was needing a lightweight coat to protect himself from the winds blowing over the city of Florence from the Apennine mountains to the East, or from the Tyrrhenian Sea to the West.

So when he arrived in Florence, after he'd booked into the Hotel Medici in the Via Ponte Vecchio, he walked to the boutiques, and bought himself a delightful light coat, the cost of which was equivalent to buying a small car in Australia. Yes, it was fabulous, yes it was the most fashionable coat he'd ever owned; but he would somehow have to hide the American Express bill from Jackie when it came in next month.

He treated himself to lunch at a delightful little trattoria close to the Ponte alle Grazi, which straddled the River Arno. As he sat, delighting in his second glass of Valpolicella ripasso from a vineyard in Verona, and looked over the terracotta rooftops of the ancient city, he thought to himself that if it wasn't for the food, the wine, the shops, the fashions, the history, the amazing buildings, the museums, the culture, the paintings, the sculptures....nobody would bother visiting Florence. Having spent most of his life in Australia, a young and modern country which venerated anything more than 50 years old, he realised how much he'd missed by not learning more about European culture.

Aboriginal culture was the oldest on earth, dating back 60,000 and probably many tens of thousands of years before that; but being a nomadic peoples, they had left no permanent settlements, no everlasting monuments. Yes, their rock art was among the most ancient in the world, but a stylization of a kangaroo or an emu or a possum couldn't be compared to the sculptured delicacy of a smile by Leonardo, nor a Venus by Botticelli, nor the fingers of God and Adam by Michaelangelo.

But through the fortuitous discovery in a Sydney art gallery, he was now knee deep in the art, history and intrigue of the Italian Renaissance, a time of chaotic politics, religious amorality and artistic genius.

For two days, David wandered from monument to monument, museum to museum, palazzo to palazzo, each one somehow more breathtaking than the previous. But the crowning glory was the Uffizi, once the offices of the Medici banking family designed by Vasari, and now one of the world's greatest museums. Unlike summer months during French and British holidays when crowds had to be constrained behind ropes and only a certain number of pre-booked visitors were allowed in according to a strict schedule, this was still the early European vacation period for Florence kept many away, and David found entry both easy and immediate.

He walked from gallery to gallery, listening to the commentary on his earphone, and staring in hushed awe at the masterpieces by Filippo Lippi, Mantegna, Leonardo, Michaeangelo, Botticelli, Caravaggio, Giotto and so many more.

Almost drunk with the heady wine of the Renaissance,

he remembered why he was in Florence, and returned to the front desks. There, he asked a young woman receptionist whether there was a resident expert on the work of the Gentileschi family. She nodded, and said in sensuously Italian accented English, "I will call our expert department and see what's there. I sure you will need a English speak. Yes?"

"Yes," said David, and watched her while she dialed the number. He thought he recognized a few of the Italian words she spoke, but when she put her hand over the receiver, she asked, "She want to know why you ask. Are you tourist? Many book in our bookshop on painters."

"No," said David. "Tell her I think I own a painting by either the father or the daughter and I want to speak to somebody."

The young woman told her interlocutor what David had just said, and the reaction was swift and positive.

"In a minute she will be arrive. She is Professor Martina Calabrese. She will land soon," said the young woman.

David bit back his smile, wondering whether she'd arrive by helicopter, but instead thanked her and waited patiently.

In less than a couple of minutes, a tall, handsome

woman, aged in her mid to late 40s, wearing a white laboratory coat, her black hair tied in a bun, and looking like a younger version of Sophia Loren, came striding purposefully into the reception area. As she entered the Uffizi's lobby, David was immediately drawn to her. And when she saw him, she beamed a smile which lit up the building.

He was the only person there at that hour, and she marched over to him. Before he could say a word, she shook her head and beamed, asking, "Is it possible that you are David? Are you the man who may have found a lost Artemisia? Tell me it's so."

Taken aback by being recognized, he shook her hand, said, "I'm David Cabot. And yes, I took a painting to the Victoria and Albert Museum, and they're examining it now. They think it may be a Gentileschi."

"Do they think father or daughter?" she asked.

"They're leaning more towards the daughter, Artemisia."

"Yes! Yes, I've seen it. A photograph. By email. And it may be. I was sent the photograph a few days ago, and I've dispatched one of my assistants to London to help in the identification. Oh my God! I don't believe that you've just walked into the Uffizi and here you are."

Still stunned, David said, "I'm sorry, but I don't have an appointment, Professor. I just wanted to find out more about the Gentileschis."

"Of course. But don't talk about the Gentileschis. Not Orazio the father. I doubt that he could have painted this work. No, this to me, if authenticated, is Artemisia. Definitely she. Artemisia. Not Orazio. Yes. Look, come with me to my office. We have much to talk about. This is amazing."

For the rest of the afternoon, Martina cancelled her appointments, and only took urgent phone calls. Instead, she cross-examined him as mercilessly and forensically as though she was a criminal barrister, asking question after question about the Sydney gallery where he'd found the painting, what other paintings he'd seen, why he was so attracted to this painting, who may have owned the painting, what was his name and any details about him.

In the end, she shrugged her shoulders, and said, "Before the authenticity of this painting is announced, I will go to Sydney and into this gallery. Who knows, there may be a couple of Titians, Leonardos or Verrocchios where you found your Artemisia."

They both laughed. "Ok, I've told you all about me and how I found the painting. Now, Professor, tell me all about Artemisia; not the stuff I can find in a book, but stuff not many people know."

She smiled. "First, Professor is not my name. It's Martina. And you are David. Second, much is known about Artemisia, but much is also not known. The Vatican Apostolic Library no doubt has much material about her when only priests and scholars are allowed to see. Much I'm sure has not been found. We have the transcript of her trial, which is amazing, but my thought is that there is much much to find. And as women discover Artemisia and her amazing bravery, what she suffered, how she stood up against men...then in this time of feminists, I'm sure she will become a great heroine."

"So you think that there might be hidden documents yet to be found?" he asked.

"Always there are documents in Italy which are suddenly discovered. We have many ancient libraries, and while the librarians know most of the books, there are always precious discoveries. These open up a new avenue to knowledge, to know more about the subject."

"But what more do you think could be known about her?" asked David.

Martina laughed. "So much. So much. Look, think about this. She was a brilliant painter. Raped. Tortured in a trial. Still she swore she was innocent, a virgin when Tassi had her. She marries a painter after the trial, a man with not a fraction of her genius, and comes to Florence to work for the Medici. She has many children. Most die in her arms. But it's as an artist where she makes her name. And not just an artist. One of the greatest of the Baroque. In her day, her name was talked about in the same breath as Caravaggio, Raphaelo, Michaelangelo. But her subjects. Oh my God, her subjects. We all know about Judith and Holofernes, but her other paintings tell such dramatic stories, which say more about her than any document. Her Lucretia, wife of Tarquinus, showing a woman who was raped, but who Artemisia painted at the moment she's killing herself, her Cleopatra who has just committed suicide, her Danae raped by the god Zeus. Painting after painting shows Artemisia's fury, her restrained anger seeping out of her brushstrokes. You can truly say that she painted her revenge.

"And after she dies, everybody assumes that her paintings have been the creations of her father Orazio, and within a generation, she's forgotten. Dismissed. Only now, only today, only thanks to the insistence of this wonderful feminist movement, are we beginning to recognize that she was one of the greatest of the great painters of the early Baroque," said Martina. "Just before, I said to you that this photograph I received from V&A in London emailed to me, depending on tests and authentication, looked like an Artemisia, not an Orazio. You have to understand that the father, Orazio, trained Artemisia to be his studio assistant, to assist him in some minor background painting, but never, like him, a true painter of faces or the focal point of a painting. She was there to grind his colours, make his paints, fill in backgrounds and landscape features. Because she was a girl, it was assumed that she could never be capable of painting subjects properly. Nor, as a girl in Italy, was she taught to read or write. She was uneducated and illiterate.

"But by the age of 10 or 11, she was already showing her brilliance and had outstripped the abilities of her three younger brothers and was so good, she was discussing form and content and assisting her father in his painting. At the age of 16, she was already at work on creating one of today's greatest masterpieces of Baroque art, Susanna and the Elders, which she finished by the time she was just 17. Did her father Orazio help her? Perhaps, who knows, but the painting is certainly in the main by Artemisia.

"It was a familiar theme of other painters, but her Susanna showed not just an astounding understanding of the female form, showing Susanna humiliated by being spied upon by old lecherous men, but showed her embarrassment, her distress because they were assaulting her, just by looking at her while she was bathing. Remember that she was only allowed to paint female, not male nudes, yet somehow, she understood the moves and shapes of the human body as well as any adult painter. The painting was so extraordinarily brilliant, that people who came to see it refused to believe that it had been painted by a girl so young. They attributed it to her father. But some time ago, Artemisia's signature was found, very faintly, in the shadow cast by Susanna's leg. It was barely visible, but it confirmed for all time, that this really was her work.

"It was this painting of Susanna that caused the father to realise his daughter's stunning talent. But over the years her genius has been forgotten and ignored. Only recently has she been recognized as a painter of genius. Which is why I'm so excited that this painting of yours might be a hidden, lost, forgotten Artemisia," she told him.

"And you think that there might be documents to be discovered which could prove this work of mine is by Artemisia," said David.

"Who knows," she replied. "Who knows what is

hidden in the Vatican library!"

"But why the Vatican. I don't understand. The trial was for rape. That's a criminal offense," he said.

"Ha!" she laughed. "How little you understand about Italy. About the Renaissance. About the Catholic Church. The trial was more of a religious inquisition. It was a senior cleric who conducted the trial and so the records have been held in the Vatican for centuries. Many years ago, the trial transcript was handed over to the State Archives in Rome, but there may be other documents which talk more about Artemisia's life. But will they be released? One day. Maybe tomorrow. Maybe in a hundred years. The Vatican moves very slowly."

"Then there's no way we can find any proof; not from the Vatican, at least. From what I understand," said David, "you have to be a Catholic scholar to access the Vatican Library. I can't claim that," he said. "I'm just an amateur art lover and a retired geologist. There could be records of this painting in the Vatican, and I'll never be able to find them or prove that the painting is by her." He looked downcast.

Martina grinned; it was a mischievous grin. "Maybe you can't, David, but I can. But even better; one of my dearest friends is a high-ranking Cardinal in the Vatican.

Arturo de Santis. A dear man. Totally brilliant, decent, wonderful. I love him and he loves me. But no romance. He loves me like he loves his sisters. Arturo was the Professor of Renaissance Art here in the Uffizi before I was appointed. It was he who tapped me on the shoulder when I was a Professor in the Faculty of Fine Arts in Yale University, and persuaded me to come to Florence to take over his position."

"What happened to him?" asked David. "Where did he go when you replaced him?"

"Well, he is a priest, a Catholic priest, but mainly he is a brilliant academic. He's always been a teacher, so he's never had any pastoral duties. He was Professor in the Art and Historiography of the Church. He's a world-class scholar of late Renaissance and Baroque Italian art, and was appointed to the Uffizi. He didn't give up his Priesthood, but he was a Bishop without a Parish. Then in 1987, the Holy Father Pope John Paul II asked him to come to Rome to be Curator of the Vatican Museums, where he is today. Big big job. He has 20,000 paintings to curate, 700 people working for him, and seven million tourists a year visit the museums he controls.

"He was elevated to the rank of Cardinal, and is now Cardinal-Bishop of the Suburbicarian Diocese in Rome, with responsibilities to the Vatican. If I approach him in the right way, and tell him that we want access to the Vatican Library for scholarship, then he might allow us to gain access. You never know," Martina told him.

"Wow," David said. "I never expected...."

"Wow indeed. If I can persuade him. But do you know how hard it is to seduce a Catholic Cardinal, even one who adores me."

They sipped coffees and determined that it could take Martina between ten minutes and ten weeks to get permission from Cardinal de Santis for the two of them to examine the Vatican Library and Archives. As to what he could do during that time, Martina suggested travelling around Tuscany and looking at the amazing hill-top villages, each one a gem in Italy's diadem.

"Alternatively, you could easily spend a month in Florence, and see just a fraction of what our city has to offer. There's so much here, even I haven't explored everything. Did you know, for instance, that just a month after the end of the trial, Orazio hurriedly married off Artemisia to a man called Pierantonio Stiattesi. He was a nobody, a modest and totally uninteresting artist from Florence. Orazio did it both to get her out of Rome, where her name was debased, and to marry her off to whoever he could. She'd lost all value to him as a marriage prospect because she was not a virgin any more, and now with her public affair with Tassi. So he somehow found Stiattesi, and persuaded him to marry her. Theirs wasn't a particularly happy marriage, and it's known she had some affairs during it, but it gave her a number of children," Martina said.

"How can I find his works, this man Statt…Stratt… what's his name?"

"Stiattesi. Pierantonio Stiattesi. I doubt you'll find anything here by him. He really wasn't a good artist. I've never seen one of his paintings, and the only reason I know of him is because of his marriage to Artemisia. But while she was in Florence and married to Pierantonio, she and Galileo Galilei became very friendly."

"Galileo? The Galileo? The astronomer? You're kidding," said David.

Martina smiled. "Darling, you'll find that the more you know about Artemisia, the more astounding she is. She broke all the molds holding women back. But yes, her relationship with Galileo was important to her. But don't misunderstand….theirs wasn't a sexual relationship. He was old and she was like a child to him. And he was almost certainly homosexual. No, David, it was when he was at the height of his fame, and just when the Inquisition was censoring him for his promotion that the sun, and not the earth, was the centre of the Universe."

"Now that," he said beaming, "is something I'd like to follow up. I was a geologist for most of my working life, and I worked in Western Australia. They have some of the clearest skies in the world and almost no pollution because the area is almost devoid of population for thousands of miles. So I spent night after night in a tent in the wilds of the Outback alone with my telescope. I got to know the stars and the planets and I did so much reading around the discoveries of Copernicus and Tycho Brahe and the others. And yes, Galileo is one of the people I'd really love to explore while I'm in Florence."

"And here's something you won't find in the tourist guides," Marina said with a playful grin. "This was told to me by Cardinal de Santis. It seems that when he was a young man, in the late 1580s, Galileo was an instructor in the Accademia della Arti del Disegno, the Academy of the Art of Drawing. He taught perspective and chiaroscuro. And in about 1615, our very own Artemisia was the first woman, ever, to be inducted into the Accademia. You can't imagine the compliment they paid her by doing this. It was public recognition of her genius, but also her acceptance by members of her profession, that she had achieved greatness.

"Of course," Martina continued, "the question on my mind is, did she meet Galileo there when she first arrived in Florence? I doubt it, but it's another amazing coincidence. And they did correspond and exchange ideas. There are even aspects of her paintings in which she is indebted to Galileo. You may already know this, because it has been written by art experts, but the blood which spurts out of Holofernes' neck follows the arc of a parabola, which hadn't been realized before by previous painters. Galileo discovered this as part of his work on the anatomy of the human being, and it's just the sort of thing that she would have asked, and he would have told Artemisia.

"She painted a second version of Judith much later when in Florence, in which she shows the arcs of blood. We have this painting here in the Uffizi; it's larger, and I think better than the original one she painted, which is in Naples. Interesting, no! Artemisia also used one of Galileo's instruments in a painting, " she said.

David frowned. "Really? I haven't seen that....which painting?"

"When Artemisia first arrived here in Florence, you

have to remember her state of mind. She'd just won the case and her honour was in theory restored. But in reality, she actually lost her reputation of a good women because of the trial of Tassi in Rome. Yes, he was found guilty, but not punished. After the case was decided, her father forced her into a marriage with a man far below her intellectual and professional level because he had to get her out of Rome.

"Here in Florence, probably unhappy and very angry, she met Michalangelo Buonarroti, no, not the real painter, but the great nephew of the genius. This man, Michalangelo the Younger, recognized Artemisia's genius, and commissioned her to paint the Allegory of the Inclination on the ceiling of the Casa Buonarotti, which was a home dedicated to the genius of his great uncle. At this time, she was very heavily pregnant with her new husband's child, and so scaling a ladder and lying on a plank of wood on her back, at ceiling height, must have been incredibly uncomfortable. Of course, the painting is oil on canvas, and so she probably painted it at ground level and then it was affixed to the ceiling, but I like to imagine that, like Michaelangelo the Great hanging by a thread painting the Sistine Chapel, this is what Artemisia did as a paean to the Master.

"The picture was completed in 1615, one of a series of fifteen allegorical representations of his great uncle, the real Michaelangelo Buonarroti. And because he wanted her to collaborate with him, Michelangelo the Younger apparently paid her three times more than any other artist who was working with him on these frescos. The Inclination has the face of Artemisia, and she's holding a brass compass, which in those days was revolutionary. It was almost certainly loaned to her by Galileo. Amazing, no?" said Martina.

"Where can I find out about Artemisia's relationship with Galileo?" asked David. "You've really sparked my interest. When I first came here, I thought that she was just a great, but unacknowledged painter, but now I'm beginning to realise what a phenomenal person she was."

Martina nodded. "And let me assure you that while our generation, people today, have never heard of her, in future generations, say the middle of the 21st Century, she'll be recognized as one of the greatest artists of all time."

The interview over, Martina apologised that she had to finish some work, and assured him that they would meet again. David suggested dinner one night in Florence with her and her husband. She smiled, and said, "Sadly, my husband is no longer. When I went to Yale, he didn't want to go, and so he divorced me. No loss, but that means that dinner will be just you and me. And yes, let's make it tomorrow night."

As he was leaving, as she walked him to the front doors of the Uffizi, David asked, "One thing that's intrigued me about her, is her name. It's such an unusual name. Does it mean anything?"

Martina said, "Oh yes. I could be wrong, and there are no factual grounds for saying this, but I think that the name was given to her by her mother, Prudenzia. She gave birth to Artemisia first, and then to three boys, but she must have been delighted when Artemisia popped out first. I'm sure she had great hopes for her daughter, and so she named her after a couple of amazing women named Artemis. One was the Queen of Caria of ancient times who fought for the Persians in the sea Battle of Salamis. The other was a later Artemisia who built the Mausoleum of Halicarnassus in honour of her husband, King Mausolus. It was one of the seven wonders of the world. Their names come from Artemis, who was the Greek goddess of hunting and purity. She was the daughter of Zeus and the sister of Apollo. She was the goddess who protected women during childbirth. The Romans knew her as the goddess Diana.

"But the reason I think she was named after Artemis was because this goddess was a woman of power, influence and strength, in a world dominated by men. Which is what Prudenzia hoped her daughter would become. If only she'd lived long enough to have witnessed her daughter's genius."

David said softly, "But could a mother have lived through the horrors of the trial and the torture her daughter was subjected to?"

Martina nodded. "That's a thing of the past. You and I, David, have to deal with the reality of the present, on behalf of art lovers of the future."

When David left Martina and the Uffizi, he wandered around the medieval streets of Florence, delighting in the architecture, the little cafes, the boutiques and the trattoria. He checked his watch and realised that it would soon be time when he could phone Jackie in Sydney and fill her in on the excitement of what had happened that afternoon. But when he got back to the hotel, he was having second thoughts about phoning Australia. It was 7.45 in the morning, and Jackie would be up having breakfast and reading the papers. So he just decided to send her a text, telling her that he was in Florence and doing well in his search.

But as he held the phone in his hands, he couldn't stop thinking about his meeting with Martina. As a Professor of Art at the Uffizi, she was at the top of the intellectual tree, but there was more to her than that, and he felt annoyed with himself that he was objectifying her. She was a lovely middle-aged woman, tall, slender, and with a sensuous body, lustrous gleaming black hair, a delightful voice and perfect English, even though some of her phraseology was at first confusing, but especially he couldn't put her beautiful face out of his mind. She had a mature woman's face, but utterly beguiling in the way that an older Italian filmstar's face electrified the screen.

For some reason, not talking to Jackie felt like an act of infidelity. In all of their years of marriage, despite being separated for weeks at a time when he was working for a mining corporation or a government doing his geological work, he'd never ever been tempted to seek female companionship outside of the boundaries of his marriage. And he hoped that he wouldn't make his first mistake with Martina.

While he knew that many of the mine workers, assistants, drivers, cooks and bottle-washers left the camp at sundown and drove often dozens of miles to the nearest town or township to visit the brothels, he'd never been tempted. He and Jackie had four wonderful children, now all adults, and two had graced him with beautiful, sensitive and boisterous grandchildren, and his family had meant everything to him. And still did.

But as he lay on his bed, musing about the new woman who had suddenly erupted into his life, he felt as if he was walking on quicksand. He took a deep breath before he allowed himself to think further, using the same analytical techniques he used when looking at the results of a survey and determining whether to recommend spending huge amounts of money of digging experimental holes in one location or another

Here he was, a middle-aged, retired, greying, balding, paunchy married man, comfortable but not wealthy, sexually unadventurous for the past forty years, and the object of no woman's fantasy. She, on the other hand, was a world-class intellectual, in one of the top jobs in a hugely competitive profession, beautiful, with a magnetic personality, vivacious, charming, sensuous without realising it, and available.

And in their three hours together, she'd not said one word, nor given the slightest indication, that she found him interesting beyond his ownership of a potential masterpiece.

Then his cellphone rang. He instantly felt guilty, and as he reached over to put it to his ear, he practiced a few words of excuse to Jackie for not phoning her earlier.

"David? Is that you?"

It wasn't Jackie, but to his surprise, it was Martina's voice.

"Hi Martina."

"David. Tomorrow I won't have dinner with you in Florence."

His heart sank. "Ok. I understand," he said.

"No, you don't. Tomorrow, I have dinner with you in Rome. I've just spoken to Cardinal Professor Doctor Arturo de Santis, and he is very very excited to help us. I give him full title because I don't know what you will call him. I call him Arturo cara mia, but you mustn't call him that."

David laughed. "I'll begin by calling him 'your eminence' and then he'll tell me how he wants to be addressed. That's amazing and wonderful news, Martina. How and where do we meet? Shall I hire a car?"

"No, there are very good trains, and we'll stay where I always stay when I visit Rome. It's a lovely hotel near to the Vatican called the Roma Giustiniano on the via Virgilio. We at the Uffizi get special rates there."

"No, I'm happy to pay. This is so good of you."

"Why waste money, darling. I'll book us in and I'll get the tickets for the train. Let's meet at the station fifteen minutes before the departure. I'll get my secretary to phone you with the details. So, until tomorrow, *addio per ora.*"

That night, and for the first time since leaving Australia, he found it hard to get to sleep. His recurring thought as he lay in bed was the nature of the room or rooms she'd be booking. A large suite with two bedrooms? Two single rooms? A large double room with a king-sized bed? But he had to be professional, as was she.

He was being stupid, acting like a schoolboy. He needed sleep if he was to function properly in the morning.

# PART, THE FIRST
### Artemisia Gentileschi…by my hand.

---

**In my beginning,** God created a girl child who commanded the earth and strove to reach upwards to the heavens. It would not be too boastful to claim that, even as a youngster, I had prodigious talent drawing and sketching, mixing amazing colours for my father and his students, and conceiving of how a passage from the Bible or some other aspect of our history could look when captured by the eye of an artist and made live on a canvas.

For years, I sat in my father's studio in the Via Corso in Rome, which was also our home. From here, and from time to time when he wasn't employed by other artists, he would teach his students how to draw or mix paints, to understand light and shadow, and how to create a smile or a frown by the merest inflection of a brush.

He would be commissioned by other painters, better

known men, to assist them complete their works. There, he was employed to paint figures of saints and other worthies on the walls of churches or huge canvasses for important people's houses. But from time to time, his status as an artist would be recognized by one of the worthies of the city, and he would be commissioned to paint a work for a nobleman. When that happened, he would be paid a large initial stipend, and we would buy wonderful things for the family home, as we knew that in a month or two, another part-payment would be due and when it was paid, then that was the best time of my young life, a time I relished both because I was with my father, and because I was painting. Of course, for my parents, it meant cloths from the Orient, meat and wine, imported French cheeses, and the freshest of fresh bread. But for me, my father's painterly success meant that instead of doing household chores, I could be free to practice my art.

It was also a time when I met and was taught by Michelangelo. He was a wild man, a drunkard, and in later life, he was accused of murder. But there are two men who enjoy the same forename, both artists of the highest calibre, both men who changed the very nature of the art of painting. Yet one who became a sculptor who rivaled and even exceeded the genius of the ancient Greeks. I talk not of Michelangelo Buonarroti, the sculptor who painted the ceiling in the Sistine Chapel and created the amazing figure of David which now stands in a square outside of the offices of the Medici family in central Florence. When my father worked in Florence, he visited their Uffizi to pay for a debt he owed, or sometimes to receive money from them, and I loved to go with him, and see from where the very wealthy Medici ran their businesses.

This isn't the Michaelangelo of whom I speak, a man who died two generations ago, more famous even than the man to whom I refer. Indeed, he was one of the three pillars of the house within which artists of today live and work. The others, of course, were Leonardo da Vinci and Raffaello Sanzio da Urbino, known then and now as Raphael. Indeed, although there were many great artists who lived and worked beside these three giants, without them, art today would be very different. Their vision, their genius, their way of capturing emotions through the inclination of an eyebrow, through a frown, through the gesture of a hand, was more than an inspiration to artists who followed them. It was a bible of artistic skills which those of us who followed could access merely by observing how they did what they did.

Even to this day, I cannot say whether I love greater or lesser the works of one of these compared with the others. Each has their place in my heart; each has infiltrated my mind. But of them, by far the most accessible is the work of the divine Michaelangelo.

Which is not to say that the sculptor was a greater artist than the painter, for the Michelangelo of whom I speak, the man who, along with my father, was my guide and mentor in putting true, unadorned feelings into my paintings, was not Buonarroti, but the other Michelangelo. His name is Caravaggio. Perhaps not as famous, but as painter, he was more innovative, more daring and vastly more confronting than Buonarroti. Visitors stare upwards at the Sistine Chapel and marvel at Adam and God and the angels and saints; but anybody who has seen Michelangelo Caravaggio's paintings, the agony in the faces, the dramas in the lighting, come away with feelings which transcend the human and approach the fire and light of the Divine.

The Michelangelo to whom I refer is the ruffian, the murderer, the beautiful and brilliant Caravaggio, a miscreant and ne'er-do-well, a drunkard and a violent man, who was also one of the most miraculous artists of his—and any other—day. It was he, the genius, who taught me the importance of chiaroscuro, using piercing light and menacing shadows to cause faces to be transfixed in an instant of fear or joy, hope or pain, making even the most ordinary objects gleam and command attention in blinding shafts of light. But he took chiaroscuro to new heights, creating an extreme of the technique which he called tenebrism to transfix the viewer and define the emotions in the faces of his subjects. When Caravaggio was painting his canvasses using this new and miraculous technique, it caused a sensation. Viewers were transfixed as they stood and stared. It was almost as though the figures in his painting, their faces lit by the most dramatic, arresting and invasive light, were about to jump out of the canvas and fall to the ground at the feet of the audience.

He was an amazing painter, a dear and valued friend of my father, and he became a loving and useful guide to me in my quest to become an artist. Yes, I was only eight or nine, possibly ten or slightly older when he first instructed me, but Caravaggio looked at my style and my ability to create figures, and helped me understand perspective, vectors, light and shadow. I think my father was uneasy at the closeness which Caravaggio and I established. He was my father's friend and confidante, and yet he spent much time with me, sitting cross-legged on the floor beside me as I sat on my stool, my canvas standing on an easel before me. He would watch me closely as I copied precisely what my father was painting. And as I applied brush to canvas, I could sense, from his body stiffening or from the softest "tut!" that I was about to paint incorrectly. I would look down at him, and he would use the subtlest movement of his finger, or even a nod of the head to tell me that my line wasn't accurate and would lead to an exaggeration; or he'd comment softly that my colour wasn't quite correct, or that my angle was wrong, or the line I was intending to use for a shoulder or a leg was too high or low on the canvas to represent the model lying there.

Perhaps it was because Caravaggio could see the impassioned potential that he was willing to give so much of himself. I don't know if my father was protecting my modesty or my talent from the voracious hands of Caravaggio, but from time to time, when he heard Michelangelo talking to me, he'd turn his head and look at us, our heads close together in secret conclave; then he'd walk over to where I was seated, leaving his model to lay still as a marble statue, look at my painting, and he'd criticise my work, or otherwise comment upon the advice Caravaggio had just given to improve it.

My father and I were as close and loving as a father and daughter can be, but when my mother died suddenly, we became closer. His encouragement of my art and my talents were only bounded by his demands of modesty, not allowing me to paint or even see nudes in his workshop. He said that it was because of the orders from the Vatican about a young girl painting naked men and women; but even if that were true, he imposed their rule harshly and acted more like a prison guard than an encouraging teacher. What he didn't know was that I was behind a curtain, peering through a tear, doing what his students were doing.

But it was not only concerning subjects for my paintings where he took on the role of a stern and censorious parent. Shortly after Mother's death, he also became quite strict in terms of my friendships. Some girls were allowed into my company, but if a boy, or a young man seemed interested in me, he would view our conversations suspiciously and if he thought that they were becoming intimate, he would suddenly come between us, often sending the poor youth slouching off in shame like a dog with his tail between his legs. So for much of my childhood and adolescence, my company was almost exclusively with my father, my brothers, our servants, and his artist friends.

And now I come to the moment when I must unveil a particular friend of my father, a painter, confidante, and mentor to him, and the man whom once I loved, but now I hate and detest with a venom which threatens to poison even me.

Agostino Tassi was a collaborator with my father when we lived in Rome. An painter of average talent, he thought he was a far greater artist then ever he was; a man who employed my father to paint the figures in his landscapes, especially those in the Palazzo Rospigliosi. It was a magnificent building on the Quirinal Hill, where the Baths of Constantine once stood, owned and paid for by the immeasurably wealthy Borghese family and taking pride of place in the centre of Rome. My father was immensely proud of his work in the Palazzo and also in the great hall of the Quirinal Palace itself, and considered those commissions as some of his finest productions.

Why do I mention Tassi, when my father worked with many painters, associated with others, and had students often in and out of the studio? And why have I already revealed the outlines, the ghostly images of my detestation of him before I've defined the cause of my fury? Because although I have previously and quite deliberately not mentioned his name, it was Agostino Tassi who raped me!

Once he'd *performed* the deed, once he'd *known* me, he told me he'd done it because he loved me. He promised to marry me. I was a woman of 18 but what did I know of love? I had lived in a cage since my mother died, and my father had the key. I knew so little of life. I would have married him, despite his having ravaged my innocence, until he reneged on his word a year later. That made my father furious, for my value as a bride had diminished. My father began proceedings in court to force this man to make good on his word, to restore my honour, and to redress the injustice which he had perpetrated.

These are all the things which I wish to tell you in this, the book of my life. But I race ahead. In those early days, my father was kept very busy, and Rome was a magnificent place for us as a family of artists. Though I was born in Rome, whenever I could, I accompanied my father to Florence where he had been born and sometimes had business, for I considered Florence my spiritual home, even if it wasn't the city of my birth. It was breathtaking and whenever I stayed, as often as I could, I would visit all of the glorious art which adorned its walls and piazzas.

In Rome, the city of my birth, as I lay in my bed, I would dream about returning to walk once more among the buildings of Florence, revel in its grandeur, its piazzas and squares, its churches and mansions. I wanted these as much as I did its verdant hills, its flowing rivers and the purity of the Florentine air. But Florence was also over-endowed with the greatest of artists, geniuses working as painters and sculptors, and so my father's decision to move to Rome meant much more work for a man like him. To have lived in Florence would have meant competing for commissions with the likes of Gian Lorenzo Bernini, Guido Reni, Andrea Pozzi, Guercino, and many more. At least the competition would have been fair and among equals. But that wasn't the competition he would have had to indulge in. No, in Florence, unlike in Rome or Pisa, one had to compete with ghosts.

For how could men today compete with gods whose ghosts still inhabit the salons and halls, the piazzas and frescos of Florence, and especially the minds and hearts of the inhabitants? Artists of a previous ago, such as Leonardo da Vinci, Michaelangelo Buonarroti, Sandro Botticelli, Giotto...need I say more? When those artists fill the minds of patrons and they expect their money to purchase a painting or a fresco or a sculpture as miraculous as those created by the gods who once walked the halls of art, then who among us is able to compete? And so my father, on a commission from a wealthy patron, left Florence for Rome.

While he lived in Rome, where I was born, father painted frescos and other works in the churches of Santa Maria della Pace, San Giovanni in Laterano, and most wonderful of all, the church of Santa Maria Maggiore. I was so proud of his work, and would watch him for hour after hour as he worked on instruction from some Cardinal or Bishop who demanded that he capture the essence of the biblical sentence selected, so that he could create it on canvas or as a fresco. Often the allegories he was commissioned to paint said more about the cardinal's personal preferences – his love of little boys or his hatred of women, or even his desire to harm a competing prelate – but none of that afflicted my father, for his income was derived from painting what he was told to paint, and not argue the theological importance of a mural or a fresco or a canvas.

He worked hard on his commissions, often discussed the ideas he had for representing the allegory on canvas with his students or, to my unending joy, with me. And then I would watch in amazement at how that wisp of an idea from the Cardinal transformed to became an actual image which his skills converted into a living and breathing drama in the lives of the subjects.

Later in his life, when I was a grown woman and his fame extended beyond the borders of the cities in which he worked, he was commissioned by Kings and Queens to visit their countries and paint for them. One of them was none other than Marie de Medici, the second wife of King Henry IV of France, who paid my father a fortune to go to Paris where he spent a couple of years. One of his paintings, the Public Felicity Triumphant over Dangers, defines happiness in the human spirit despite the menacing of storm-clouds in the background of the painting. It now on the walls of the Palais du Luxembourg. It is a glorious painting which shows woman proud and dominant and conquering her own deepest fears; as to whether it was painted from his memory of my unhappiness which transmuted into the woman I became today, I do not know.

Unlike his painting of happiness, father was unhappy at the court of Marie de Medici, and was glad to accept a fresh and exciting challenge from England. It was his crowning moment when King Charles of England employed him to become one of the Royal Painters.

How did this happen? Well, some time after he'd was employed by Marie de Medici, in 1626, he and my three brothers left Paris for England and became members of the household of the King's first minister, the Duke of Buckingham.

That was a happy moment in my life as well, for the King, an avid collector of art and patron to fine artisans, also invited me to join my father, and together we painted some wonderful pieces, some of which became part of the Royal Collection of both His Majesty himself, as well as his wife, the Queen.

His commissions came from Queen Henrietta Maria, the King's wife. He painted many fine works which the Queen was happy to hang in her palaces. Sadly, he died there thirteen years later. I'm sure he would have preferred to have been buried in his native Florence, but because of his status as Painter for the Royal Family, he was given a sumptuous farewell, and his body lies in the cold and unfriendly earth of England.

But I pace ahead. I am still at the moment when I transmuted from girl to woman. Not that I wish you to think that all my father's life, unlike mine, was an upwards trajectory of fame and fortune. There was a time in Rome, not long after he'd taken our family to live there, that our lives nearly collapsed into a state of anarchy and chaos. And it was all because of the company of artists and other reprobates with whom he associated.

Only a few years after we arrived in the city, while my beloved mother was still alive, though showing early signs of the illness which was to take her life, my father fell foul of the laws of the land. It was in August, 1603, and my father, in company with Michelangeo Caravaggio, Ottavio Leoni and some others, were carousing in an inn, drinking to the point of insensibility, that they stupidly and recklessly wrote some poems about some third-rate painter named Giovanni Baglione. Indeed, so bad was he as a painter, despite being commissioned by a number of wealthy worthies in Rome, that he eventually gave up painting, and instead became the writer and recorder of the lives of truly great artists, one of them being none other than Caravaggio himself, despite having taken this very man to court for offensive writing.

I don't wish to diverge too much from my own story, but what happened to my father and the other reckless artists gives you an indication of the life he lived. The already-mentioned Baglione had recently completed an altarpiece of the Resurrection of Jesus in one of the Jesuit churches, and somewhat stupidly went around saying that Caravaggio was insanely jealous of his work; Baglione even boasted that because of his genius, as great as that of Leonardo or Michaelangelo, it was he who had been favoured with the Jesuit's commission, and not the more famous Caravaggio. It was well known in our circles that Baglione had copied Caravaggio's style in his paintings, having little to contribute from his own talents.

Nonetheless, Caravaggio and my father and the others wrote these scurrilous poems about Baglione's lack of originality, deficient talent, limited capacity and miniscule aptitude, which they circulated among their friends. Of course, they were much ruder than I've suggested, and incorporated many of his body parts into their rhymes.

Yes, it caused great hilarity, but when the poems came to the notice of Baglione, he was furious, and needed to secure his reputation against the libels. So he took Caravaggio and my father and the others to court, citing slander because all of the scribes, and especially Caravaggio, he boldly claimed and affirmed before a Judge, were all jealous of Baglione's talents.

Of course, it was one thing to poke a vicious dog with a stick, but simple naivety not to expect it to attack you and bite your leg off; which is precisely what happened in court. Despite asking many artists to stand and give character evidence on his behalf, acclaiming him to be one of the most brilliant artists of his day, nobody, not one renowned artist, would stand up in a witness box in court, and aver that Baglione was as great an artist as was Caravaggio or my father Gentileschi. Quite the contrary; the fact that nobody would speak on his behalf was the greatest indictment possible against his talent as a painter.

But the man was utterly damned when some of the accused took the stand, and told the Judge just how bad was Baglione's work. While standing in the dock and giving testimony, Caravaggio said that he knew of no painter, of any repute, who thought that Baglione was a good painter, and that his altarpiece was a clumsy piece of work. He told the court it was the worst thing the tenth-rate painter had done, and that despite many painters of repute having seen it, not one, not a single person, had sought the good will to praise the painting.

But being the main instigator, and because Baglione was favoured by those who were important patrons in Rome, Caravaggio was found guilty, and sent to Tor di Nona prison after the trial as punishment. My father and the others were also found guilty and fined a paltry amount.

Of course, when he was released from prison, Caravaggio, joined by my father and the others, overnight became the heroes of the artistic community, as well as many in the public square. They were feted, and constantly surrounded by their peers, invited to gatherings in inns, and begged time and again to recite their slanders. All of this was too much for the chagrin of the victim of their ridicule. Despite crowing like a cock that he was the man who'd caused Caravaggio to be imprisoned, he soon realised that he was a figure of ridicule, and so withdrew into his house and was rarely seen in public.

So what was the extent of the courtroom victory for Baglione? Well, he was so damaged by what was said in court of his ability and works, that he received only minor commissions after that, which so diminished in a short amount of time, that his livelihood as a painter ceased, and he became a scribe to the genius of other artists. One of the lives he wrote was that of Caravaggio and although he was generous in his statements about the painter's genius, one could tell by reading his words that Baglione still harboured a deep and abiding hatred.

Of course, my father and Caravaggio were more than just drinking companions and artistic friends. My father, generous and open-minded, recognized the eternal and universal genius of the younger man, and sought to learn from him, to improve his art and to quietly learn the lessons which he absorbed from the way in which Caravaggio created his works of art. He paid full obeisance to the younger man's talents, asking questions which revealed new techniques and methods which my father than incorporated into the use of light in many of his paintings.

And I, too, as Caravaggio's student, watched in amazement at the deftness of his hand, his use of colours I'd never have dreamed about using, and his bold yet delicate brush strokes to create a glance or a smirk, an arched eyebrow or a frown which gave a Saint's countenance an unworldly, yet knowable expression. At this time, since his creations of the two major works about Saint Matthew in the Contarelli Chapel of the church of San Luigi dei Frencesi, he was the most famous painter in Rome, possibly in the whole of Italy, and he was bombarded night and day with commissions, most of which he rejected.

And from him, from dear Michelangelo Caravaggio, I learned to create drama in my subjects. It was he who taught me the importance of observation which I used in my later life as a painter. From his instructions, I learned to look not at my subject's faces, but into them, beyond them, into their minds and thoughts to highlight the depth of emotional intensity when they were *in extremis*—at the point of cutting off a man's head and serving it up to her community on a platter, at the point of killing a man for the crimes he had committed—and all of this was accomplished because I painted not my subject, not the model, not even the moment, but the anger and disgust which was formed in her mind in those precious seconds before or as she committed the act of violence and revenge.

For a number of years, Caravaggio and my father enjoyed a deep and abiding friendship, interrupted only by the younger artist's times in prison or escaping the authorities or hiding in the villa of some patron. Yes, he lived a wicked life, always fighting, duelling, drinking, carousing, and causing mayhem in the city. It was only because of his angelic genius as a painter that he somehow stayed alive and wasn't murdered by some jealous husband or aggrieved citizen.

Why? Because he was protected by his patrons, who knew well of his faults as a man, but who were desperate for his talents as an artist. When he was in a fight, or he'd thrown a plate of artichokes over a waiter in fury at some minor disrespect, he would draw his sword, fight whoever was at hand, and then escape through a window or back kitchen and flee to the gates of his latest patron, begging the guards for protection.

Yet all of this came to an end in May of the year 1606 when an incident occurred, punishment for which not even Caravaggio could avoid; and the punishment would have been death! Perhaps it was a gambling debt, or perhaps it was because the two men were in love with the same prostitute, Fillide Melandroni, but Caravaggio engaged in a duel with the scion of a wealthy gangster family, Ranuccio Tommasoni. The two men hated each other and had fought many times in the past, but this time, Caravaggio went just too far, and not only did he triumph over Tommasoni, but as the man lay on the ground, his arm wounded and blood pouring out onto the street, Caravaggio lost all reason, and took down the man's trousers and castrated him. Screaming in pain and fury, Caravaggio then pierced his heart with the sword, and left him to bleed to death in the street. Perhaps Tommasoni was the whore's pimp and it was a question of money, or perhaps it was because of love. I have no idea. They also say that it was politically motivated because the Tommasoni family was notoriously in favour of the Spaniards who were threatening Rome at the time.

I repeat that I don't know. But it caused a tragedy in my life, because Caravaggio was forced to flee Rome for

Naples and then Sicily, and I never saw him again.

Which, although I've avoided it to this moment, brings me to Tassi and what he did to me.

The following morning, at just past 11.00, they arrived in Rome's Termini railway station. As they walked down the length of the platform, David kept wondering about the sleeping arrangements they'd have tonight in their hotel, although any hopes he might have had of an intimate dinner evaporated when Martina told him that she'd invited Cardinal de Santis to join them, and he'd eagerly agreed.

"Shall we taxi or walk to the Vatican?" David asked.

She looked at his two heavy bags, full of clothes for an indefinite stay in Europe, and without replying, headed for the taxi rank. "First the hotel to deposit the bags; then a walk to the Vatican, which is only ten minutes away."

As they waited for a taxi to arrive, he said, "You'd think that with their creative flare, the Italians could have come up with a better name for a station than 'terminus'. Rome's airport has one of the most charismatic names

-Leonardo da Vinci. Why wasn't your central railway station named after a famous Roman, like the Medici when they were Popes here, or the Orsini or the Colonnas... or maybe even the Borgias. Now there's a name for a station....Stazione Borgia. Or do you think people would be too scared to use it?"

Martina smiled. "Actually, the train station already has a wonderful name. It's called after the district, and the district took its name from the Baths of the Roman Emperor, Diocletian, which were across the road from the entrance. In Latin, the word for hot is *'thermae'*, which was corrupted into terminus, which means 'the final destination'. So the name of the station is, all at the same time, geographical, eponymous and descriptive."

David smiled. "Remind me never to be smart with you. You know too much."

She laughed. "Only my field, darling. Take me into the West Australia desert, and ask me to identify a rock, and I'm useless."

A taxi arrived and they journeyed to the hotel. At the reception desk, he tried to understand what she was saying, but with his few words in her language, and because she spoke Italian so quickly, he was lost. He tried to look at the pieces of paper she'd just signed, but the receptionist whipped them away before he could see what types of rooms, or room, they'd been given. The porter took the suitcase into a luggage room so that they were there for the evening when they returned from the Vatican. And as they began to walk through the streets of Rome, David wondered whether he dare ask what the sleeping arrangements were for that, or any other evening while he was in the city. But he decided that he'd find out soon enough.

Regardless of whether she wanted a romantic liaison with him, or he with her, or whether it was just a purely professional meeting, or whether he should try his luck with her….regardless, he vowed that nothing would affect his relationship with Jackie. What happened in Rome, stayed in Rome. She was certainly an exceptionally attractive woman, but his attraction was as far as he could allow it to go. She was a professional….and he was there for a purpose. But….

It was a short and invigorating walk from the hotel to St. Peter's Square. But instead of crossing the Square, full of tens of thousands of tourists, they instead walked to the right of the vast St Peter's Basilica. As they crossed, Martina said, "His offices aren't in St. Peters or the ecclesiastical offices, but on the Viale Vaticano on the northern side of the city. Just around the corner from the entrance to the Vatican museums. The Vatican Art Gallery used to be in the Borgia apartments, but Cardinal Ratti, Pope Pius XI, ordered a new building just before the Second World War, because the collection was so vast."

David was confused. "You said Vatican Museums. There are more than one?"

"Oh my dear, you have no idea. It's the biggest collection imaginable, housed in 54 separate museums, some small, some immense. It houses 7,000 pieces of matchless paintings, frescos, sculptures and more...so much more."

David asked, "So who created the collection?"

"It was the inspiration of Pope Julius II. The Warrior Pope. And it was a single sculpture which was his inspiration. Some workmen were digging to plant new vines in gardens of the Santa Maria Maggiore at the beginning of the 16<sup>th</sup> Century. They dug up the amazing sculpture of Laocoön and His Sons. It's a huge statue, a masterpiece of sculpture from the ancient world, from the island of Rhodes. The sculpture shows the Trojan priest <u>Laocoön</u> and his sons Antiphantes and Thymbraeus being attacked by sea serpents. It's breathtakingly brilliant and was even mentioned in praise by Pliny the Elder.

"Anyway, Pope Julius asked Michaelangelo Buonarroti to examine it and determine whether it was worth keeping. He was amazed by it, and strongly recommended that the Pope bring it to Rome to become a centerpiece for the new St. Peter's Basilica. The Pope put it into a room, with other sculptures he liked, and that was the beginning of the Vatican Museum," she said, just as they approached the front door of the offices of the Museum.

Martina asked to be announced to His Eminence, Cardinal de Santis. Moments later they were escorted into his office. He was wearing trousers and a black shirt with a clerical collar, a huge pectoral cross, and a Cardinal's red skullcap. As they entered, he stood from behind his desk, and walked around to greet them. Martina kissed his ring, and then he gave her a giant bear hug, kissing her on both cheeks.

"My dearest friend. How are you," he said in perfect Italian-accented English. "And you must be the man who discovered what we hope and pray is a lost Artemisia."

David walked two steps forward, grasped his hand and kissed his ring.

"Eminence, I'm David Cabot. And yes, I discovered what I hope is an Artemisia in an art gallery in Sydney,

Australia."

"Come, my dears, sit down, and tell me all about it. From what Martina told me, David, it's currently being authenticated in London at the Victoria and Albert."

David nodded, but before he could explain, Martina said, "I've sent over Dr. Francesco Marinelli, who's an expert on early Baroque."

"Ah! Yes, Francesco. He was one of my students. Very good. Bright. Well, he'll be able to determine its authenticity. I assume that other experts from other countries have been sourced," said the Cardinal.

"Yes, of course. From France, England and Germany. The people in the V&A want a panel of experts to determine it."

The Cardinal nodded and turned to David. "And if it's authenticated, what will you do?"

"I've given it a lot of thought, Eminence. I could hang it in my lounge-room in Sydney, but then only my wife and children would see it, which would be criminal—"

"No more criminal than what the Borgias and the Medici did when they commissioned a painting. It was just for them," he said.

David nodded. "Or I could put it out on loan to a museum, and then the world could see it."

"Better, much better. Or you could sell it. You must have thought of that, David," said Martina. "It's like winning the lottery. You bought if for a handful of dollars, and if it's genuine, it could be worth hundreds of thousands of dollars; maybe even millions."

"True, and of course I've thought of doing that. Except that we really don't need the money, and to be honest, I really like the idea of owning it. I'd never even heard of Artemisia before I bought the painting, but now, well frankly, I'm in awe of her. I want to see all of her paintings and see where mine fits in the scheme of her work," he said.

"And then as the owner, you'll feel like a Medici or a Borgia. How many of us can say we own an Italian masterpiece? Except me, of course. I guess I'm lucky," said the Cardinal. "I own over 7000, but then as Martina will tell you, I've always been a bit greedy."

"Talking of greed, are you still able to come to dinner with us tonight, Arturo cara mia?" asked Martina.

"I would love to join you. My secretary has taken the liberty of booking us in to a charming little restaurant which serves the best food, and has a small but immaculate wine list. I hope that's alright."

They both nodded.

"Now," said the Cardinal, "How can I help you? You said, Martina *carissima*, that there could be documents in the *Biblioteca Apostolico Vaticano* relating to Artemisia. Yes, there could be. And they may or may not be accurately documented. We may not even know of their existence. Many of our most ancient documents are sitting there, piled one on top of the other. One day we'll sort them out, but for a church that thinks in millennia, and not days, it's a big job.

"And you can't enter our Library and just start searching. You have to know what you're seeking. We have over a million books, nearly 100,000 Codices, vast collections of letters to and from Popes. Our collections date to ancient times, but the real library has been collecting and keeping records and documents for over 600 years. Can you give me an idea of where to begin looking?"

David couldn't think of an answer, but fortunately, Martina said immediately, "If we go chronologically, then we could start at her trial, which was in 1612, but that's probably too early. We know that she was illiterate, and only learned how to read and write as an adult, presumably long after that, when she was in Florence. Or perhaps Naples. She died around 1652 or 3, and was in decline mentally and professionally. So if we begin the search in, say, 1640, when she was perhaps still at the top of her game, and she might have been in a reflective mood, we could find something. No?"

The Cardinal shrugged. "Who can say what's in the Archives. But we will look."

"We may have your permission, Arturo *cara mia*, but do we also need permission from the chief librarian?" asked Martina.

The Cardinal smiled. "Better you leave him to me. I've already asked him for permission, which he has granted. Frankly, I doubt he would give you permission if you just approached him. He's a very difficult man. Very Conservative."

Frowning, Martina said, "Cardinal Tisserant? But he's a beautiful old man. I've met him many times, and he's always been open and willing to discuss my researches."

"Regretfully," said Cardinal Santis, "my dear old friend Eugène Tisserant passed away last year, and was replaced by His Eminence, Cardinal Antonio Samorè. Not the most cooperative of my brethren on the Sacred College of Cardinals. He was all set to become the Patriarch of Venice following the death of Cardinal Urbani a few years ago, but was pipped at the post by Bishop Luciani, which nearly drove him crazy. It was a roadblock in his path to the Papacy. In a fit of pique, Samorè resigned as Prefect of the Congregation for the Discipline of the Sacraments, a post he'd been appointed to by Pope Paul, so to mollify him, he was named as Librarian for the Holy See. So he sits in his library, brooding and plotting his vengeance, scheming and lobbying his brother Cardinals, and just waiting for His Holiness to meet his maker. Then he'll lobby like crazy to become Pope, just like the Renaissance Popes. And if that happens, God help Catholic women around the world."

Stunned by the Cardinal's frankness, David said, "Will we have problems when we're in the Library, despite your imprimatur?"

"I don't think so. He's far too important in his own mind to bother with what scholars are doing, unlike Cardinal Tisserant, who would sit and talk to the scholars and suggest ways in which the Library could help them in their studies," said Cardinal de Santis. "But regardless of him, Cardinals and Bishops and Priests are always sitting in the Library, doing their research, so if I come in and sit with you, he won't pay any attention. Also, I know most of the library staff, the custodians, and I have a good relationship with many of them, so he won't present us with any problems.

"So," continued the Cardinal, "let's talk about what you hope to find about Artemisia in our Library. We have, as you know, a copy of the record of her trial and Inquisition. But what more could there be?"

"That's what we don't know. But once she'd learned how to read and write, there's every likelihood that she could have written letters to Princes of the Church who might have commissioned her to paint for their palaces. Also, we know from her paintings, done after the trial, that she was still in a state of anger and fury at what had happened to her. So there's every chance that she's written a philippic, which might be buried somewhere in the Archives," Martina said.

"A what?" asked David.

"A philippic. It's a bitter denunciation against somebody, usually somebody in power," said the Cardinal. "It's a term which was introduced into the language after the Greek orator Demosthenes denounced King Philip of Macedon for his imperialism. The Roman orator Cicero also used it."

David shook his head. "I'm so out of my depth among you two."

"Stop it David. You're a man of the earth, of rocks

and soils. Arturo and I have spent our lives with the language of painting and literature. What's that American expression…different folks, different strokes."

"Yes," said Cardinal de Santis. "I can see somebody like Artemisia writing a philippic. But what worries me is that because she will probably be railing against men, or the Catholic hierarchy because of what she's suffered, the leading men of her day in the Vatican might have destroyed her letters, or hidden them out of sight, or worse, much worse, they might have slotted them into the pages of some book which hasn't been opened for nearly 400 years," said the Cardinal.

"And that's another thing which concerns me," said Martina. "I've been thinking about this since we decided to come here to Rome. Paper was incredibly expensive in those days. So was parchment. Her original work could have been buried by somebody later in a palimpsest."

"That thought occurred to me," the Cardinal said, "and if so, finding it will be like finding a needle in a haystack."

"Sorry to sound like a broken record," said David, "but what was that word you just used?"

"Palimpsest. A major problem for historical researchers. Because paper and parchment was out of the reach of ordinary people, they were often reused. So a letter or document would be written, and then later on, maybe years later, somebody comes along, scratches out what was originally written, and then writes his own document on top. All that scholars can usually see is the quill marks of the original. Often we can determine what was first written, but it makes life very difficult for the researcher."

Depressed, David said, "I hadn't realised how difficult this was going to be."

Martina smiled. "And when you go into the desert to find gold, is there a map which points to the exact location of the lode, or do you have to do a lot of research and soundings before you start digging?"

"Fair point," David said. "OK, so when can we go into the library?"

"Tomorrow. There is a limit to the number of scholars at any one time. Appointments have to be made, even for a Cardinal. So, off you go, children. Go and become tourists in the Museum or the Art Gallery. Relax and tonight we dine and relax."

It was, indeed, a perfectly relaxed and enjoyable afternoon, followed by a gloriously resplendent and delicious dinner in a charming little restaurant close to the Vatican.

The afternoon had been spent by David and Martina walking the corridors of the Vatican's art galleries. She acted as his personal tour guide, explaining the heritage, histories and place in the pantheon of art of each of the paintings, telling him stories about the artist who'd painted it, the circumstances of its creation, the nuances of technique and style that separated this artist from that, this time period from others. Unlike a tour guide whose spiel allowed little divergence from what had been memorized, Martina's knowledge of the artist, the time and the place was so extensive, that she was like an endlessly fascinating story-teller.

When they'd gone for a break in the afternoon at the Vatican's café to enjoy a coffee and a pastry, she asked him frankly whether she was giving him too much information.

"I am a bully when it comes to art," she said. "It's such a massive subject that sometimes, I forget that not everybody eats, sleeps and breathes Michaelangelo and Versace, Leonardo and Caravaggio."

He laughed and reached across to hold her hand. She squeezed his and smiled. "You know," he told her, "a couple of years ago, my wife and I took a trip to the island of Indonesia. We hired a car and drove down the entire spine of the island, from west to east. With us was a guide, an expert on the island. We called it our NAFT tour."

"NAFT?" said Martina. "What's NAFT?"

"This guide insisted that we stop every five minutes to examine another Hindu shrine or religious monument, climb all over it, and he'd spend all his time explaining why on this temple the elephants were pointing this way, whereas on the previous temple, they'd been pointing that way. It was so detailed, we called it our NAFT tour..... not another fucking temple."

Martina snorted out laughing, causing people on nearby tables to turn and stare.

"The point is, Martina, that what you're telling me is endlessly fascinating. I feel I'm getting a tutorial on art from a brilliant tutor, and I can't tell you how much I appreciate it nor how thrilled I am," he said.

She squeezed his hand again, and then continued to drink her coffee. "Good. I'm glad. Because we've only explored three salons. We still have dozens to go, and we're only up to the 16th century. And we're not leaving here until I've shown you the ceiling of the Sistine Chapel."

Later that night, they arrived at the restaurant without returning to their hotel. The meal was the very best of Italian cuisine. Simple, straight forward, but superbly crafted and utterly delicious. They both allowed Cardinal de Santis to order for the table.

During the main course of the meal, David said, "Eminence, I'm a bit concerned about going to the Library tomorrow. My presence is unnecessary, as both you and Martina are the experts. And isn't it possible that Cardinal Samorè will wonder what an Australian geologist is doing, looking for information about Artemisia?"

Cardinal de Santis shrugged. "That doesn't worry me. He won't be interested in you if he sees me with you. No, my friend, what worries me is not the Samorè of the Library, but the Samorè of the Sistine Chapel. What he will do when the Pope dies and we Cardinals are in a Holy Conclave. My issue with that man concerns the current health and welfare of the Pope. His Holiness is now 79 years of age, and far from a well man. His papacy has been full of tensions and traumas, and being Pope has not been kind to his health. I fear he won't last much longer before he ascends into the arms of the Almighty.

"And His Eminence, Cardinal Samorè is the first to

recognize this and to take advantage. He's like a hyena on the African veldt, waiting to feast on the flesh of a weakened creature, circling and keeping his distance but always looking....looking. His eyes are everywhere, and anywhere. His running of the Library doesn't concern me....his running for elevation to the Papacy before the present incumbent is dead, does. The man is so conservative, so rooted in the Church standing her ground against the demands of modernity, that the world will march forward while the Universal Church is stuck in the 13th Century."

Martina said, "But when His Holiness passes on, nobody in the Sacred College would elect such a conservative; surely! And isn't the question whether he has sufficient support in the Sacred College of Cardinals. If you, as a Cardinal, have been able to recognize how he would hold the church back, and the damage it would do, then surely your brothers can see the same deficits and understand why he wouldn't make a good pope."

Slowly, sadly, Cardinal de Santis shook his head and said softly, "Regretfully no. Many of my brethren are little more than myrmidons, living out their lives and protecting themselves and supporting the man they favour to be elected as the next Pope in the hope that he will return their favours by preferential treatment. It saddens me to say, but...."

"I'm sorry, yet again and I know I must sound like an ignoramus, but that description you just used. Myrmidons? What's that?"

Martina explained. "In Homer's Iliad, the Myrmidons were the soldiers of Achilles. They were loyal automata, men who killed mercilessly, and never questioned orders. Today, they're best described as robots."

"Which describes perfectly many of the older cardinals. All they want is the comforts of a quiet life, which my brother Cardinal Samorè has promised them if they vote for him," said Cardinal de Santis. "I don't doubt that most of them are fervent Catholics with the best interests of the Church in their hearts, but at their ages, they haven't got the ability to see the world beyond themselves and their needs. The younger ones, the African and Asian and South Americans all have the universal view of the Church; they see the plight of the vast numbers of impoverished men and women and especially the children in the Third World, and wish to relieve their suffering, using the Church as the instrument which will encourage their governments to take action. These newer Cardinals have zest and spirit and courage;

but the older Italians and Germans are hide-bound in tradition, steeped in two thousand years of history and are like the immovable rock. And sadly, these people tend to hold sway in the Conclaves."

"Are you in the running to become Pope?" asked David.

The Cardinal laughed. "I would immediately reject it in the unlikely event that it was offered. I have no pastoral experience. I could be a wonderful Pope for the Universal Art Gallery, but not for the Universal Catholic Family. Outside of the art community, I'm barely known. I have no support within the College. I'm not a politician. How could I be persuasive when I'm dealing with the sorts of ignoramuses my position means that I have to deal with, like some of the world leaders elected to run their countries. How could I talk to them? Oh my God, listen to the way I'm speaking. What if I'm overheard? So undiplomatic. Another reason I must never even contemplate being Pope. I'd say things which would start World War Three."

Martina laughed. "Yes, you've never been a diplomat. I remember once you saying to an artist who was seeking your imprimatur, '*Have you thought of becoming a house painter?*' I agree, dearest Arturo, that as an academic you're peerless, but putting your backside on the throne of St. Peter would be a disaster."

"Agreed. So to answer your question, David, no, absolutely not. God forbid the Holy Spirit descends on my brethren in Conclave and whispers my name in their ears," he said.

They walked back from the restaurant to their hotel, just fifteen minutes away. Rome was cold, but the warmth of the food and the wine stayed with them on their journey.

After Martina had hugged and kissed Cardinal de Santis goodbye at the steps of his apartment, David and she wandered through laneways, avoiding the main roads. They talked about her love of the Cardinal as a father figure and mentor, and about David's work as a geologist. Yet she didn't ask him about his wife, his family, leaving David to wonder if the omission was deliberate.

As they walked, she linked arms with him as she chatted. It was a natural, fluid, and very European move, probably the sort of things most Italian women did without thinking. But it touched David deeply and he wondered what would happen when they reached their suites.

Their bags had already been taken up to their rooms,

which were adjoining. He wondered whether or not there was an interconnecting door.

"Well," she said, fitting the key into her lock, "it's been a wonderful day. Thank you, David, for being such a charming companion. I hope you sleep well, darling, because tomorrow is going to be full of excitement and adventure, in between hours of boredom."

She kissed him on both cheeks, entered her room, and closed the door. It was so finite, so defined by the loud click of her door's lock, that all he could do was to phone Jackie, and then go to sleep.

# PART, THE SECOND

———◆———

**Tassi…** my brain feels it's going to explode when I even think of the name of the man to took my innocence and spent a year engaged to me to stop my father from prosecuting him. Only when we found out that he was already married did we begin the prosecution.  Years ago, many men tried to seduce me because I was a handsome woman, with a fine body, an attractive face, long and luxurious hair and a smile which was like the light of a dozen candles. But I always managed to ward off their advances, their exploring hands and diverted their seductive intentions.

Let me repeat, reader of the future, that I am writing of my life today, and I don't know when in the coming years, it will be read. So let me tell you of the Italy into which I was born, an Italy which, I sincerely hope, is very different for the lot of women than Italy today.

In my day, sex, for most men, and for a small but renown number of girls and women, was the easiest available and certainly the cheapest commodity in the large cities. Some older and uglier women were called *Pani* because a night with them was as cheap a loaf of bread; others were respectable women during the night, but added to their family income during the day when their husbands were at work.

Prostitutes were available at all times of the day, either in bordellos, or, for higher class women, as mistresses with their own separate apartments, and in the most elevated levels, with their own servants and retainers. Of course, I'm talking about the mistresses of Dukes and Counts, of Cardinals and Bishops and, in the days when the Borgia and Medici controlled the catholic church, of Popes themselves.

But for the religious faithful, and the priests who led communities, these were also the awful days of the assaults by the protestant preachers in the North who were constantly assailing the Papacy for crimes and sins against God, the people and Nature. Their attacks were relentless, loud and damaging. As word slowly spread to the common people about what the priests in charge of our Faith had been doing since the crucifixion of our Lord, widespread discontent had grown and grown. Before the denunciations by the protestors of the North, nobody had dared to question the priesthood, nor to ask "why" when a new ecclesiastical tax was imposed. But then the protestors from the lands of the Dutch, the Germans and the Swiss demanded answers from prelates and bishops who were answerable to nobody. And the hierarchy of the Catholic Universal Church didn't like it at all.

The greatest complaints of all were made against charging impoverished believers for Indulgencies, where money was raised from the bereaved to pay for the departed's path to Heaven. God only knows whether He raised a soul from Purgatory into Heaven, but without question, the money raised the dome of St. Peters in Rome close to the skies.

No wonder the Northern protestors against the Papacy railed against the immorality and venality of Rome. Indulgencies paid for the wastefulness, the immorality and the lusts of Pope Leo X, Giovanni de Lorenzo de'Medici, the most inglorious and disgusting Pope since the time of the Blessed St. Peter. It was he, Giovanni de'Medici, who said on his elevation to the Chair of Peter, "*Since God has given us the Papacy, let us enjoy it.*"

He needed a lot of money to enjoy it, and so he let

loose Johann Tetzel, a Dominican friar who travelled throughout the world selling these Indulgencies. His rallying cry was '*When a coin in the coffer rings, the soul from Purgatory springs.*'

And by God, did those coffers ring. I don't know if any souls sprang into Heaven when their poverty-stricken relatives dropped their hard-earned coins into his grasping coffers, but the money given to the Church paid for the building of St. Peters Basilica.

So the priests and the vast structure of the Catholic faith set about securing their position in the holy order and mounted a defense against the accusations, which then became an attack against those who spread the information.

It was, and still is, called the counter-reformation, a time when the Catholic Church reacted with determination, violence and vengeance against the reformation, especially those in lands such as Holland and Denmark, England and Germany, where preachers accused the Pope and the Cardinals of theft and sexual amorality, of simony in their promotions, and rapacity against the people. But what brought everything to a head were these indulgencies. These were slips of paper on which was written a promise by the Pope that a dead relative currently in Limbo or Purgatory, would be raised by the payment of a sum of money inscribed on the paper, into a level closer to Jesus, God and the angels in heaven.

No wonder that the northern priests were furious with the Pope, especially when his agents were going around cities with their collecting cans, fooling the gullible, and reciting rhymes to convince the faithful that their payment would go directly to the benefit of their dead mothers or fathers, wives or husbands, sons or daughters.

Of course, the Church putting its bony fingers into the pockets of the poor and gullible was nothing new. Five hundred years ago, in the times of the first Crusades against the Musslemen of Arabia, the church had used promises of benefit in the afterlife and remission of worldly sins to men who were willing to take up arms and fight. But needing more money to fund its wars against the followers of Mohammed, it told those unwilling to become soldiers of the Cross that they could pay for their unwillingness to serve, which would still remit their sins and even they, on payment, could enter the Elyssian Fields of Heaven.

And so it went on. The church continued to claim that it, not prayer or goodness, was the gateway to the remission of sins. It announced that it had a treasury of indulgences, the merits of Christ and His Saints, which only it, the Catholic Universal Church, could dispense to believers. Pope Clement VI, in 1343, even said that *'the merits of Christ are a treasure of indulgences.'*

And the money rolled into its coffers until a monk put a stop to it. A monk abused by the Church as I was abused by our courts of justice.

Because these indulgences were nothing more than a money-earning scheme created by the Popes, somebody had to take a stand, and say "Enough!" A man who realised that while the Church gave people hope for the final destination of their beloved dead, they were also robbing the poor blind. These benighted people were paying good money to the Church, even if it meant going without food or warmth in winter. So a century ago, this monk called Martin Luther wrote a document which he nailed to a door of some church, and the words he wrote, in his native language of German, have spread throughout the other nations, translated into French and Italian and English and Spanish....and what he said had caused the greatest consternation in all of these lands.

You may wonder how I know all of these things. After all, for much of my life, I was illiterate and my words were inscribed in the faces and bodies of my paintings.

I could not read more than a few words, until I was in Florence, and a pamphlet written by Luther was read to me by a Priest, who stood there and told us that the words he was reading indicated that Luther had recanted his heresies, and that this pamphlet was proof that he had seen the light.

But did he tell the truth, or was he lying about the words he was reading? There was no way I could have known, and so I paid a school teacher to come to my house and teach me how to read and write; which he did, and I have been doing so ever since.

And my greatest moment of glory was to read the very same pamphlet which the priest had read to me, and realised that he had lied in what he'd said. The pamphlet laid more accusations against the Pope and the College of Cardinals, but now that I could read, I doubted everything which any churchman said to me.

Perhaps it's because, as a literate and capable woman, I am still devout and a passionate student of the Faith. No, I'm joking. Indeed, it's quite the opposite. For since my rape and the injustices of what happened to me, I have turned my back on my religion, denied my faith, and become a non-believer of such passion and militancy that I will not allow a priest onto my property, nor will I allow a crucifix into my house. My paintings tell stories from the Bible, but that's what they are – stories.

And so, in my adulthood, I have read all of Luther's writings translated into my language, and marvel at their simplicity, their elegance, and the genius of a man who had the courage to stand up and proclaim to the world, while being judged so unfairly by the Inquisition, *"here I stand, I can do no other, God help me."*

Luther established what true repentance was, and denied the link between the Pope's power as a representative of God, and his inability to grant remission of sins as the Vicar of Christ. He said that the canons of the Church apply only to the living and can't be extended into purgatory on behalf of the already dead. And that while the Pope and his Priests can intercede on behalf of a dead person, remission is dependent on God's will alone, and nothing that the Pope can do or say can make a difference. But what he said which struck a chord of glory with the populace, was that the indulgent nature of indulgences renders them contrary to true repentance because they dull the conscience.

Oh Glory to great Martin Luther. Wonderful man that he was. That for me was the stopper in the jug of wine, the full stop at the end of a written letter, the last and most accurate brushstroke to perfect a subject's face forever on a canvas.

And so, years after the injustices perpetrated against me, I entered into a feeling of grace with myself, a grace absent of God and Angels, or the remission of sin and the need for expiation. The fury remained, as did the paroxysms of indignation, but any feeling of shame and self-abuse I felt evaporated when I read and studied what Luther had written all those years ago.

Of course, the Church was a fifteen hundred year old body which had suffered assaults from the Romans, schisms from within, attacks by Mohammedans, wars and revolts; and even though this was a serious offensive against its authority, when a body's history is as long and intense as that of the Church, it has many resources upon which to draw.

So the church rose up as a united body and damned and condemned and created an entire army of priests whose job it was to undermine and answer and refute the claims which Luther and the other protestants made. And the militancy of the counter-reformation spread into the towns and cities of the land, so that any adverse comment made about a drunken priest, or a groping Bishop and choirboys, would be reported to the ecclesiastical authorities, and some Jesuitical person would visit the miscreant's house like the Angel of Death and utter the sternest of warnings.

So even though sex and drunkenness and licentiousness were as prevalent today as they were fifty year ago in the days of the Borgia and Medici Popes, it was more subtle, better concealed, and less overt.

The main complaint of the Protestants was against the wealth of the Cardinals and the Pope himself, as exemplified by the magnificent palaces in which they lived. And with what were their walls and ceilings adorned? By the very paintings which they paid artists like my father and Caravaggio, Donatello, Titian and Bernini to create. So indirectly, my father and his colleagues were being accused of theft from the public.

Which is why sex and drunkenness, amorality and other antisocial and reckless behaviours, were so greatly condemned by the priests in their churches, who were encouraged to do so by their Monsignors, who in turn were instructed to do so by their bishops, who had been ordered to do so by their Cardinals from a demand for obedience to the Magisterium of the Church as mandated by the Pope. As I remember, the pope in those days was Alessandro Ottaviano de'Medici, who was also called

Papa Lampo – the Lightning Pope – because he died of chills only four weeks after his election.

Or no...wait...I don't think it was him after all. My memory is strong, but the numbers of changes of Pope over the past hundred years, confounds even the most committed of faithful. So if it wasn't the Lightning Pope, then it must have been the one who followed, Camillo Borghese, Pope Paul V; yes, it was he, for he reigned for sixteen of the most tumultuous years the Papacy has ever known. Not the kind of tumults caused by the Medicis or the Borgias, who were immoral, and turned the Basilica of St. Paul and the Vatican itself in Rome into little more than a brothel, but the tumults I've already mentioned – against the majesty of the Faith.

The tumult which was caused by Paul V was because it was he who put poor Galileo Galilei from Pisa on trial before the Roman Inquisition. Apparently, Galileo had written documents in which he claimed that he had measurements and observations which proved, like other astronomers before him, especially those from the North, that the Earth was in perpetual motion around the sun. This was, in the eyes of the Inquisition, a reinterpretation of the Bible, a violation of the tenets of the Council of Trent and as close to Protestant heresy as possible. To have demoted the Earth, on which the Christ once strode, to the same status of a planet like Venus or Jupiter or Mercury, was a heresy which could not be tolerated by the Church. Christ and the Earth on which He walked, had to be the centre of the universe, or else what was the Catholic Faith? An afterthought among the stars?

So the Pope told him that his support of Nikolei Copernicus could not be tolerated, that the earth was the centre of the Universe and that the Sun travelled for all eternity around us, paying obeisance on its journey because Christ the Saviour had been born and was crucified here. The Sun and the other planets, both near and far, travelled around the Earth on Aristotle's Crystalline spheres.

But the trial and findings against Galileo by the Inquisition caused him to be locked under house arrest, unable to speak to people or publish his work, and even forced him to recant his scientific findings. I had already met him in Florence, but it was when he was under house arrest, that I wrote to him and began a correspondence which opened my eyes about the veracity of measurement and calculations, of science and method, and the inaccuracies, errors and imprecisions of faith-based facts. After all, to say to a student of Nature such as Galileo, that God was correct in absolute when He wrote in the Bible that He created the heavens and the earth, light and dark, the waters of the deep and the stars in the firmament, all in seven days, and that this must be true because it was a matter of Biblical fact, was simply ludicrous. Galileo's measurements proved that science was right, and the Bible was wrong. The earth was not the centre of the Universe.

Even when he was forced, upon the threat of the pain of torture, to recant his conviction in print, that the earth moves around the sun; even when he was forced to deny his calculations, his theses, his teachings and concede that the earth is not the still and silent centre of the universe, around which the sun and the planets rotate, he said, as he was leaving the priests and bishops and Cardinals in the Court of the Inquisition, *"Yet still….it moves."*

I howled in laughter when he responded to me in one of his letters that this was how he left the Inquisition, and entered house arrest. He even managed to smuggle out of house arrest one of the compass instruments he used in his measurements, in order that I could use it as an artifact in one of my paintings, *The Allegory of Inclination.*

I still treasure Galileo's letters to me; they are so full of thought and consideration, of his view of the universe not as the product of a deity, but as a vast and indefinable machine, perfectly oiled and moving without the friction which causes earthly machines to grind to a halt.

But there's one letter of his which, though I kept, I will never show to another living person. In the days when I was writing to him, I was already famous as an artist, both in Rome and Florence and other cities. I sent my paintings to kings and queens for their approbation, and hopefully for their purchase. Many wrote back to me, praising me for my skill as a painter, even though I was a woman. I wrote this to Galileo – yes, it was a hubristic and unwise thing to do; I now realise that one does not boast before a man such as Galileo, a genius of near god-like intellect. I forgot to think before sending my letter that this was a man condemned by those very mighty people who were praising me – and in my letter to him, I said how I had seen myself honoured by all the kings and rulers of many lands to whom I sent my works, and who sent me great gifts and compliments.

But he wrote back to me, and said that such gifts might be precious to me, but were mere baubles to those who sent them, and the words they wrote about me would last only as long as the ink, before it faded and became illegible. But he continued that, unlike kings and queens and Popes, as a scientist, he could not send the products of his mind, nor the paintings of his imagination, for his eyes saw the infinity of the universe, and the universe was unlike an artist's model. It was in constant motion and could not be captured in anything more a moment of existence, even by the most gifted of artists, for that moment represented nothing more than a shimmer in the eternity of the firmament.

He was right, of course, and though it made me feel uncomfortable and less than happy, it was an object lesson in vanity which burrowed deep into my heart.

But I digress. This is the part of my life concerning the rapist Tassi and his assault against me. And what all of this new and uncomfortable militancy by the Church, defending itself against protestant assaults, meant for us, the people? It meant that the citizens of Rome and Florence, Pisa and Urbino as well as all the capital cities of the different provinces throughout the land, were now under the merciless scrutiny of the Universal Church, and sex and licentiousness were no longer as free to indulge in, as once they had been. The authorities who were assigned the mission of ensuring the unwavering adherence to the doctrines of the Catholic Church employed spies and agents in the cities to report to them any criticisms of the government of the Church.

Conversations which were held in private, or drunken braggadocio made in inns and public houses, restaurants and meeting halls, were all grist to the mill of these listeners. Even whispered between brothers or spoken inadvertently in unguarded moments by husbands to wives, could be reported to the authorities by jealous men and women, or those who sought revenge but were too cowardly to wield a sword.

When this happened, and the authorities were notified by their agents, the repercussions would be merciless. A visit, a beating, a few days in the darkness and dankest cell of a prison without trial or the benefit of lawyer, were all it often took to return the miscreant to the straight and narrow path of the righteous. So in those days, and even today in the midst of the Counter Reformation, we still had to be careful of what we said and what we did.

But what has all this to do with Tassi. In those days of my late childhood, when I was on the cusp of womanhood, I still had to ward off boys and young men who approached me when my father's back was turned, or when he was away from the house working on a commission in a church or a palazzo. The nature of the church might be changing, but human nature remains the same, and young men still lusted after girls as much as older men still lusted after wine.

Which brings me, inevitably, to Agostino Tassi. I could begin my description of him by imagining him as one of the subjects I paint. As an artist, this is how I would create him; firstly, I'd draw a faint charcoal outline of his face, filling in details of his nose and lips, his eyes and mouth. Then I'd step back and view my work from a distance, because outlining the features of the face simply defines the way a person looks, but says nothing of the person's character. No, to create a whole person, one has to see behind and beyond the visage the man or woman presents to the world, and look at what the eyes are saying, what the brow is expressing, and how the shape of the mouth conveys a thought. Then I would pick up my paintbrush, and use a suitable colour for this skin, for the shadows the light creates beside his nose, his brows, his beard. And then, finally, when his face is recognizable, I would look beyond the face into the very heart and soul of the man, and I would use my talent as an artist to portray him as good or evil, kind or offensive, with intent to be generous, or to deceive. Through my eye for line, for the depth of a shadow, through the inflection of an eyebrow or the shape of the mouth, the very character of the man would be displayed for all to see.

That's how I would portray Tassi; as a violent, malevolent, lying, deceiving, wife-killing, incestuous malignant presence. So if I were to tell you that Agostino Tassi was, from the very beginning, a fraud and a counterfeit, you would understand why I was so easily taken in.

Fraud? Counterfeit? Yes, for his name, his very name, wasn't Agostino Tassi but Agostino Buonamici. Which means The Great Good Friend. That's like saying that Nero was a good friend to the Christians, or that the Vikings only wanted to be good neighbours.

And that wasn't his only deceit, because although he was born in the unsophisticated provincial town of Perugia, he told everybody that not only had he been born in Rome, but had been adopted because of his physical beauty and talents as an artist, by a noble family whose *pater familias* was the Marchese Tassi. Yet when the truth about him came out, it became known that he was merely the son of a furrier, a man who skinned and sold furs or made them into the trimmings for dresses or capes.

What a sublime contradiction of name and manner! What an abuse of meaning! His name would better have been Agostino Rotten Enemy or Agostino Liar and Thief of Happiness. So do I begin at the beginning, from when I first met him, back in those days when I was a child and too young and certainly too naïve to have understood the nuances of what he whispered to me when we were alone, or the hidden meaning of his comments, or even the looks he gave as I entered a room.

He was in his early 30s and I was a woman-child of 18. I say "woman-child" because at the age of 18, I was already some years older than the age at which Italian girls traditionally were married. By 18, many young women had already been married for five or six years and had two or four or even more babies in their clutch. But my father considered that my talent as an artist was worthy of study and concentration, and was more important than finding me a suitable husband who would be wealthy enough to look after me and my children, and not demand too rich a dowry.

Unlike Caravaggio, who was always in and out of our house in Rome, Tassi simply dropped in one day. He had employed my father to paint figures in a work which was a landscape of architecture – columns and architraves and arches – on the walls of one of the rooms of the Palazzo del Quirinale which he'd been commissioned to complete by Pope Paul V. Within the archways were dozens of people, which Tassi couldn't paint properly, and so he asked my father to paint them.

It was the first time I had met him, and in those days, as a young and impressionable girl, I was attracted to him. And why not? He was at the height of his fame as an artist, although other artists of his day—my friends and friends of my father—often ridiculed him because all he seemed to paint were large murals and frescos of seascapes and fishermen in extremis, and murals which looked more like a draftsman's concept of a building. He could not draw a human figure and so employed my father and other true artists to paint them into his frescos and murals.

But he was certainly a handsome and dashing man and when he came to our house, my heart raced as I looked at him and saw that he was staring at me. The other thing which attracted me to him was that he was a protégé of the Pope himself, and so mixed in a circle of men who lived in the very highest levels of Roman life.

He had a violent, aggressive manner. This was a man whom other men feared, a man who would fight with his fists or draw a sword if there was the merest suggestion of disrespect, a man who used his fists so often when he was in his cups. He spent as much time in prison as walking the corridors of the City. He was a man of fierce passions and I was drawn to him like a moth to a flame.

Please don't misunderstand me, reader of this, my life. My father was a gentle man, as were my brothers and most of our friends. But there are some in our circle, such as Tassi and Caravaggio, who have taken the passions of Art into their breasts, where it beats in their hearts like a drum, loud and insistent. Their mood is fiery, their temper always at the edge of control, their passion at boiling point. And Tassi was one of them.

I would have married him in an instant, and I know that I would have had a difficult but amazingly exciting life. And I know as a certainty that he felt the same way about me. Indeed, according to my bosom friend – in those days - Tuzia Medaglia, he was obsessed with me. And as soon as she told me of his obsession, I observed him more closely, and realised that he was following me everywhere around the house, the studio and the precincts. When other students came up to talk to me, he would somehow find a reason to intervene and interpose himself between the two of us. It was as if he was jealous of me giving my attention to somebody else.

Even after he raped me, I didn't fall out of love with Tassi. Yes, this sounds strange and absurd to me today, as I'm sure it sounds to you. But he said that the rape was caused by his passions overwhelming his decency, and that he would repair the insult to my body and the devaluing of my worth when he robbed me of my innocence. How? Simply by marrying me. He would buy me a ring, and arrange the wedding. Ha!

Even when he became my tutor, I was showing great promise as an artist. I had already shown immense talent by this young age when my father was my mentor, my tutor and my greatest advocate. In truth, even at the age of eight my canvasses showed a sophistication which was admired by many of my father's students. Even though I was so young, when I was eleven or twelve, students twice my age would gather around my stool and view my technique with amazement and envy, asking me how I had managed to convey this or that emotion, or how I'd used light in such a way as to add additional drama to a character's reaction.

This both amused and bemused my father who was, after all, their teacher as well as my own. He would listen to their comments but more insistently attend to my answers and the erudition my immature self used in answer their questions.

One evening, when the studio was empty and the

last student had gone home, he said to me, "You know, Artemisia, one of the tragedies of art is that you were born a girl, for if you were a man, one day, and with sufficient practice, I'm certain that you would take your place in the pantheon of the great artists."

He was devastated by the death of my beloved mother, as were my brothers and I, but as is the case of almost all people, we slowly recovered, and viewed our lives in the future as a somewhat greater challenge.

In order to make ends meet, finding income in Rome in those days often difficult to obtain, my father rented out part of the upper story of our house to a young woman several years older than me.

Tuzia Medaglia and her one-year-old son arrived five years after my mother died, when I was 17. In the beginning, we formed a close and intimate bond. I never truly knew how old Tuzia was, but from the way she behaved with a number of the students who were always in our home, I assumed that she had already seen twenty or more summers. She was especially friendly with my father, and whether or not she was more than a companion to me, but to him also, I neither know, nor would care to speculate. My father was a widower; Tuzia was a single mother.

Tuzia was employed by my father to be my companion, to ensure that I remained chaste until my marriage, and to be a duplication of my beloved mother, guiding me in the arts of womanly behaviour, ensuring my modesty, protecting me from those dangers which were ever-present, and against which my busy and often-absent father was not capable. But she soon became for me as much as a faithful companion as a mother, more of an older sister, really, and we shared secrets and hopes and desires.

And in those days, my desires were flourishing. Since the death of my mother, my father had kept me largely confined to the house, the studio, and only rarely allowed me out into the city, but then accompanied by him or an older brother. Yet the house was full at almost all times of the day and night with his students and other artists, who would look at me and notice me, smile at me and try to engage me in conversation. This often annoyed my father, and were it not for my budding talent as an artist, needing the freedom of a studio and access to models and paints and solvents, I would have been packed off to a nunnery as soon as he saw a boy talking to me.

Which at last, brings me to Agostino Tassi and the day on which he raped me. The year was 1611, the month was May. The day was the seventh of that month. The hour was noon.

Tassi and my father were working together inside the Palazzo Pallavicini-Rospigliosi. Their job was to decorate the walls of the vaults of the Casino delle Muse. According to my father, as he was creating imaginative faces and bodies, Tassi put down his brushes, and stood looking in admiration at the painting.

Then he walked over to where my father was standing, working on a particular angle of some character's stance, and Tassi said that he had to return to his home, as he had left an important document which he had to give to the officials who were overseeing the commission. Thinking nothing of it, my father continued working, while Tassi washed his hands in the basin, quaffed some wine, and then ran up the steps to the outside of the Palazzo. He mounted his horse, and rode straight to my father's house. No, that's not quite correct. First, he rode to the home nearby of Quorli, his friend, who worked as some minor official of the Pope within the Apostolic Palace. Tassi remained mounted on his horse, and shouted to him to follow immediately so that the two of them could enjoy some time together. Like a lap-dog, Quorli followed on his horse, and the two braves arrived at my door.

I heard the banging, wondering who it could be, but I was in the middle of a canvas and didn't want to be disturbed. At this moment, I was painting Tuzia and her beautiful, angelic son, capturing them on canvas as a Madonna and child. All was going well, but the knocking was insistent, and because my father was working with Tassi, there were no students who could have obliged us to answer the door.

So I sent Tuzia down the wooden steps from my bedchamber where I was painting, to the front door. Moments later, I heard noises inside the house.

But my mind wasn't aware of what was happening. I was concentrating so deeply on realizing a particular lighting effect in order to touch, like the kiss of an Angel, the face of the infant Jesus, that I didn't recognize any of the voices. Perhaps they were whispering, or just speaking softly, but I remember hearing some laughter; perhaps drunken laughter; I don't know. Tuzia didn't return, and once I'd mastered that particular blend of colour, depth and intensity with the light – again thanking the Almighty for the help which Caravaggio had given me in understanding the potency of brightness and shadow – I was beginning to become annoyed that my Madonna hadn't returned. She was needed, and although the Infant

Jesus was sitting quite still, I could see that he was about to become tearful for the absence of his mother.

So I put down my brushes, and for the first time since the knocking on the door, I paid attention to what was happening in the house. I could hear movement on the stairs coming up to my bedchamber, whispers, muted suppressed laughter. I didn't know what was happening. Perhaps some students had arrived and in the absence of my father, were daring each other as to which of them would invite me to lunch somewhere; I truly didn't know, until Tuzia suddenly opened the chamber door and stepped boldly inside.

"Artemisia, dear, some people have come to see you," she said, almost casually. I should have been more alert, for as a member of the household, but not family, her normal address to me would have been, "*Artemisia. At the door is Signore So and So, who has called and wishes to pay his respects.*"

But my mind was still in the land of the Bible, where the Virgin Mary and Her Son Jesus were in a stable in Bethlehem. Yet I turned around, and saw two men outside the door, waiting admittance. One I knew well, my father's partner in painting, Agostino Tassi. The other man I didn't know. And again, because I was so immersed in the subject matter of my work, thinking about a dramatic chiaroscuro treatment for the brow of the Madonna, it never occurred to me that Tassi shouldn't be here at all, but should be at work with my father.

I nodded to them, and was about to leave my painting and my bedroom to take them to another part of the house. There I would find out the purpose of their visit, for it was not appropriate for them to enter the bedchamber of a young woman, even a chamber used as a secondary studio to which I was exiled because my father was painting nudes in his studio. I put the brushes into the jar of solvent so that they didn't solidify while I was away from my painting, and turned to leave the room.

But Tassi was already just inside the door, blocking my exit. Tuzia moved further into the room to make way for them, which I remember struck me as odd. Surely, Tuzia wouldn't have allowed Tassi to enter.

And once he was through the door, effectively using his large body to make me step back into the room, his companion Cosimo Quorli walked brazenly inside. I was dumbstruck, offended, and said curtly, "Gentlemen, please follow me to a more suitable room, where Tuzia will serve you refreshments."

Tassi said, "No, this room is good for us. I'm here to tell you that your father has employed me to tutor you on painting techniques, and to determine other talents you may have."

For some reason, his friend Cosimo giggled.

Tassi continued, "He says that while you are good, indeed brilliant, you still need to learn the techniques of the painter."

Two years earlier, I had painted entire canvasses, which had been viewed by well known artists and judged to be wondrous. And truth to tell, I often helped my father at night with figures in his paintings, because he grew easily tired and commissions had to be completed.

So informing me that Tassi was to be my tutor was, to be frank, quite shocking. I had been taught by none other than the greatest painter of the age, Michelangelo Caravaggio, as well as by my father, and to think that a man like Tassi, one who painted architecture and waves and boats could teach me about the subtleties of capturing allegorical moments, times of intense passion, whether from the Bible or from ancient myths, I found oddly insulting.

And it was even more odd when he looked at my unfinished picture of the Madonna and Child, and said,

"Enough painting. Come, lay with me and we'll talk about what it is that I can do for you."

His companion, Cosimo, giggled again, like some silly schoolboy who'd just heard a dirty word, and it annoyed me. But what both upset and worried me was that my companion, Tuzia, was also smiling, as though encouraging Tassi to continue in his rude manner.

So I slipped past him, and retrieved my brushes from the jar, and said, curtly so that the import of my words wouldn't be lost on him, "Sir, forgive me, but I must ask you to leave my bedchamber. This place is not suitable for your presence....or that of your giggling companion. I have work to do. I must finish my Madonna and Child while the images of her are still in my mind."

At that, he became angry and an image of fury suddenly appeared in his face. "Not so much painting! Not so much painting! Put down the brushes. Now! That is my order."

I was taken aback. I kept the brushes firmly in my hand, and was about to demand he leave my room, when he strode over, grabbed the brushes from my hand, and threw them to the floor. Shocked at his violence, I didn't know what to do. He was towering over my head and menacing me. I turned and looked at Tuzia, my face begging her to intervene. But she didn't. Instead, she looked at me and laughed, and then at Tassi and said, "Go on, Master. Go on. Make a whore of her. Teach the spoiled bitch what real women do for their men. Go on!"

I looked at her in horror and disbelief, not knowing what to do or to say. Then Tassi grabbed me by the shoulders, and I screamed. What did I scream? "Tuzia! Help me!"

But she didn't. Instead, she walked over to her infant child who had just begun crying because of the raised voices, picked him up, and walked out of the door.

Alone now with the two men, Tassi pushed me towards the bed, thrusting me forward, so that my shoulder painfully struck one of the bedposts. I cried out, and for reasons I'll never know or understand, called out "Tuzia. For the sake of God, help me." It sped into my mind that my companion of these past two years had just revealed her true face and the depth of her feelings of jealous towards me because of the difference in our stations.

Something in her silence suddenly sharpened my senses. I stood up from the bed, and faced the man who had just thrown me down. No longer immersed in thinking about my images of the Madonna and Child, no longer terrified by this tall man and his ridiculous companion threatening me in my room, I was suddenly angry. Angry beyond reason. How dare he enter my chamber and throw me down on my own bed.

I have my father's temperament, and when things go awry, his first reaction is to anger. As was mine now. I was furious that the sanctity of my room had been violated, that these men were intruding on me and my presence, that my time to paint my portrait was being abused, and that I was in peril of their abuse.

All these emotions suddenly erupted in my being and I became as hard as iron in my anger and resolve. How dare these two ruffians, these *canaglia,* these *delinquenti,* assume that they could rob me of my innocence, my purity, my art, without consequences? So I grabbed a knife from my easel, one which I used to sharpen my charcoals and held it to Tassi's breast.

"Get away from me, you *teppista,* or I'll skewer you. Back, I say, or you'll find this knife in your guts."

Shocked, and obviously worried about having a knife sticking into his breast, he laughed. But it was a nervous laugh. "Well, little one. For weeks, I've been secretly admiring you. I am even willing to marry you. I think I love you, little one. But your father keeps you under lock and key, and this is the only way I can be with you."

I was stunned. He was a business companion to my father. I had spoken to him, perhaps, three or four times. Yes, I was attracted to him, and knew of his powerful connections, but this was a new Tassi, an ugly and violent Tassie, and I knew nothing of his obsession.

And then he said, "I've had you followed by my servants wherever you've been and they've reported back to me about the men you've spoken to; the men you've slept with, the company you've kept. But they never told me you were a *toporagno,* a little shrew with a knife."

"What?" I yelled. "I have never ever been with any man in my life. I remain innocent, untouched."

But he wasn't listening. Instead, he looked at his ugly, giggling companion, standing by the door, and said, "What say you, Cos.? Shall we...."

It was my mistake, and one which cost me my virginity. As he began talking with his companion, I was distracted, and I looked around, giving Tassi the opportunity to grab my hand with the knife in it.

But the moment I felt him pull my hand away, something made me plunge the knife forward, and it cut through his jerkin, through his shirt, and I felt it enter his body. It came to a stop when it hit a rib or his breastbone, I'm not sure which, but it caused him to jump backwards in pain, and to yell out. I looked at him, and saw that his shirt was suddenly bloody, which made me feel impelled to wave the knife in his face, and say to him, "The next time, this blade will be in your heart or I'll cut off your manhood, you *pezzo de merda di cane*. The decision is yours."

Cosimo, from the doorway, burst out laughing, and said, "Dear me. Listen to her. A so-called lady calling the great Tassi a piece of dogshit. How rude." And he continued to giggle, high-pitched, like a girl.

But I wasn't listening to that idiot. My real battle was with the taller, stronger and more menacing Tassi. I screamed at him, "Get out of my bedchamber immediately, or the next thing this blade will bite sits between your legs."

What shall I tell you about the next moments? Do I need to paint in words what actually happens when two men overpowered me, pulled up my skirt and raped me; well, I say two, but it was one man in truth, because although Cosimo's eyes spoke of his lust, his male member was incapable of standing to attention, and try as he might, encouraged by Tassi who held me down so that his friend could have his way with me, Cosimo was incapable of entering my body. My legs were held open by Tassi, and

Cosimo kept trying to enter me, pushing and groaning and cursing me for being cold and heartless, but unable to thrust his manhood into my body.

Not so Tassi. Oh, he was in full force, despite my injuring him once again with the knife, striking out in defence of my honour, and cutting into his arm and his shoulder. But they were mere flesh wounds, I'm sorry to say, which will heal easily, and which were not sufficient to stop him from violating me. And violate me, he did. Twice, and then once more when Cosimo found that he couldn't do it. There was no holding back this man. Tassi was so much in the throes of lust, that he was like a buck rabbit in season. When he tried to enter for the third, or fourth or fifth time, I was so incensed that I reached between his legs, grabbed his member by my hand, and used my finger nails to score deeply into the flesh. He yelped in pain, and thumped me hard in my stomache, causing me to cough and choak, knocking the wind out of me and causing me to lose consciousness for a moment.

I write now with the hindsight of history. It is three decades since I was raped, and much of the horror of that day has become muted in God's graceful light. But although I've recounted what happened like a storyteller, I still feel the overpowering anger and powerlessness I felt when they were using me as their plaything. Any control I had of my life was ripped away from me. It isn't easy to retell these painful events, but I hope you, my reader, can feel the anger which coursed through my veins.

And when it was over, I lay on my bed, blood from my abused womanhood staining my white sheets. I lay there, my breasts exposed, my legs splayed, incapable of moving. I was in such pain, I didn't know if I would ever feel normal again. My head hurt from where he'd banged it on the wooden bed frame to make me keep still; my shoulder hurt from where it had collided with the bedpost; my lips hurt from where he'd kissed me so violently. But worst of all was this enormous ache from inside my body.

Full of unexpected emotions – excitement, apprehension, fear – David Cabot walked quickly to keep pace with Martina Calabrese as they strode towards the Belvedere Courtyard, the entrance to the Vatican's Apostolic Library.

Over breakfast that morning, she'd reminded David of the enormity of the library, and that if they found nothing, he wasn't to be disappointed.

"The Library is one of the oldest existing libraries in the world, and scholars have been pouring over its contents almost every day since it was opened by Pope Sixtus IV. That was way back in 1475. It contains 75,000 historical documents and well over a million and a half books. Scholars come from all fields of knowledge, from history, religion, law, science, philosophy, theology and more.

"But that doesn't mean," she added quickly as she saw the disappointment on his face, "that discoveries aren't made. Not often, but when they are, it is major news. And remember that much has been hidden from view by previous popes, librarians and curators. If you don't want stuff to be found, but it's too important to destroy, there's no better place to hide it than a large library. And we're not only talking about Popes and Princes from centuries ago in the ancient history of the church. If you want to find out about the details of the dealings which Pope Pius XII had with the Nazis in wartime Europe, you have to have the rank of a Bishop to be given permission. No scholar may view them. Perhaps one day, but not now. And because of the amount of documents, their cataloguing and assessments are decades behind schedule. The librarians themselves have no idea what's hidden here."

"Then how the heck are we going to find letters or documents or manuscripts which Artemisia might have written?" asked David.

At first, Martina shrugged. Then she said, "First we look for her name. Remember that she's barely remembered these days. Very few people other than art historians would be researching her. Then, if we find nothing, we look for the people we know she associated with. Her father Orazio, Michaelangelo Buonarroti the Younger, Galileo Galilei, her husband Pierantonio, the Duke Cosimo Medici...all the people with whom she worked or associated. They might have left clues, if any of their works are in the Library. If they are, then in their books or letters, there might be reference to Artemisia, which will give us a clue to what she might have written and where she might have left it.

"You must remember that for much of her life she was illiterate. She learned to read and write when she went to Florence, because there, she was mixing with highly educated people like Galileo. But we have no idea of how literate she was as an adult. Perhaps she was only able to write down a shopping list. If so, then on the chance that we find something of hers here, it could be nothing more than a note or something like that. But as scholars, anything we find can illuminate our objects of interest."

They were met at the doors of the Library by Cardinal Arturo. Because they were in public, both kissed his ring.

"Well, my children, this is the day when big things may happen. Or not."

He grinned as they walked into the Library.

By now, David was getting used to buildings which

were designed to astound and belittle normal people. Cathedrals had been built on the vastest scale which could be created not to house large numbers of people, but so that city dwellers and visitors from other countries would be stunned when viewed from a distance. Churches, even in remote country towns, had ridiculously tall bell towers so that peasants working on the land would know that the priest, and God above him, was looking down on his labours. And the vast scale and size of palaces were planned by their owners to cower those who stood before them.

Which was precisely the effect that the Vatican's Apostolic Library had on David. Not its size or scope, but the amazing art on every wall, every ceiling, every cornice, every column. He followed the Cardinal and Martina and wished that she was holding his hand, because it was difficult looking upwards and sidewards at the art, while trying to follow their direction.

Soon they were seated at tables reserved for scholars. Martina whispered to David that she would go and find out what texts they had which were either written or referred to Artemisia Gentileschi.

Half an hour later, she returned and told him, "Not much. Records of her trial, references from works about other painters, a few things such as that. The Librarian will bring the works to us."

David looked around at what other scholars were doing. Many were older men and women, studiously examining texts and making notes. He assumed that these were university researchers, possibly professors or leading academics. Some scholars were much younger, probably research students doing masters or doctoral degrees, writing furiously and not wasting a moment of their precious time. He remembered back to his university days when he was studying Geology at the University of Western Australia. They were halcyon days, but he was so fixated on getting a good degree that he failed to participate in much of university life. He's always regretted it.

He whispered some things to Martina, but the Librarian arrived with a dozen or so books and manuscripts which she gave to the Cardinal, who thanked her profusely.

None of them, of course, was available to David, as they were in Italian or Latin. But Martina and the Cardinal pored through them, whispering to each other as though they were in secret conclave. David was desperate to ask what the books and documents were, but didn't want to interrupt their time in the library.

After an hour or so, in which he'd watched them confer, agree, disagree, make notes, get excited and rifle through tome after tome without any reference to him, and during which he said not a word, David determined that this would be a good time to make his presence felt. While both of his colleagues were discussing hotly something in Italian and Martina was writing copious notes to the Cardinal's dictation, David said, "Would you like me to get you both some coffee?"

It was a facetious remark, and Martina immediately realised the intent behind it, saying, "Oh darling, we're really sorry, but there's so much here, and it's all in Italian and Latin. It's written in the same style of language as Shakespeare wrote for his plays for an Elizabethan audience, and so Arturo and I have been discussing the precise meaning of words and what they might have meant when the document was written. He and I, right now, are talking as though we're living in, and speaking the language of, 17th Century Florence. I know we've been excluding you and we apologise, but if you can't speak modern or Renaissance Italian or ancient Latin, you won't understand what we're trying to discover in these documents. Please, dear, have patience and we'll tell you as soon as we leave. Just let us get on with it."

So he settled back in his chair, and wondered whether the Library had any good books he might read while he was waiting. He'd brought a cell phone, laptop, and Kindle to Europe, but had left them in his hotel room as he assumed that he'd be involved in the search. After a further few hours, during which he stepped out to walk around Vatican City, he returned to find them outside of the Library, still in heated discussion.

"Well? Any major discoveries?" he asked.

"Yes," said the Cardinal.

"And no," said Martina. "We found just a single letter of interest. There's quite a lot written about Artemisia in the Library, but just referring to her biblical paintings. However, there's a Cardinal from her time, and in his papers, we found a very interesting letter, which was written by Artemisia. It really caught our eye, but you need to be something of a detective to understand what she was actually saying. Some really interesting stuff, which we'll talk to you about over lunch."

She linked her arm through his, and the three walked away from the Library. In the streets adjoining Vatican City, they found a quiet restaurant, where once again the Cardinal ordered for the table. David was happy to let him, as his choices yesterday had been delicious.

Sitting at the table, Martina continued, "As I said before, there are a number of references to Artemisia in letters to Cardinals and even Popes from people like Michelangelo Buonarroti the Younger, praising the work which she did on the allegorical painting in the Casa Buonarroti in Florence. The Allegory of Inclination shows a nude female representing the interior nature of creativity and scientific and artistic ability. She's seated on a cloud holding a compass. You can tell Galileo's influence because above her in the sky is the star which guided the Magi to Jesus. The reason the letter was in the Archives is because at that time, probably in the year it was written, Galileo was being examined by the Inquisition."

"And," said Cardinal de Santis, "apart from the detailed written record of the trial of Tassi under the Inquisition, which is well known and available, we also found a truly enigmatic note. This is the letter which Martina told you about before. It was written by Artemisia to a Florentine nobleman named Francesco Maria di Niccolò Maringhi. Neither of us had heard of him, and so we'll investigate him further. But somehow, this letter between Artemisia and this Maringhi fellow came into the possession of one of the then Pope's most senior Cardinals, Guido Bentivoglio who died in 1644. We were lucky to find it, as it's but a brief annotation in the Vatican's Index of Contents. All it said in Latin was *"Epist. No. 258 Ex. A. Gentileschi. Ad. Sg. FM Maringhi.* In English, that means it was letter number 258 from Artemisia to Signore Maringhi. That's all it said. We only looked at it because it mentioned Artemisia's name.

"How or why they came to be in Bentivoglio's private papers, is a mystery. There's no other reference to it at all in his papers. It could have been that Bentivoglio was a supporter or patron of artists, and we do know that he was an avid collector. Yet somehow, for some reason, he collected letters as well as paintings. He never became Pope, but he was a powerful member of the Curia. There's a portrait of him painted by van Dyke in the Galleria Palatina in Florence.

"Now we won't know for certain until we do much more detailed research into the good Cardinal Bentivoglio, but from the brief material which Martina and I have read, it appears that he was appointed Nuncio by Pope Paul V, but on his return to Rome, he purchased Cardinal Borghese's palazzo on the Quirinale. He was passionately interested in art, and became patron to the painter Claude Lorrain, who had studied under Caravaggio, who was the teacher of Artemisia. It all seems to fit, somehow."

"But the note? What did the note that you found say?" asked David impatiently.

"Well, my dear, as neither Martina nor I have ever heard of his man, Francesco Maria di Niccolò Maringhi, we need to know a lot more about him. But the note was to thank him for continuing to offer her friendship, even though their relationship finished many years earlier. I think it means that they had a passionate sexual affair when she was living in Florence, even though she was still married to her husband, a minor artist called Pierantonio Stiattesi. Also in the note, which was really quite surprising to find here in the Apostolic Library, she thanks him for supporting her financially and praises her husband for knowing of their affair, and not standing in her way. As she put it, "*one of the few decent things he did in my life, even though it was founded on his indecent love of the money you gave me, and which I brought home to support my family.*" She's very forthright," said Cardinal de Santis.

"Is that all?" asked David, his frustration growing.

"No, darling," said Martina, knowing that Cardinal Arturo would still take ages to get to the point. "In the letter to Maringhi, she said something about a book she had written. She calls it the book of her life. If we find it, it will rewrite history.

"Everybody assumed that she was illiterate, certainly when she lived in Rome and before she went to Florence, but this letter she wrote to him was well composed and she used both Italian and Latin. So she was far from illiterate. She's remarkably intelligent, and the fact that she was writing a book, says that historians have been very wrong about her intellect. Yes, she learned to read and write in Florence when she was married, but she gained the skills very quickly, and became as proficient as anybody else, judging by the letter she wrote to Maringhi. But what's truly fascinating is that she gives a clue to what this book is all about and where she's hidden it. It's a book which recounts her life history. But when she describes it to Maringhi, she changes from Italian into the language of the Church. Which is very strange. She's written it in Latin, and we don't know why."

"What does she say?" asked David.

Martina glanced down at her notes, and read, "*De cursu vitae meae librum scripsi ; res gestae in quo narratae ad usum omnium mulierum valde sunt exponendae. Me mortua, quaeso, hunc librum reperi, ede, emitte foras. Vita mea patefacta est, sicut in tabulis inscripta, ad memoriam patris carissimi consecrata.*

"Meaning?" asked David.

"Meaning, and I'll translate it into English, "*I have written a book about the course of my life; the experiences related in it must definitely be set out for the benefit of all women. When I am dead, I beg, find this book, publish it, send it out. My life lies revealed, just as if written in…..*""

Martina frowned, not sure of how to translate the next part of Artemisia's sentence, and showed the document to the Cardinal, who looked at the word, struggled for a moment, and then said, "I think she means in the public eye…."

Martina nodded, and continued, "*My life lies revealed, just as if written in public records, consecrated to the memory of my dearest father.*"

David frowned. "Sorry, I'm not seeing where you're both going with this. She's written an autobiography, and she's dedicated it to the memory of her father. How does that help us?"

The Cardinal smiled, and said, "This was a clever woman. She knew the meaning of metaphor and of allegory. Just look at her paintings. Judith cutting off the head of her enemy is feminism writ large. So her use of words would have been very precise. The word she used wasn't what you said. The word you used, dear David, was 'dedicated'. She used the Latin ecclesiastical word '*consecratam*,' which in English means 'consecrated.' That is the clue."

Still clueless, David looked at Martina for help, so she said, "The other thing she said later in this letter was to tell this man Maringhi that he would have to travel to find the book. She wrote in Latin that if he'd heard that she had died, he was to travel to a distant cold land to retrieve her book. She said, again in Latin, "*Meis verbis diligenter perlectis, quo tibi eundum sit certe scies.*"

"In English, that means '*Having read through my words carefully, you will know definitely where you must go.*' So the words she used are very important and carefully written. And she wrote them in Latin, and not in Italian so that few people, other than an educated Bishop or Cardinal, maybe not even a lowly priest in those days, but one to whom the letter was written, would be able to understand the meaning behind her words. Only this man Maringhi, who we assume was her lover. To understand what she meant properly, we can't think with our heads today, but have to put our heads back and think like somebody from the 17th Century."

Just as she said it, the waitress walked towards their table, and began putting down plates of steaming spaghetti and bowls of minced meat in spicy sauces.

"Anyhow, let's eat our lunch, and you'll see where our logic leads us."

While Martina and Cardinal de Santis ate, David, still impatient, asked, "Ok, now explain what's so important about her use of the word 'consecrated' instead of 'dedicated'?"

Martina remained quiet as Cardinal Arturo poured generous glasses of a light red wine. "To understand the difference, it helps to be Catholic."

"And to speak Latin," added Martina.

The Cardinal sipped the wine and smiled at the taste. Then he said, "Normally, a book is dedicated to a patron or a parent or a husband or wife. Yes? But in this note which Artemisia wrote to Signore Maringhi, and which somehow found its way into the collection of Cardinal Bentivoglio, she instead used the word 'consecrated'. And then she adds the word 'permanently' immediately afterwards. So we must ask ourselves, why?

"The consecration of a building like a church or a person – say a Bishop – is a sacred ceremony. Yes, it's a form of dedication for a carefully designed purpose. You wouldn't for example, consecrate a toilet for the purpose of relieving yourself. But you would consecrate a church or a cathedral and make it holy so that believers can pray in a building associated with God Almighty, and feel a closeness and intimacy to the Father, the Son and the Holy Spirit. The word consecrate means in Latin to associate the blessing or the gift with the sacred, the Holy, the divine.

"Then we must consider the word 'permanent' which she uses after she talks of consecration. Why permanent? What's permanent? A Church? No, for they come and go with time and fashion. A Cathedral? Perhaps, but most last only five hundred or a thousand years. And people certainly aren't permanent," said the Cardinal.

Martina took up the conversation. "So what's permanent, David? What will last forever and ever and ever? And remember her words to Maringhi, that it was in a cold and distant country...."

He thought for a moment, and shrugged his shoulders. "Death, I suppose. And a grave is cold."

"Precisely," they both said together.

"Death, but not the coldness of death; she was talking about cold in reference to a distant country," said Marina. "So she obviously wasn't talking about her death. She may have been living in London when she wrote that letter, or she may have been in Naples, a warm city, but one which was suffering terribly from the plague, which would have killed thousands of people. We just don't know. And she couldn't forecast her own death with any accuracy, but she did know of the death of somebody close to her, whose date and place of death we know from our records."

"Her father, Orazio," said David, "who died in London. Cold, miserable London."

The Cardinal and Martina looked at each other, and beamed smiles at him. "You should have been an investigator," said the Cardinal. "Exactly what we thought. We checked. Her father's grave is beneath the high altar in Queen Henrietta Maria's Catholic Chapel in Somerset House. But why would a painter, in those days little more than an artisan, have been given one of the most important burial sites? Well, you have to appreciate that the Queen was only a girl of 17 when she arrived from Paris. Orazio was the court painter in France to Henrietta Maria's mother, Queen Marie de Medici and she had sent her young daughter over to England to marry the High Anglican King Charles 1st.

"Many people thought that he was secretly a Catholic and hated poor young Henrietta Maria when she arrived in London. So when the Catholic Italian and friend of

Popes, Orazio Gentileschi, arrived in England, she was thrilled to have another person of her faith associated with her intimate circle, and welcomed him like an old friend from home. Which is why when he died in 1639, 13 years after he arrived in London, she gave him such a prestigious burial site.

"At the time of his death, he was working on commissions for the King and Queen. We know that Artemisia visited London in 1639 to assist her father in his work, for by then he was an old man. Artemisia herself was 46 years old, which was the age that many people died in those days. And remember that she had given birth to a lot of children, very few of whom had lived. So her life expectancy wouldn't have been much longer. It's possible, and I know we're speculating, that she wrote her life story in London. We can speculate that she was still angry about her treatment as a women by the male-dominated world of the Italian church and state, so the book could have been a denunciation, a philippic. It could have been too controversial, too damning of the Church or the ruling families of Italy, to have been published in Italy. We don't know and won't know until we find her manuscript.

"But what we do know is that her father Orazio died

in London and was buried in Somerset House. I'll bet that Artemisia hid the book in his grave, and left a note for her lover, after her death, to go and retrieve it. Its contents must have been so scandalous, and made her so concerned about it falling into the wrong hands, that if it was found in her lifetime, she would have been burnt at the stake."

David thought for a moment or two, and then said, "I can't fault the logic, but you're making huge leaps and assumptions. And why is this book so important? It's her life story. Ok, but how does that prove that my painting is a genuine Artemisia?"

The Cardinal reached over, and grasped David by his shoulder. "My son, we are the pawns in history's great game of chess. But even when we move one seemingly insignificant square forward, we can dramatically alter the game. Only by searching, researching and questing, will we find the truth. In her book, Artemisia might mention that she painted this work you found in an art gallery in Sydney Australia. Or she may not. How it got there may be part of the story. But what's most important, my dear, is that we uncover this book, this story of Artemisia's life. Her story is one of power and revenge following her rape and degradation and torture. Against all odds, when virtually any other woman would have been cowed by the events of her youth, Artemisia stood up, and made a name for herself. She's utterly remarkable. So even if this book doesn't prove your painting's provenance, be assured that if we find this written work, it will be a huge triumph in the history of art and culture. All thanks to you."

Martina nodded, and said, "And don't forget what she wrote to Maringhi....... *res gestae in quo narratae ad usum omnium mulierum valde sunt exponendae .... the experiences related in it must definitely be set out for the benefit of all women..* She was a feminist. As Arturo just said, all you have to do is to look at her paintings.... Judith and Holofernes, for example. This woman could be the figurehead for a worldwide movement of female consciousness. She could stand amidst the ranks of great women of the past who railed against the treatment of their sex, women such as Christine de Pizan, Mary Wollstonecraft, and Simone de Beauvoir. And you, David, could be the man responsible for bringing this fabulous woman back to life."

Martina and Cardinal Arturo looked at David, who sipped his wine, and wondered what his wife would say when he called her tonight.

# PART, THE THIRD

———◆———

I remember lying there long, long after they had departed. Their laughter still filled my mind. But as consciousness returned to my injured brain, I listened carefully to see if they remained somewhere in the house.

I could hear no sounds in the house. But I think that's because the blood rushing past my ears seemed to remove me from my present. When I closed my eyes, and listened more acutely, more consciously, the only sound I could hear was my heart thumping in my chest.

Lying on the bed, my body now numb, and no longer throbbing in pain, my thoughts began to clarify, and I remember – although this was many many years ago – thinking to myself, *What if Tassi's seed grows in me and I become pregnant? What if he goes into an inn and boasts that he's taken me? What will become of my reputation? My father's reputation? What man will want a used woman, now that I'm ruined?*

These unanswerable and insuperable questions were the landscape upon which my violation was portrayed. My future, once exciting and replete with potential as a woman, an artist, was suddenly bleak and uncertain. I was now, thanks to my violation, a fallen woman, little more than the whores men like Tassi visited in the brothels. My honour had been stripped from me, my value to my father had been destroyed, and the composure which an artist needs when painting, had been shattered.

So I lay unmoving, silent, listening to the heartbeat of the house in case Tassi and his lapdog reappeared, wanting to have more enjoyment of me and my body. But the house remained quiescent, motionless and lifeless. And it seemed strange to me that not even Tuzia, my treacherous, perfidious and disloyal servant and companion, was moving around.

I fell asleep. When I opened my eyes, the sun was already deep into the West and the dark of night was beginning to cloak our city like a blanket. I sat up, and listened. And I heard movement in the house. I heard my father's voice coming from his studio; he was speaking to Tuzia. And in my waking state, I also think I heard the voice of another man, but I couldn't be certain.

So I quickly stripped off my bloody dress and undergarments, poured water from the jug into the basin, washed the dried blood from between my thighs, and sought in my dresser for a rag to place between my legs to soak up the poisons which continued to exude from my body. Then I dressed and, supported by the walls, I walked on unsteady legs out of my bedchamber and down the stairs to the central house, where my father was in his studio.

My mind was reeling. What would I tell him? How could I tell him that his beloved daughter had been violated, and her virginity taken from her? How could I admit my shame? Tassi had used the inside of his hand to strike me and so apart from a redness which had now disappeared, there were no marks to show and speak of my shame.

The first person I saw was Tuzia, standing in the hallway, who greeted me with a smile, and said, "Oh, good evening, Artemisia. How was your painting? Would you like a glass of mulled wine? I'm just getting one for your father?"

But before I could answer her, she turned her back and walked towards the kitchens. I watched her retreat. I wanted to follow her and strike her down, but my legs wouldn't move and I was incapable of speech. It was as though the afternoon hadn't happened, as though the rape of her friend, the daughter of the household, the young woman entrusted to her to be her companion, had been nothing more than a figure from a scene in a painting, hanging on the wall of a gallery.

Was I going mad? Had I imagined the whole thing? But no! The blood! The pain in my shoulder! Tuzia was the instigator, the facilitator of my rape, the woman who had encouraged Tassi to violate me. Yet she spoke to me now just as she did yesterday and the day before.... servant and companion, not facilitator of my disgrace.

I stood there, rooted to the spot, in utter shock, until my father called out from his studio, "Artemisia, dear one. Come and greet your father. There's a visitor who'd like to speak with you. And I want you to tell your father how your day has been. How is your development of the Madonna and Child?"

And then, almost as an afterthought, he repeated, "Come into the studio, because an important gentleman is here to meet with you. Come child."

Still I didn't move. I was in a dream. I was no longer human, no longer woman, but had become a shadowy figure in the background of one of my paintings. Silent, immobile, fixed, the afterthought of a creator; yet I was crying out for attention. I didn't understand what was happening.

Moments later, my father said, "Come, girl. Your father wants your kiss and to see you."

And from the kitchens came the cry, "Artemisia, dearest, go to your father."

The longer I stood there, the more the certainty dawned on me that I was no longer a person, and nothing more than a shadow in a painting, a character in the background, a hapless maiden incapable of moving because the artist had drawn me in a position fixed in space and time. My legs wouldn't move; my arms were leaden, hanging by my side; and my mind felt as though waves from the sea were crashing onto the shore. I was swept by emotions of incredulity, and felt as though the nightmare of just hours ago had been nothing more than my imagination. Yet the blood, the poisons, still drained from me. My body ached from the violence.

Slowly, I forced myself to walk towards my father's studio, determined by what I had to tell him. I stopped before I entered the portal, suddenly unwavering in my resolve that first person I would confront with her guilt would be Tuzia. I would be the Prophet Isaiah, pointing my righteous finger at her and casting her into the depths of Hades; and only then would I be more prepared to tell my father.

But it didn't transpire in that way, for my father came to the door of his study and saw me walking slowly, painfully, towards the kitchens.

"Come daughter. We have a visitor. We want to see you."

I turned, and encouraged by his smile, walked towards him. But my steps were painful, because of the violence done to my body, and I looked more like a baby toddling on chubby little legs, than a grown woman used to striding through town.

My dress caused him not to notice the pain of my walk, gripped me lovingly by the arm, and leading me into the studio.

And there sat Agostino Tassi, one leg over the arm of the chair, the other splayed on the floor as though he was a Lord of a Palazzo.

I looked at him, and he smiled as I entered, and said, "Ah! The beauteous and talented Artemisia. Your father and I have been talking about you."

Too stunned by his appearance in my home, by his seeming lack of apology or remorse or even acknowledgement of his crimes against me, I just stood there dumbfound, looking at him.

"Dearest," said my father, "Maestro Tassi, as you know, is a business and painting colleague of mine. We work together on his commissions. And he has agreed to become your tutor in landscapes and backgrounds. But more than that, dear girl, he has been observing you for some time, and has come to admire you greatly. So much so, dear one, that he has asked my permission to take your hand in marriage and for you to become his wife. And bearing in mind Master Tassi's wealth, position in Roman society, his excellent connections and prospects, especially with the Pope and the Cardinals of the Vatican, I have willingly given him my approval."

He looked at me, not to seek my approbation, but to encourage me to go over to Tassi, take his hand and kiss his ring as though he were a Cardinal or a Bishop, and I, a mere supplicant. But I did no such thing. My mind was reeling.

This afternoon, he and his lapdog friend had done foul things to me and left me hurt and injured in my bedchamber. Yet, as though in a dream, this evening, that very same man was seeking to restore my honour and make amends for violating me by making me his wife. It was absurd, stupid, and in that moment, I was bordering on insanity. If two guards had appeared at my door and said that I was an escapee from a madhouse, I would have agreed and willingly gone with them.

I looked at Tassi, then at my father, then back at Tassi. I opened my mouth, but no sound came out. Tassi laughed and said, "Speechless? I'm not surprised. We hardly know each other, Lady, but I'm a painter, a man of impulse and passions like Titian, Caravaggio and Michaelangelo. I see something of beauty and I have to paint it, to possess it for all time, to capture it, and never let it leave my mind. I have seen you many times, Madonna, even though you haven't seen me, yet you are inscribed on my heart. You are in my eye, whether it's open or closed. I see you all the time. And I want to make you mine, to share with me all of the joys and excitements of life. Your father has already given his assent, and so all that remains to be determined, is the date of our wedding.

"However, as I said to my friend and confrere, you father Maestro Orazio, you are old enough to be wed, but still young enough to need time and to develop skills as an artist. So we think that our engagement should remain a secret from society, but last for a year, and, perhaps on the feast of Saint Valentinian on the third day of November next year, we will become man and wife. This will allow us time to know each other."

I nodded. I heard the words which were being said, but I was fighting against vomiting. Here I was, standing in a studio with my father and my rapist, talking about marriage. The word "bizarre" doesn't even begin to define the circumstances. There were so many things I could have done. I could have told my father what had happened earlier in the day, upstairs in my bedchamber. I could have picked up a knife from the table, rushed over and stabbed Tassi in the chest and watched in unconcealed happiness as the blood spurted out and the life drained from his body. Or I could have seen the offer of marriage to this man as his way of begging my forgiveness, a heartfelt and sincere apology for what he'd done.

So what did I do? I could not bear to break my father's heart by telling that his beloved daughter had been defiled, her value to him diminished. Nor could I murder Tassi, for then I would have been imprisoned and because Tassi was a protégé of the Pope, I would no doubt be dragged before the Inquisition, tortured and broken on the rack.

So my only way forward was to nod quietly, like a mute, bow in obeisance, and use the time of my silence in trying to understand what was happening. Which, to my eternal shame and contrition, is what I did.

But silence was no longer an acceptable response. For it occurred to me that my father would expect me to say something, never having been silent or reticent in the past, and so I said, "Thank you, Maestro Tassi, for the generosity of your offer. My father has accepted your proposal, and as his daughter, it is my duty and obligation to acquiesce. However, in order that we begin to know each other, I would beg your indulgence and ask that you spend some time with me in modest conversation. And I would hope, provided that my father trusts both you and me, that our time together may be private and not invaded by a chaperone. For there are things which a modest young woman should say to an older and more experienced man who asks to be her husband, things which I would be embarrassed to say in front of my father."

My father smiled, and stood, saying, "I have a feeling I understand what you mean, daughter, and therefore I will go into my bedchamber to read. But since the death of my beloved wife, I have been both mother and father to you. And I know that at this moment, were she with us, she would advise you. So I say this to you, my beloved daughter; there is only one thing I you must remember.

Getting to know your husband's body, and him knowing yours, are the very core of marriage. Love may or may not come, though it would be a benefit to you both, conferred by the Almighty One. In the case of your late beloved mother and me, God smiled upon our union and our love was strong and enduring. But don't be afraid of the reality of carnal knowledge. You will soon get used to it and, who knows, one day, you may enjoy it as much as your husband will enjoy his knowledge of you.

"Now, daughter, ring a bell when the two of you are finished your conversation. But for the sake of propriety and your modesty, daughter, speak in a hushed voice, but keep the door open."

And he left. Tassi and I were together. Suddenly the studio, the friendliest and most familiar room in my house, became full of menace and foreboding. For several moments we looked at each other without words.

"Well," he said, eventually, "you truly are a good actress. Even I was convinced. Not a word to your father. That's good. I had an answer, of course, in case you entered the room full of fury, but there was always the chance that he may not have believed me. However, this quiet assignation between us will clarify things."

"Clarify?" I said in amazement, holding in my anger

and refraining from launching myself bodily at him and beating him to death. "Clarify? You raped me this afternoon and proposed marriage this evening. How is that a clarification of anything?"

He seemed unperturbed, almost nonchalant as he considered my comment. "I am here, dearest Artemisia, to offer you my hand in marriage. To give you a ring. Yes I forced myself upon you during lunch, but I was overcome by love. I have loved you from afar, and now that your father has admitted me into your household, I shall love you from a-near."

I was almost too stunned by his arrogance to speak. But speak, I did. "You dare talk to me about love, Signore Tassi? Love? Love is an act of gentleness, an act of grace and kindness, not an unleashing of lust and violence. If you loved me, why did you bring that dog, Cosimo, to join you in your act of violation?"

"Ah! Yes, that was a misguided thing to do, and for that, if nothing else, I owe you an apology. I was drunk at the time, and the wine robbed me of the conscience which is the cape worn by my better self. Still, as it turned out, he wasn't capable of doing anything, so rather than an act of violation, he was party to an act of indecency. And as to your claim that you were violated, Madonna, let's just say that it was more in the way of an audition for your role as my wife, than the desecration of a religious icon."

He could see the fire and fury light up my face, and realised that what he'd said, to the victim of his violence, was like taunting a caged bear by poking him with a stick. My fists tightened, my body clenched as thoughts of stabbing him with a knife flew through my mind.

"What I mean, dearest Artemisia, is that I could have made love to any woman in Rome, but instead, I chose to come to your home, and make love to you. I favoured you above all other women. Is that so wrong?"

"Yes!" I hissed, deliberately keeping my disgust from leaving the room. "Yes, it's wrong. For in your act, I was reduced to a sack of corn. I was a nonentity, robbed of the ownership and authority I used to have of my own body, forced to deny you your carnal desires. By your strength, your power, you stole my body from me. I didn't want to give my body to you. I was a virgin this morning, yet tonight I am defiled. I am battered, bruised, and bleeding. My head, indeed, my entire body, aches," I said through clenched teeth.

"But doesn't the offer of marriage, a sincere and loving offer made in the sight of heaven, mean nothing to you?"

he asked. "It means a great deal to me! And as the Pope's protégé, when the moment is right, I will ask His Holiness to officiate at the ceremony; we will be wed in St. Peter's Basilica. Any bride would love to do that, surely."

I was so stunned by his lack of understanding, by his blinkered vision, that I could barely say the words which were forming in my mind. But when I did, it began as a trickle, and ended as a torrent.

"Yes, Tassi, most women would regard such a wedding as wonderful, but why do you think for a single moment that such wonder would apply to me... and to you? After what you did to me this very day? And speaking of days, a wedding is but one day in our lives. And a single day, no matter how magnificent, doesn't equate to a lifetime together. But the question you will have to account for, whether I marry you or not, is whether a marriage can be built on the foundations of the disparagement and vilification of one of the parties by the other?"

He was about to answer, but I spoke over him, "Could Beatrice have loved Dante, had he violated her? Could Heloise have loved Abelard if he had raped her? Yet you sit there, arrogant and self-righteous, having taken my precious virginity, and instead of begging my forgiveness, instead of being terrified that I will report you to the authorities, you think that I can be mollified by your talk of a wedding in the Vatican. What? Do you think that being married by a Pope will stop me from seeking vengeance? Or that it will turn my head and make me happy and compliant so that I'll live the rest of my life with you?

"Well, Signore Tassi, let me tell you what I am thinking. I'm wondering about how I will live for the rest of my life in the knowledge that my first experience of sex was merciless and violent. Instead of being with a man I loved, a man who adoringly opened my body to the joys it should by rights know, a man who loved me as much as I love him, instead of being gentle and loving and gracious in the eyes of Heaven, I was beaten and assaulted. I'm wondering how I will ever sleep again, knowing that, because of what you have done, for years and years I will be suffering from nightmares; spectres will play in my darkened mind ever time I close my eyes, and I will see and smell and feel your body forcing its way into mine. I'm wondering if I will ever stop hating you? And what I wonder most of all, Signore Tassi, is if you have any true understanding of the consequences of your actions today? Because if you do, then you think that your promise of marriage shows that it is merely your road to salvation; that it is the way you think will prevent me seeking revenge and punishment against you."

Again, he opened his mouth to speak over me, but undaunted, I continued, "Not so, Signore, for my wrath is mounting by the moment, my anger has grown since I was violated, and I am at a stage where I will go to the roof of my building, and scream out your name, and that of the dog who was with you, so that all of Rome will know that you are a coward, a rapist, a liar and a scoundrel. That, Maestro Tassi, is my answer to your proposal of marriage."

He looked at me, frowning. It was not what he'd expected. He had anticipated that because my value as a bride, now that my virginity had been taken, was so greatly lowered, that I would be quiet and thankful for his offer of marriage, and that I would be complicit in his duplicity against my father's goodness. He drew several deep breaths, and said softly, "A pity, Madonna, for not only will you ruin your own life by this course of action, but also that of your father. For as a man beyond reproach, and a protégé of His Holiness, when I defend myself against your accusations, and tell the world of the liaisons you have had with numerous married men, when I speak of the whorehouse I've seen you enter and leave, then not only will you be ruined, but not one worthy in Rome or Florence, Pisa or Venice will commission Orazio to paint for them ever again. And your career as a painter will be dashed on the rocks of hubris.

"Think carefully about your next actions, Artemisia, and the dirt you will throw at me. My standing in Rome makes it simple for me to brush off your accusations like dust on a velvet jerkin. Your righteous anger will destroy not only yourself, but those whom you love."

I was about to say something, but he continued, "There are two options open to you. The first, and most beneficial, is for you to remain silent, because then you will wear a ring on your finger to show the world that you are a woman favoured by one of Rome's leading citizens; but the second option is that you speak out as you've threatened, and all the catastrophes of the world will rain down upon your head, and the heads of those you love most. Wear the ring I will buy you, and next year you will be wed to me, with all the benefits I will provide; but speak out against me, and you will be wed forever to perdition."

And with that, he stood, walked past me, shouted a good farewell to my father, and left my house. Leaving me gape-mouthed, startled and shocked.

Did I go into my father's bedchamber and tell him what had just transpired? Did I confess to him that I had been defiled, devalued, dishonoured? And did I tell him that the offer of marriage was not because Maestro Tassi was overwhelmed by his love for me from afar, but was his way of deflecting my accusations of rape? No. I knew that my father would want to know the nature of my discussions with Tassi, and if I retired to my bedchamber, he would pursue me and ask. It was for that reason that, instead of going to the kitchens and berating Tuzia, instead I walked up the stairs to my father's bedchamber and knocked gently on the door.

He opened it, and immediately asked, "Well?"

"Father, I have suddenly had the offer of marriage thrust upon me. I need time for the idea to form in my mind."

"I know that, dearest daughter," he said, "but such offers don't come along every day, and remember that you're no longer a child of thirteen, but a woman of eighteen. Most women of your age are married by now, and tending to their husbands and children. Many of my students look at you when you work with us, and I know what's in their minds.... *Why isn't Artemisia married yet? What's wrong with Artemisia? Why is no man interested in Artemisia?*"

I didn't want to disabuse him of his thoughts, but the truth was that when he was out of the studio and I was alone with his students, some of the more adventurous ones would gather around my easel, and make pointed suggestions as to what they and I could do together by the banks of the Tiber.

But I let him continue. "You see, Artemisia, men like Tassi are like wild horses. Once broken in, they become amenable, quiet, and domestic. Tassi feels that it's time he settled down. He's lived a wild life. While we've been working on some of his large canvasses together, he has told me something of his earlier life. He learned his painterly skills in Florence, but committed some offense against the Grand Duke, and so he was made into a slave on some of the Duke's convict galleys; that's where his interest in seascapes and men at sea originated.

"And yes, truth to tell, he has known many women, but has always behaved properly, as befits a gentleman. So when he marries you, he will instruct you in the arts of lovemaking of which you know nothing. As I said earlier, dearest daughter, had your beloved mother not died five years ago, she would have undertaken the duty of instructing you, so that on your wedding night, you would have been prepared for what will happen to you. I attempted to introduce you to these necessary conversations, but I'm not as equip as would be a woman. I shall ask the wife of one of my friends if she will have a conversation with you about what is expected of you on your wedding night," he said.

"But why do I have to get married, father?" I asked, with a tone of desperation in my voice. "Many women go through life without a husband."

"Yes, and they're sent to be cloistered nuns in a nunnery. Is that what you want? I was going to do that when you were a girl, but your skills as a painter, and your mother's insistence, stopped me, so that the world could see and know your talent, and you, your paintings and your talent would not be sequestered, out of the sight of the world, inside the cloister walls. But is that what you want? Do you want to become a nun, for as I see it, Artemisia, it's either a nunnery or marriage. There are no other roads available for a woman in your position, a woman without means, without income and without sufficient in an inheritance to make her own way in life."

"What!" I said, suddenly angry. "Were I a man, I could remain single, and be a painter travelling from palace to palace, court to court around the world, being commissioned to create works of art, and live the life I want. Like Leonardo da Vinci. Why can't I live that life?"

"Because you're a woman!" he shouted, now getting angry. "No woman of standing, of stature, ever, has travelled the roads of Italy, France, and other countries, selling her talents, alone and unaccompanied, like the peripatetic Scholastics. It's unheard of. If you remain unmarried and ply your trade as a painter, then who will support you if great men won't commission you?

"And be assured that they won't, Artemisia, because no Pope or Cardinal, Bishop or Prince will tap you on the shoulder and say, '*Come into my Palazzo and create this or that for me.'* Men who commission these paintings want naked figures of gods or nymphs, satyrs or satyresses. And nobody will allow you to paint nudes from living models. Nobody! So if nobody will commission you, then when I die and this studio closes, how will you live? Your brothers may survive, but what will become of you?

"No, Artemisia, the decision has been taken. The offer has been made and accepted. It is a good match, and when you are happily ensconced as his wife, you will thank me. You will be wedded to Agostino Tassi. You will have a life of comfort. You will give yourself to him freely and willingly. You will! Your father demands it."

And he dismissed me, with a wave of his hand. I left his bedchamber, and stood in the hallway, breathing deeply. Not only had I been violated by Tassi, but now I was trapped into an evil marriage forced upon me.

As a daughter, I had to do what my father ordered me to do.

As a woman, I had no means of escape. I would be destitute unless I agreed to marry Tassi, for my father would undoubtedly disown me.

But as an artist, I could use my characters to define the iniquitousness of my situation, and what had happened to me.

———

It was close to eight in the evening when David and Martina arrived back at their hotel. For Martina, it had been an exhausting, but unexpectedly successful couple of days in the Apostolic Library. For him, days of waiting and feeling useless. At the elevators in the lobby, they waited for their ride up to their floor, when Martina turned to David, and said, "Do you want to go up to our rooms, now? I'm so animated, so full of Artemisia, that I'll never be able to sleep. Fancy a drink in the bar?"

"Thank heavens you suggested that. I was going to ask you, but didn't feel it was appropriate," he said.

She laughed, and hit him on the arm. "Don't be so stuffy. You're a typical Aussie gentleman. Full of bravado, but too shy to ask a lady out."

They walked into the bar and took a table overlooking

River Tiber and the Sant'Angelo Bridge. The waiter took their orders, and they settled back to reflect on the events of the past couple of days.

"Is there any doubt that Artemisia could be referring to having placed this document in her father's grave?" asked David. By mutual agreement, their conversation was carried in an undertone, as in Rome, one never knew who might be listening.

She shrugged her shoulders, and leaned closer to him. "There's always doubt. We don't know the state of her mind when she wrote the letter. We don't know if her cryptic reference meant England. We don't know if the meant Somerset House in London. There's so much speculation. But when we try to fit other possibilities into the puzzle, none of them fits as well as Orazio's grave under the altar of the Queen's private chapel in Somerset House.

"The problem is," she continued, "that we don't know if the grave still exists. Remember at the time that England was under the authoritarian reign of King Charles 1st. There were religious wars between Catholics and Protestants, there was civil unrest in England because Charles thought he was in charge by the Divine Right of Kings but Oliver Cromwell believed that the people ruled through Parliament, and because Henrietta Maria was a Catholic Queen and hated by the population. I've checked the history of where Orazio was buried, in the Queen's Catholic Chapel in Somerset House, and it was attacked by a mob in 1648, but we don't know what was destroyed. We know that they ransacked the chapel, burnt the fittings and with a pike stabbed the altarpiece, which had been created by Rubens, but we don't know whether they went beyond and desecrated the grave.

"We also know that Artemisia left England in 1648 when the Civil War ended. Or she may have left at the beginning of 1649 when he was beheaded, which really was the end of the fight between Charles' Royalist' forces, or Cavaliers as they were known, and the Parliamentary army of Roundheads. By his execution, it was proof positive that Parliament was the supreme government of England. Artemisia may have dug up the book and taken it with her, or she may have left suddenly and hoped that it would stay safe. There's so much we don't know, which is lost in the mists of history. That's the problem of being an historical researcher," said Martina, sipping her drink.

"By the way," said David, "I'm not shy. You said at the elevator that…"

"Yes, I thought you were shy. In Italy, men are much

more inclined to touch and kiss a woman when they meet. But all you do is shake hands. I thought for a moment that you didn't like me."

Surprised, he said, "No...no, quite the opposite. You're an amazing, fabulous, beautiful and brilliant lady. I admire you greatly. It's just that I...."

She waited for him to finish what he was going to say, but he lapsed into silence. She found it bemusing. So she continued, «I know I'm talking about things the way they were 30 years ago, but in those days in Italy, a girl learned from an early age that when she walked through the streets, the wolves would whistle and pinch her bottom and do everything to make her want to make love to them. It never worked of course, but that sort of thing has been going on since the time of the Caesars. They used to do it because it's the manly thing to do. When I was in America, the approaches men made to women were far less subtle....and today, with so much dating on social media, I'm really out of touch."

David burst out laughing.

"......everybody thought that because you spoke with an Italian accent, you were fair game. Even when I said 'no' very firmly they assumed I meant 'yes.' A couple of academics in America are still nursing very sore balls when they kept trying, so I made it plain that I wasn't interested in sleeping with them. In America, only a kick in the balls will convince people you mean what you say."

David burst out laughing again, and raised his glass to toast her.

"So, David, what did you think of our Cardinal?"

David thought for a moment, and replied, "He's amazing. Such a brilliant universal mind, such a depth of knowledge, such an elevated position in the Vatican and the Catholic Church, and yet it's all bound up in such modesty."

Martina nodded and sipped her wine. "Yes," she mused. "That's as accurate a portrait of my beloved Cardinal Arturo. You know, if he wasn't a cardinal, and wasn't so old, I would have married him. When I was his student and he recognized my interest in art, he nurtured me, lovingly as a father. But there was a part of me that loved him like a man. My husband, my ex-husband, wasn't jealous, but then he was off living his own life with women, so when I got a chance to go to America, it was both a relief and a way out."

"And in America," David asked, "did you find any love interest?"

She shook her head. I was working so hard, teaching

in a second language and at a different university, and all the politics. It was all I could do keep my head above water."

"American men didn't do anything for you?" he asked, but immediately realized that it was a leading question, and he'd only known Martina for a matter of a few days.

"Sure. Some were very attractive, some not, but I'm a European and I dance to a different drum beat."

He didn't answer immediately, but nursed his drink. "It surprises me that you weren't....forgive the expression, but hit-upon. You're a beautiful Italian woman. I'm surprised that people didn't....."

She smiled, and interrupted him. "Of course they did. But I had a way of handling it. I was always friendly, but made people realise where my barriers were placed. I went over to work and build my reputation, not to have stray liaisons with academics. And what about you? Have you had stray liaisons in your work as a geologist? You must have travelled a fair amount," she said.

He laughed. "I did a lot of travelling, but mainly into deserts and deep valleys or high mountains. To be honest, when you're working 15 hour days, seven days a week on location, it's so good to get a good night's sleep. And when I got home from my explorations, my wife and I had so many wonderful times together."

She smiled, and wanted to tell him that he was doing a pretty good job of underselling himself. But she was entranced. Italian men outside of the University or academic environment were so sure of themselves, so dismissive of women like her, women who could hold their own in any educational and intellectual realm. Which is why she liked David. He was modest and thoughtful, didn't boast or brag or try to impress. And he was good looking, which was a bonus.

She wanted to interrupt, but she looked at him, deep in reflection, and remained silent. He continued, "You're so brilliant, you know so much; I feel so out of my depth when I'm with you. The woman I'm married to is lovely and intelligent, and we're really comfortable together. But we talk at night about the kids and politics and television and sometimes we discuss the books we're reading. But I listen to you and the way you talk to the Cardinal, and it's a level and depth of intellect I simply don't have. I'm just concerned you'll consider me a bit of a buffoon, like Artemisia considered her husband....what's his name?"

"Pierantonio...."

"Yes, him."

Martina nodded, and sipped her drink. "You're not a

fool, David. As you've just said, this just isn't your field. Remember, it was you who found the lost Artemisia. Not me, not Arturo and not a world-wide legion of brilliant art experts."

He didn't know what to say, and so he remained silent.

"I too work hard and don't have time for a social life. So if you're interested in spending some social time with me, I'd welcome it," she said.

"Social time? I'm sorry, I don't understand...."

"David, Rome is a thrilling city, with theatres, opera, the best restaurants in the world. What I'm saying is that we're going to spending some time together, and while we'll work hard, we might like some time off in the evening. I have friends here in Rome to whom I could introduce you, or we could do what I don't have time to do in Florence, and that's go out at night to dinner, like this, or go to a movie or a play. All I'm saying, darling, is that let's not spend all night in an hotel room....let's have a bit of fun. That's it."

She reached over, gave him a kiss on the cheek, and walked away.

The following morning, they breakfasted together in the hotel's cafeteria.

"Do you want to go to a movie tonight?" he asked.

Martina sipped her coffee, and burst out laughing. « I was wondering if you'd thought more about what I said. Yes, I'd love to go to a movie, or I'll look and see what opera is on at the *Teatro dell'Opera de Roma*."

She opened her computer and through habit, checked her emails. "Oh shit! Oh bugger!"

"What?" he asked.

"I've just heard back from Somerset House. I enquired after Orazio Gentileschi's grave in the Queen's chapel, and they've written back to say that it was vandalized and destroyed as was much of the Chapel in the revolutions of the middle of the 17th Century. But they say that the old Somerset House was pulled down by Sir William Chambers, the Comptroller of the King's Works, and in 1775 they began building the new Somerset house. They say that there are a number of headstones saved which weren't damaged, but his wasn't one of them."

"So that means the quest is over," said David. "If the grave has been destroyed, we won't be able to find the book."

She turned around in her seat and looked at him. "Perhaps. But she was a resourceful woman. Who knows what she did with the book. Remember that England at that time was riven by civil war. Who knows what she took with her when she left England."

She devolved into silence. He'd seen that look of deep introspection before, so he remained quiet.

"Y'know, David, there's something that's been bothering me ever since we found Artemisia's letter. Why was it in the papers of Cardinal Guido Bentivoglio. Sure, he was a collector of art, and yes, in his day he was a prominent Catholic. But he wasn't the Pope. We're assuming that he was a friend of Artemisia's lover, but we have no proof. That's a line of enquiry I'd like to follow through."

She turned to him, and said, "We're not finished yet!"

## PART, THE FOURTH

A week after I was deflowered, after a week of restless sleepless nights in which my dreams were black and menacing, I woke, dressed quickly and decided to spend the day in contemplation. I wouldn't work at my art, but instead, I would withdraw, and if I could ride, then I would take a horse into the hills, and there I'd find a pleasant rustic inn and spend the day in the bosom of Nature. Up there, in the hills surrounding Rome, where the air was pure, the silence was comforting and the peace was calming, I could breathe deeply, and reflect on the sudden change to my life.

Rarely did I leave the city; rarer still were the times when I would be alone, and not accompanied by my father, or a companion. But this was a day like no other. The previous day I'd been laid low, and then, as if by some miracle, like some *deus ex machina* from a Greek tragedy, the fates had decided to have fun with me, and lift me up so that I would be wed.

But where was I in all of this? Women have very few of the rights of men in Italy, but having been violated, I began to wonder what were my rights, my ability to make decisions, in the schemes of others? Of Tassi? Of my father? And of that duplicitous termagant, that Xanthippe, that conniving and back-stabbing Judas in a woman's skirts? That devious Tuzia?

Didn't I have a voice, an opinion? Did I not count in my father's calculations? Were I a man, I would be consulted, heeded, my opinion judged as worthy of consideration, weighed up in the balance along with the opinions of other worthies. But that wasn't allowed to a woman. A woman in Rome, in Florence, in any city of Italy, had no voice, no standing, no matter.

Just because I was born woman, did it mean that my sex deprived me of the right to do what I wanted to do? Did I not have the right to say no to my father, to Tassi? Did I have to abide by the decisions thrust upon me by others? Even those who were supposed to love me, care for me, ensure my welfare?

Sitting in the sunshine outside of the Wayfarer's Inn, on the northern route to Siena, drinking a light Chianti and eating some bread and meat, I pondered these questions, and decided that every road I could travel, other than that ordained by my father and Tassi, would result in overwhelming pain, grief, difficulties, objects which were insurmountable and ultimately my destruction. And the destruction of my family!

Yet the sunshine, the occasional friendly greeting from passing travelers, and the kindliness of the innkeeper's wife who kept coming out to me and supplying me with more wine and food, allowed the tempests in my mind to calm.

Yes, I would marry Tassi. Yes, I would remain silent about the rape, for Italian law viewed the punishment of a marriage as sufficient reparation. And yes, I would swallow my bile, bury my anger and hatred, and let it erupt from my breast, from time to time, in my paintings. And if anybody asked me in the future why my women were so angry, I would be forthcoming, but not identify Tassi as the perpetrator. The world would know what had happened to me. Just not who'd done it to me.

By the time I had settled things in my mind, it was already the middle of the afternoon, and time for me to return. I paid the money I owed for the food and wine, and bade farewell to the innkeeper's wife. But as I walked towards my tethered horse, she ran out, and begged me to wait a moment. Then she made me promise that one day, I'd return and taste her mushroom soup, which traditionally she made with a crop of porcini mushrooms she picked in the early hours of the morning higher up the mountain. She assured me that a bowl of that, with freshly baked bread from her oven, was better than anything I'd eat in a restaurant in the centre of Rome.

I thanked her for her kindness, but as I did so, there was something approaching a tear in her eye. She smiled at me, stroked my face, and said, "So beautiful."

I was shocked. This wasn't the way in which innkeepers behaved in the city. I hugged her, and asked why she was being so kind. She said that many years ago, she had a daughter who would have been my age, had she not died of typhus.

I nodded, and said to her that I had a mother who had died five years earlier, and who would have treated me with the same concerns as did the innkeeper's wife. We looked at each other for a long, long moment, joined in loss and grief, and hugged again. Then she said something which truly shocked me.

"Child, for the whole of this day, I've watched you as you sat outside and thought deeply about something. I don't know what it is, but whatever was the thing which concerned you most, remember this….we are here on this earth for a short time, compared to the rocks and trees, the sun and the sea. So you must only rely on your own self, on no one else, to go forward. Your future is in your hands, and yours alone."

I nodded in agreement, kissed her again, and repeated my promise to return. Then I rode back into Rome, and to my home, thinking about what she had said. But my future had been taken out of my hands, and placed into the custody of somebody else. My future! But not my art.

The first thing my father demanded of me when I had returned the horse to the stable, was why I had spent an entire day at leisure, and not working. But even before I could answer, he continued, "As an artist, you are tied to your canvas, like a monk chained to his Bible, or a horse tethered to a tree. You cannot spend time away from your subjects, or they will reflect your absence in the way they look and in the feelings of the painting.

"The greatest artists, men on whose shoulders you stand, Leonardo, Michaelangelo, Raffaello, spent every waking, and many sleeping moments, thinking about their paintings. Do you think that they took a day off to daydream in the countryside, when some worthy had paid them good money to finish a commission? No, of course not. So let's not have any more of this nonsense, Artemisia. It is hard enough for you, a woman, to be taken seriously as a painter. Don't make it easier for your critics to find reasons to ignore you and your work."

And with that, he returned to his studio. There was not a question about me, my feelings, my joy or doubts about my forthcoming engagement to Tassi; not a word about where I'd been, who I'd met, what I'd spent the day doing. On previous days, I would have been hurt, but today I remembered the Innkeeper's words of wisdom. *My future is in my hands. Not the hands of others.*

So I returned to my room, lifted the sheet off my canvas and looked again at my Madonna and Child. And then a problem struck me. My models were Tuzia and her infant child. Although I had spend the week in my room, or downstairs with my father, since my violation, I had hardly looked at Tuzia; and if our eyes had accidentaly met, mine were full of hatred and contempt.

Yet she was the woman I would soon be visiting in the kitchens in order to berate, to accuse, to denounce for her complicity in my rape and to dismiss her from my household. And if I did that, and she would refuse to sit for me; then I would have to abandon the painting, for to paint another model over Tuzia's face, as well as to find another cherub, would be difficult. Not impossible, but difficult; and then my father would ask why I had changed models and what would I tell him?

So despite my fury at her, in order to retain her services, I would have to pretend that I had not been violated, as I was forced to pretend to my father, my brothers and Tassi himself.

Burying the truth of what happened to me on that day was akin to burying a corpse in unhallowed ground. Soon it would rot and decompose and the stench would rise up and overwhelm me. But what else could I do? Life had to continue, and I had to put the events into the perspective of my life. What did his violation say about me, my paintings, my future as an artist, my relationships with other painters? Nothing. It said nothing about me. It said only things about the men who'd abused me.

So for me to ensure, as the innkeeper's wife said, that my future was in my hands, and not the hands of others, I had to put the violation behind me; to treat it like breaking my arm from a fall from my horse, or an attack of a disease from which I recover. I had to put the assault into a box in my mind, lock it securely away, and keep the key available so that when the moment was right I would unlock the box, let out my fury and then, like Pandora, unleash all the ills of the world upon the people who had abused me, but mainly Agostino Tassi. Prometheus had stolen fire from the gods and suffered the consequences. Tassi had stolen my virginity and my good name, and although he wouldn't know it until the time was right, I would be the eagle that would eat his liver, every day until his end.

Realizing my feelings, Tuzia kept out of my way, and when I confronted her downstairs, she quickly excused herself and said that she had errands to run. During the day, if she heard my footsteps in a corridor, she would scurry away; at night, she kept to her room, and, I assume, locked the door. So my confrontation — or my offering a hand of reconciliation — was neither given nor taken.

I didn't see Tassi for another two days. I don't know why he didn't visit, but my father continued to work with him on the vast painting they were creating inside the Casino delle Muse of the Palazzo Pallavicini-Rospigliosi. But then, suddenly, when my father appeared after work and as the sun was setting, he opened the door of the house, accompanied by Tassi. I watched their entry, hidden by a column from an upper balcony.

The moment I saw him, I felt like somebody had just

punched me in the stomach. He walked into the house, put off his cloak and hat and flung them nonchalantly over a chair in the entry hall.

My father shouted up, "Artemisia, dearest, your father and your fiancé are here. Come down and greet us."

He then called loudly for Tuzia to bring them a carafe of wine and some food as they walked into the studio. I timed my descent from my upper vantage point to coincide with the entry of Tuzia as she carried the refreshments on a tray into the studio. I wanted her to see that normality had returned to the household.

As she entered the studio, carrying the wine and goblets, and platters of meats, cheeses and bread, I ran downstairs in order to follow her inside.

Cheerfully, I said, "Dear Father, greetings. And to you, dear fiancé, I greet you also. May I greet you with a kiss?"

He was looking at an unfinished painting by one of our students, and turned in surprise at my voice. I walked over, kissed my father a daughterly greeting, and then went over and hugged and kissed Tassi. I could see the look of surprise in his eyes. I then turned and beamed a great big smile at Tuzia.

"Tuzia, dear friend. Could I impose upon you to bring

another goblet for me. I wish to drink a cup with my father and my future husband."

She wasn't as good an actress as me, and her jaw dropped in shock. But she recovered quickly and left the room.

"So, husband-to-be, what have you and my father accomplished today?" I asked.

Before he could answer, my father told me of the work they'd done that day. As he spoke, I found a chair and sat down, listening eagerly to his discourse. I turned to Tassi, who was sitting there, listening to Orazio, but looking at me as though I was Mount Etna, quietly smouldering, wondering whether this was all a playact, and whether I would suddenly explode and spew out hot lava.

When my father had finished I said cheerfully, "What a wonderful day. But tomorrow, Father, is Saturday, and I'm wondering whether I have your permission to ask Maestro Tassi if he'd like to come for a short trip into the countryside. Because he is Tassi, I won't need a chaperone. A few days ago, I rode into the hills on the road north from Rome to Siena, and there I found the most delightful inn, serving delicious food and wine. If you are free, Signore Tassi, then I would truly enjoy spending the day with you, and of course, Father, you are welcome to accompany us….as is Tuzia. The day I spent outside Rome has revitalized my spirits, and I would like my fiancé to experience the quiet and peace of the countryside."

Still surprised, Tassi said, "I would be delighted to accompany you Madonna fiancée. And to share the day of ease with you, Maestro Gentileschi, would be a delight."

"A shame," said father, "for tomorrow I have four students coming here. All have paid to attend my class, and I cannot let them down. And Tuzia will be needed here to prepare food and drink for these boys. But on the condition that I have your word that you will conduct yourself at all times like a gentleman, Maestro Tassi, then I would be happy to give you my permission."

In truth, I knew about the students, and Father's and Tuzia's inability to join us. What I wanted was to be alone with Tassi, and to determine how our futures would be drawn.

The following day, two hours after sunrise, our horses saddled and the panniers full of food and wine, as well as a blanket for us to sit on when we were in the country, we set off from my house to the Siena road. For the first hour or so, we rode in virtual silence, Tassi commenting on my riding ability, and me talking about the difference between the air of the countryside and the fetid stench of the city, especially in the summer months. He commented that at least, these days, the Tiber River wasn't full of murdered bodies as in the days of the Borgias.

But by the time we'd reached the inn where I'd stayed three days previously, we stopped, tethered the horses, and entered. At first, because the sun was already high in the sky and our eyes weren't used to the darkness of the inn, I could see very little; there were some patrons sitting on stools and benches at tables, but little more.

And then, as my eyes were beginning to adjust, I heard the innkeeper's wife welcoming me, "Oh, my dear, you've returned. But I haven't been up the mountain to gather the mushrooms."

I smiled, and said, "No matter, Madonna, I'm here with my husband-to-be to drink some ale before we continue our journey."

"Then come and sit down, and I'll fetch you the very best ale that we have. My husband brews it fresh every month, and today's is just a few days old."

We sat and she came over with two mugs and a flagon of ale. As we drank, Tassi said to me, in a voice which meant he didn't want to be overheard, "Artemisia, why are you being like this? The last time we were alone, you were threatening to kill me with a knife. Now, suddenly, you're a loyal and charming companion. Am I about to get a big surprise? Have you got a knife in your horse's pannier with which to stab me in the back when I'm not looking? I want to know what's going through your mind."

I laughed and reached over the table top for his hand. "If I was intent on murdering you, would I bring you here to a place so public, and introduce you to my new friend, the innkeeper's wife?"

"Then why has your demeanour changed so much? Why are you being so compassionate and friendly?" he asked. "You swore that you would tell the authorities what had happened, and gave me the very real impression that you sought my death."

"Because, Agostino, what you said to me then was quite correct. Though I was in pain, in real and physical pain, and my mind was in turmoil from what you and your lapdog did, as the next day dawned, and I woke up and my pains weren't as great, I realised that I could accept your forced love making as an early trial for the love making we will enjoy during our marriage, though it's certainly not how I wanted to lose my maidenhood.

So I chose this rather than the other path; the alternative would be to reject what you said to me, accuse you before the world, and then by my decision, you would bring shame and ruin upon myself and my family.

"But then you offered me marriage and a ring, both as an apology for what you'd done to me and as a punishment for the crime you committed. I know that I am below you in status in Roman society, and that you will be accused of marrying below your station. But you're not marrying a servant girl you made pregnant, one with no breeding, education or skills. I am a good painter, and men of the quality of Caravaggio have said that one day I will be counted amongst the truly excellent artists of our age. I believe that myself, and with your tutelage and wisdom, I will continue to improve.

"So rather than viewing ours as a forced marriage to expiate your sins against me, and far from a marriage below your status, I have come to terms that we are equals in our relationship, and that my talents will one day match yours. And think about this, Agostino, what great painter throughout history has had for a wife a woman who is acknowledged as being equally skilled as a painter. We will be a celebrated couple, and we may be invited into the royal palaces of Europe, of France or Germany, Italy or England or any other great nation, as guest painters on commission." I remained silent, and looked across the table at him. He was thinking deeply, and suddenly nodded. "Yes, you're correct. This is good. I'm glad that this is the way you're thinking. Very glad. Now, let's drink our ale, and ride into the hills where there's nobody around, and gently and lovingly know each other in body as well as friendship, but this time as husband and wife."

I was surprised. "But dear husband-to-be. I'm still bruised from when you took my maidenhood."

He shrugged. "What is a bruise of valour when shared between lovers? Come, Artemisia. Your fiancé requires you to follow him."

And he stood, paid for the ale, and we left the inn.

Later that morning, when the sun in the sky indicated that it was the middle of the day, we stopped our ride north, and headed across a field to climb higher and higher into the hills. As we breasted one of the foothills, we stopped and turned in our saddles. Rome, far into the distance in the south, looked as though the tops of the buildings were on fire. The sun was reflecting off the metal cupolas and rooftops of the towers, basilicas and churches like candles lighting a hallway. Further to the

East was a patch of ground where trees once stood, but now was just grassland, with a brilliant shaft of sunlight shining on it.

"There," said Tassi. "We'll stop over there and take luncheon. I feel we've ridden enough, and if we spend an hour or so there, resting, then we'll return to Rome and your house in time for supper."

So we kicked our horses and they obliged by ambling towards the large clearing. We dismounted and tethered them with sufficient rope that they could graze on the grass in a wide circle. Then we took the panniers and blanket and made ourselves a resting place.

I immediately began to set out plates and knives, followed by the cheeses, meats, olives, peppers, and large chunks of bread and freshly churned butter. When the food was out, I poured Tassi a large goblet of Frascati from the northern Lazio region, the one made from the Malvasia di Candia grape variety, robust but not overpowering. He appreciated my choice of wine, and drank the entire goblet, which I quickly refilled for him.

"Is our life going to be like this, Artemisia? Days in the countryside enjoying the sunshine and having good wine and food?" he asked.

"No, husband-to-be, for then these special times

would become commonplace and no longer appealing. Our life together will be one of hard work on painting commissions, travelling to the courts of kings and princes, and when time and commitments permit, taking days alone and together, like today."

Then the look changed in his eyes. Suddenly, instead of looking at me as a companion, something in his expression altered, and I could sense that he was starting to become passionate and desiring me again.

"I do not need to eat now, but rather I wish for us to lay together as man and...."

"Wife?" I asked.

He laughed.

"Yes," I said. "We can lay together. But first, fiancé, I must repair to the woods with a bottle of water so that I can attend to my womanly parts in private and wash so that I am untainted from the exertions of the day. Please excuse me." And I got up and hid behind a nearby tree.

Now you may be horrified by what I have just written, and by what I was about to do, dear reader. I was about to give myself, freely and totally, to a man who had raped me and stolen my maidenhood. Did I suddenly love him? Had I forgiven him?

No, none of it. I still felt anger and vengeance towards

him. I still wanted to hurt him, report him for his violations. I still wanted to bring him low. I do not ask for your judgement. It is impossible for you to put yourself in my position. This, for me, was the lesser of two evils. I had reasoned it in my mind that any such course of vengeance would have brought greater ruination on me, my father and my brothers, than giving the appearance of being a loving and devoted wife.

My time will come. And his time will come. The great Marcus Aurelius, the Stoic Roman Emperor once said that the best revenge is to be unlike him who performed the injury. So if I can live my life in opposition to the type of man Tassi is, expressed through my paintings, then that will be my revenge.

Now is not the time for vengeance. Now is the time for me to become Colombina, the naughty and mischievous servant girl who I have seen in performances of the Commedia dell'Arte, playing tricks upon her master and fooling him in different ways. So now is the time for me to be a player.

And now it is Tassi's time to be the man he sees himself as, even though it is through the mirror of my eyes. Now I must spend my time cautiously, making him think that he can ease himself into a life of happiness in me, not knowing that he has harboured a viper in his bed; so now is the moment to make this our time. The time to be man and wife. No matter how I seethe inside my guts; no matter how my heart aches when he touches me. In order to protect myself and my family, I had to become an actress; I had to become Colombina, his little dove.

So when I had finished my ablutions behind the trees and I returned to him, having discarded the rag and buried it beneath the leaves and detritus of the forest, I wore a loving smile on my face. I lay down with him in the shaft of brilliant sunshine. And he moved over and took me for a second time. He took me gently, softly, gradually. He took me as he would take his love and lover. As his fiancée. As his future wife. As the mother of his future children.

And me? I lay there and received him. I smiled and thanked him. But I was absent from the entire engagement. So I took him not as a woman, nor a fiancée, nor a wife, but as a viper, coiled, prone, watching - waiting for my moment to strike.

The table was laden with empty crockery, like an archaeological dig for ancient relics. Half an hour earlier, they'd been full of olives, pasta, bruschetta, and bowls of ribollita, the speciality of the restaurant. One dish remained, a few slices of the Cardinal's favorite pizza, which he was slowing and singularly consuming. Martina and David had both surrendered, saying they couldn't eat another mouthful.  Now, watching Cardinal de Santis as he relished every mouthful of the pizza, David was reminded of the Second Deadly Sin, Gluttony.

The Cardinal noticed that David was looking at him eating, and somehow seemed to read his thoughts.

"First Corinthians, David, Chapter 10, Verse 31. *'Therefore, whether you eat or drink, or whatever you do, do all to the glory of God.'* It was the Almighty that guided the chef's hand to make a pizza as delicious as this. I live as sin-free a life as possible, but when I eat, I try to glorify God in my choices. The moment it comes to food, the flesh is willing, but the mind is weak."

David remained quiet and smiled. He'd been forced to limit the amount of food he was eating since he'd come to Italy. But whenever he ate with the Cardinal, David slept badly that night with a seemingly immoveable stomach full of carbohydrates. And he was suffering flatulence from all the pasta he was eating in Italy. He wondered why the Italians didn't spend their days farting.

Indeed, since the Cardinal and Martina had dived back into the library two weeks before in order to study Cardinal Bentivoglio's letters and documents, he'd done little but act as a tourist in Rome, travel down to Naples, explore the Amalfi Coast and the divine hilltop towns along the way, and return at night to a tired but tender Martina. He'd phoned Jackie and suggested that she jump on a plane and join him, but she had too many commitments. And in truth, he enjoyed his time alone at night dining and laughing with Martina. It was always a friendly but professional dinner, talking about anything and everything, and he was drawing closer and closer to her. But even though she touched his arm and held his hand at dinner, when they returned to their rooms, she always kissed him on the cheek, and then retired to his room, leaving him wondering whether she wanted him to push their relationship further.

He felt he was being lazy by not participating more in the research, but both Martina and Cardinal Arturo assured him that they were engaged in major historical and linguistic research, the sort of investigations which broke new academic territory. And because he spoke neither Latin nor medieval Italian, his use to them was little more than ensuring they had adequate supplies of coffee when they took a break. So for the past two weeks, he'd played the part of a tourist, until they emerged that night from the Apostolic Library. Martina had phoned and left a message on his cell phone while he'd been in an art gallery, knowing that he'd return to the hotel before her. She said they had some interesting news, and to meet them in a restaurant close to the Vatican.

It was the first time that David and Cardinal de Santis had met in two weeks. He and Martina had been immersed in the Apostolic Library, morning, noon and on many nights, examining, translating and interpreting the precise meaning of words, expressions, phrases, and greetings in literally hundreds and hundreds of letters which had passed between Cardinal Guido Bentivoglio in Rome, and his correspondents in many Italian cities, as well as in France, Germany, Holland and England. Most of them were Church or State matters, and could be safely ignored, but a good number were copies and responses of letters sent to painters to discuss their work for the Vatican. The only one they had found that was out of the ordinary was the letter from Artemisia to her lover Maringhi in which she told him to recover her book. For some reason they didn't yet understand, the letter had found its way into Cardinal Bentivoglio's papers.

Others of his non-ecclesiastical letters referred to the Vatican's art collection, but the vast majority were dealing with matters concerning his role in the Vatican as Cardinal, Statesman and historian, between the years 1621 when he was made a cardinal, and 1644 when he died suddenly at the age of 65. According to Arturo, he died shortly after a Papal Conclave in 1644.

"It's likely," said Arturo, eating a third slice of pepperoni pizza, "that the Conclave killed him. There's cause to think that a lot of older Cardinals were utterly terrified and their lives may have been shortened by that Conclave."

David frowned. "A Conclave? But why should a Papal

Conclave be terrifying? It's only to pick a new pope, isn't it?"

Both Arturo and Martina smiled. "Darling, picking a pope in those days was vastly more intense and much more dangerous than today being a member of the Praesidium and choosing the next Russian president. Vast sums were hurled around to buy votes in the Conclave. Factions among the Cardinals often came to blows, even in the Sistine Chapel. But the 1644 Conclave....you have no idea," she said.

Arturo continued, "About thirty cardinals were locked up in the Sistine Chapel. The Protodeacon, Cardinal de Medici, tried to get an Italian elected as pope. He was opposed by Cardinal Mazaran who was supported by the French Queen Mother, Anne of Austria, who wanted a French Cardinal appointed. They were opposed by Cardinal Francesco Barbarini, who sided with the Spanish Cardinals, and wanted one of their number elected. Vast amounts of money and preferments were offered, but they were deadlocked week after week. Eventually, Barbarini threatened to keep all of the Cardinals in the Conclave locked up and still deliberating so that the older Cardinals would die and hopefully the numbers would change and benefit one side over another. Remember that in those days, the Sacred College was much smaller than today's College, so the death of one or two could have changed the vote dramatically.

"And while all this was going on inside the Vatican, on the streets of Rome, mobs of gangsters, half of whom were paid by the French and the other half by the Spanish, were roaming the streets, looting and beating and causing deadly mayhem."

"Good heavens," said David. "So what happened?"

Cardinal de Santis said, "Well, eventually, the Spanish and the French armies began to move towards Italy and there would have been a full-scale war. The Conclave lasted for about five very long weeks, but eventually, terrified by outside forces and no doubt falling ill and exhausted, the Sacred College elected Cardinal Pamphili, an Italian, who became Pope Innocent X. Both the French and the Spaniards lost out. However, it's said that our friend, Cardinal Bentivoglio was a very strong contender for the Papacy. And here's where it gets very interesting for you and us," said Cardinal de Santis.

"In the correspondence we looked at this morning, Cardinal Bentivoglio sent a letter to Pope Innocent just before the Cardinal died. In it, he said that his health had been made poor by the Conclave, and so he had drawn up his last will and testimony, which he registered with the Secretariat of the Sacred College of Cardinals. But he begged His Holiness to accord him one last wish. He asked Innocent to ensure that when he died, his formal possessions, books and letters and papers, were to be kept in the archives of the Apostolic Library as they were official Church documents. Remember, David, that he was also an historian and knew the importance of official documents. But he asked that his private, non-ecclesiatical, books and letters and papers were to be sent to his home. Both Martina and I know this place, but only as visitors. It's the Castello Estense, the Este Castle in the city of Ferrara. Sometimes it's called the Castello di San Michele, or St. Michael's castle. It's beautiful. In the middle of the city of Ferrara, surrounded by a moat. And if we're lucky, that's where the Cardinal's papers are to be found."

"But Artemisia's book?" asked David.

Both Cardinal de Santis and Martina shrugged. And Arturo reached across the table, and finished the last slice of pepperoni pizza.

"You know," Cardinal de Santis said, "this style of pizza is never eaten in Italy. It's only made for tourists. Such a pity. I love it."

# PART, THE FIFTH

---

Never, ever, will I enter again the month of May without my head feeling as though it's exploding. For in the month of May, my private anger became my public shame. It was the time of the trial of Agostino Tassi for raping me. The trial began at ten in the morning on the fifteenth of May, 1612.  I will never forget this moment when my private anger became my public shame. It's inscribed on my soul, painted into my canvasses, etched forever onto every mirror in which I look.

The Judge had assembled a subordinate judge and six jurors, only men of course, to hear the trial. My father and I entered the courtroom, and I knew that my fate was sealed, regardless of the outcome. Tassi wasn't on trial for raping me, but for financial restitution to my father and brothers for having stolen from them. His taking of my virginity had reduced my value as a marriageable commodity. They wanted either a large dowry from Tassi, or a contract of marriage.

But I jump forward too much, over-eager to come to that moment in my story. So I must begin in the previous year, when my father was working with Tassi, who he was certain would soon become his son-in-law.

It happened that as they were working on their mural, a woman came to the Palazzo Pallavicini-Rospigliosi to seek out Tassi. She was led by the guards, down into the Casino delle Muse where they were painting. My father told me that when she appeared, Tassi was shocked. Mortified. He shouted at her to leave the Casino immediately, but this angered her, and she began to shout. She said many ungracious things to him, horrible things. She sounded like a fish wife. Tassi hurriedly put down his brushes, and rushed to grab her by the arm and march her out.

Alone, except with Tassi's servant, Giovanni, my father turned, and asked the young man, who was the Lady.

"No Lady, Maestro. Be assured that Madonna Tassi is no lady," he said.

My father was surprised. A relative? Too young to be a mother and too old to be a daughter, he said to Giovanni,

"Madonna Tassi? A sister?"

"Sister? No, Master. That's the Maestro's wife. That's Sophia Tassi."

"His....?"

"Wife," said Giovanni. "They've been married these past fifteen years. Not happily, though. She's a....well, I shouldn't speak ill of her. And the Master must have the forbearance of Saint to put up with her. I hear tell that he wants her gone, but she won't go, and because they have a son and a daughter, and even though he's the Pope's protégé, nobody will believe that the marriage hasn't been consummated. So no divorce. But I shouldn't say anything, because the Master has told me to remain quiet about his private life."

"His.....wife?" said my father, suddenly needing to sit down. At that moment, he had two options. The first was to await Tassi's return at which time he'd confront him and deal with the *pezzo di merde*. Alternatively, he could leave the commission, return home, say not a word to me, and send out some servants to investigate whether what Giovanni had said was true. Perhaps a divorced wife? Perhaps a mistress who called herself wife?

He decided upon the second option. And the following day, two of our servants returned to inform him that they had visited the area where Tassi lived and talked to shopkeepers and the local priest and others. And all of them returned later in the day with news which they told my father in the confines of his studio. They all confirmed that Tassi was, in fact, married to Lady Sophia, though all acknowledged that the marriage was miserably unhappy.

I had no idea what was happening, although the atmosphere in the house seemed to presage a storm. My father asked one of his servants to bring me to his studio. I followed, and when he asked me to close the door, I knew, deep in my heart, that something was terribly wrong. His studio was usually like a piazza in the centre of a city, always open with people coming and going, food and drink constantly available, and conversation always heard. Today it was menacingly silent.

"Daughter," he said, sitting in his chair with a cloud of doom above his head. "Has your fiancé ever discussed his home and family with you?"

"Sometimes. Not often. I know he has two brothers, but he always tells me that we'll all meet before the wedding. Why?"

"Has he ever mentioned his wife?"

"Wife!" I remember laughing. For a moment, I assumed he meant me, but when I saw the look on his face, I knew the true depths of the problems surrounding me. Suddenly, the floor felt as though it wouldn't support my weight, and I grasped at the arms of a chair so that I could sit down.

He said nothing further, but just looked at me.

"Wife?" I repeated. The word felt bitter in my mouth. "Wife! Tassi has a wife?"

My father nodded. "Yes! He's married....my men confirmed it today. I met her yesterday when she came to the Casino where he and I were working. He bustled her out of the door, but his servant Giovanni told me, and I sent my men to his neighbourhood to confirm my worst fears."

"Wife!" I now shouted the ugly word, a dagger in my heart. "He has a wife?" I realised that I was screaming.

"For months...and months....I've asked him when the marriage contract he promised, will be finalized. He continued to tell me that because he and the Pope held their relationship, because he was His Holiness' protégé, the issue of a contract in marriage was complicated; he said that his financial affairs were being separated from those of his brothers, and he was waiting on the Notary to finalize the distribution of their parent's inheritance. Month after month; more and more excuses. All seemed reasonable. But now, these stories he told taste like ashes in my mouth." My father had to sit, he was so overwhelmed by the enormity of the revelation he'd discovered.

I was gasping for breath. My mind was reeling. It was as though there were two Artemisias…one young woman sitting here, staring at her father, learning the hideous news about her future husband's deceit. But there was another Artemisia in my mind and heart, this one laying on a rug, high in the hills above Rome, drinking Frascati and making love under the burning sun to a lover she planned to marry and then destroy. Which Artemisia was I? What had I allowed myself to become? And all at the behest of men…my father, Tassi, and others who looked upon me as an item of merchandise, and not as a daughter or wife….or artist?

And then my father asked me a question, which was more like a sentence of death than an enquiry. "Tell me honestly and truthfully, girl. When you and Tassi have been alone together, when you've been for rides into the country, has he behaved like a true and proper gentleman? Are you still a maiden?"

My momentary hesitation and the look on my face told him what he needed to know, but not the entire story. And despite the cruel news he had received about the man he had welcomed into our home as his son-in-law, now was the time for me to unveil the truths I'd hidden from him for much of the past year.

"I feared as much," he said.

"But there's much you don't know, father," I told him. "Worse, much much worse than you can imagine."

He shook his head sadly. "How much worse could it be than the fact that your maidenhood has been sullied; that you are no longer a virgin who can be offered to a future husband; that your value has been…."

"Value?" I shouted. "Value! Is that all your daughter is to you. A painting to be sold to the highest bidder? A piece of pottery you sell in the marketplace? I am your daughter. I am Artemisia. My value is who I am, not whether I am intact."

He was shocked by the tone in which I addressed him, but instead of berating me, he shook his head sadly, and said, "Unfortunately, child, this is not how a future husband will view you. The man I want you to marry will be seeking a chaste and untarnished wife."

"Like the Virgin Mary? Come, Father, do you really think that every woman who marries a man goes to the altar in a state of innocence. You may think that, as do many of the men who seek a virgin for a bride, but women have tricks which fool husbands on their wedding nights. Their sheets in the morning may be stained red, but that's because they've secreted vials of goat's blood into the marital bed. Do you think that young women about to get married don't discuss these matters, especially with their maids and servants? Do you think we don't ask advice?"

He opened his mouth, but no sound came out. And after several moments, he said, "You said that your intimacy with Tassi was worse than I could imagine."

I nodded. "On our first occasion, when he took my innocence, he burst into my bed chamber upstairs, along with a companion, locked the door, and raped me. He took me by force. He...."

But it was too much for him to bear, especially after realising that Tassi already had a wife.

"NO!" he shouted. "NO! You lie. Not even Tassi...."

"He did! I swear it on the grave of my blessed mother. I was innocent until then. I had known no man. I was pure in mind and body. And then he burst into my room, forced me onto the bed, and he and his friend raped me. Raped! Your own daughter!"

I stopped talking, because of the look on his face. First it was a look of disbelief. Then shock. And then his brow creased, and he began to shake his head.

"No! No, this cannot be, Artemisia. When did this… this…take place?"

"When he first sought your permission for me to be his wife. He raped me at lunch time on the very day he asked you for my hand in marriage."

"No! I say again, no! Your mind is afflicted by what I told you about his having a wife. He could not have raped you, child, because I remember that day. I remember it clearly as a day of celebration and happiness. It could not….did not…happen. You are deluded. A fever afflicts your brain. You must be ailing from the news that he has a wife. Let me remind you. He and I were painting all that day. At night, I brought him home. You came into the studio…here…this very studio….and you were warm and friendly and accepted his offer of marriage with grace and dignity. Was that the attitude of a woman who had been so grievously wronged?"

I had to drive the issue home. I had to tell him the truth, now that he knew some of what happened. Now I had to expose Tassi's duplicity, as well as his violence. "Was he with you at lunchtime on that day? Or did you lunch alone?"

Father thought back, and suddenly, his face seemed to

drain of blood. He became silent.

I continued, knowing that he now knew the truth. "You ask why I was happy that night. What recourse does a woman have who has been raped, Father? If I had complained to you, you would have beaten him; perhaps even slit his throat. So what would that have achieved? Because he is protected by the Holy See, you would have been arrested and condemned to death.

"Or if you hadn't attacked him. Instead, think what would have happened if you'd decided to use the laws of the land on your behalf and we'd gone to the courts. Then my name would be known throughout the land, not as a defiled women, not as merely a victim, but there would be gossip everywhere saying that I led him on. I couldn't pass by people in the streets without them whispering about me, calling me 'whore' behind my back, knowing that I had been defiled. In the eyes of the street, father, I would have been the guilty party. And Tassi? He would have been slapped on the back, called a rascal, and people would toast him in pubs and inns. And worse; he told me that if I reported him for the assault, he would both ruin me, and you. He would tell lies in public, and they would be believed because he was a protege of the Pope."

My father continued to shake his head in disbelief,

and I know he wanted to contradict me, but I continued, "You have no idea what he said to me when I confronted him the next day, threatening him with the law, even contemplating using your palate knife to skewer him. He stressed that as a protégé of the Pope, as a man of high society, he would ruin me if I reported his crime; I could tolerate the ruination, but I would not allow him to ruin you and our household. He would rain devastation down on us; you would never again be commissioned to work, as neither would I....."

In anger, my father shouted, "Why would I care about that when my daughter...."

So I shouted back, "Because your daughter was the victim, and it was my decision as to how I would respond. And I decided to keep the matter to myself in order not to bring ruin to my family."

He began to speak again, "But why didn't you tell...."

"Because to make amends for his crime, he said he would marry me, make me his wife, and then all would be forgotten and forgiven. Which is what our lives have been during this past year. And so with those options clearly set out before me, I decide to save my pride, save my family, to bide my time, and that any punishment I meted out against him would be done in the cold and harsh light of revenge, and not in the heat of temper. I was willing to wait a year, a dozen years or more if needed, until I wreaked revenge on him for his crime. Or until the white heat of my anger had cooled to cold embers. I made the decision when I was of rational mind; it was a cold and calculated decision, father, but one which would have succeeded, had you not just told me that he has a wife. Now his schemes have been exposed, and my submission to him and his lies has made me into mockery."

I remained silent, as did Father. He breathed deeply, and I could see rage in his eyes and I imagined what he was thinking. He would kill Tassi with his bare hands; no, he would get servants to lay in wait, and they would cut his throat late one night as he walked home; but no again, he wouldn't resort to violence; instead, he would go to the Vatican and seek the assistance of the many Cardinals who hated Pope Paul, to expose his protégé as a rapist and criminal and lecher; and then no, again, for that would make him partisan in the politics of that holy rat's nest, so instead, he would take no action, continue as life had been yesterday, but demand a full explanation from Tassi as to what his plans were in consideration of me.

Of course, I do not know his true thoughts but at

that moment I wished his thoughts turned to vengeance as mine had been for these past months. I was praying that whatever course of action my father took, would be coldly considered, icily calculated and politically careful.

After a long and agonising silence, my father said, "The first thing I shall do, is to do nothing. Nothing other than demand an explanation of why my daughter has been placed in this hideous predicament. Depending on his answer, I will then decide what action to take; it may be to prosecute him in a court of law, or it may be...."

I interrupted him. "A court of law? On what grounds do you feel he can be prosecuted? For violence? For his offense against my person? For lying about his marital status and making me a false promise? You have no grounds to prosecute this miscreant, Father, and even if you had, such a public accusation would require me to be exposed to all of the evidence which will need to be given. It will ruin me and damage you. I would become a laughingstock, the cause of gossip, a figure of ridicule. Think carefully before you take this step, for you may do more damage to those you love than you do to the man you hate."

"No crime?" he shouted. "No crime! But he forced you. He raped you!"

"Which is not a crime in Italy!" I said, as softly and gently as I could.

He sat and continued to shake his head in disbelief. "Surely you can have recourse...."

"No! I have no remedy available to me to punish this man. That's why my first instinct was to use a knife as my judge and jury. But why should I face death because of what he did to me. So becoming his wife was an alternative. And believe me when I say that never would there have been a more shrewish wife than I would have been. Once I was in possession of a ring, and a priest had sanctified our marriage, I would have led him a merry chase. But the ring was never forthcoming, despite my having demanded it month after month. And now I know why."

"But he has robbed me of your value. He has taken your maidenhood, robbed me of your worth as a bride. Where once you could have married into the society in which I walk, now, ruined, you can only expect to marry a stonemason or a fisherman, a lowly farmer or an elderly olive merchant." He continued to shake his hands, surveying in his mind the ruination of all of his plans. Where once he saw his future tied to the trajectory of Agostino Tassi's fortunes, now he saw his life as supporting his unwed daughter, a burden, an encumbrance.

In his thoughts, he left me, and wandered through dark and cold corridors, where all of the doors were bolted against him. I could have argued; I should have berated him for thinking of himself and his fortunes, and not of me and my wounds; of the wrongs done to me. But it would have been of no value, and so instead, I stood, kissed him on his forehead and returned to my room.

I sat, staring at the finished picture of the Madonna and Child, looking at Tuzia's face, and wanted to rip it to shreds with a knife. I had considered taking it in a week or so to the Orsini palace to see whether the Duke would like to purchase it. That would have given me sufficient to money to open up my own studio, and possibly have my own students. If they said no to the Madonna and Child, then perhaps I could travel to Florence and see whether the Medici might consider a purchase; but a young woman, alone on the road from Rome to Florence, was extremely unwise.

How the fortunes of my life had changed. Yesterday I was contemplating the value of my painting and what could be done for my life by selling it. Now I was contemplating the value of my life and whether the only way I could earn money was by selling my body.

As I sat in my chamber, I heard my father leave the house. I assumed that he was going to an inn to drown his sorrows and drink away the disappointment he felt in his daughter.

And me? I lay down on my bed, and burst into tears. I think I cried until morning.

# PART, THE SIXTH

---

Father sought advice from friends and fellow artists, and had consulted a Magistrate who had told him the same things as I had said earlier: that the offense of rape wasn't a crime in the eyes of the law, only in the eyes of society. But he agreed with my father that the offense against his daughter was a matter of commerce, for if the rape was of a virgin, one whose value as a marriageable commodity was based on her maidenhood, then her worth was reduced when her purity had been taken. So my father could prosecute Tassi for the reduction in my value as a bride.

I had begged him not to proceed, for how could I prove that I was a virgin when I first met Tassi. Father assured me that many people would come forward to attest to my character as a young woman of good faith and sober habit. I said that regardless of what people said of me, all Tassi had to do was to say that after his insertion, there was no blood, and my case would be ruined if the judge believed him. And the judge was much more likely to believe a protégé of the Pope, and a man, than the word of a women born of an artist whose reputation was as much that of a drunkard and carouser, as a painter.

So how did I arrive at the door of the Town Hall where a court of law was assembled to hear my father's claims against Tassi. It was in part because the day after my father discovered the existence of Tassi's wife, he sent a servant to command that Tassi appear at his home, and when he did, he was the antithesis of apologetic and repentant; and it was also in part because he told my father what would happen to him if he was unwise enough to follow through with his threats of legal action; but mainly, it was because when my father went to an inn and was in his cups, he was encouraged by his friends, who assured him that Tassi would never appear in court, but would settle for money beforehand, as being the Pope's protégé, they were certain that he would be able to dip into the treasury of the Vatican.

On the day after my father found out about Tassi's wife, he returned with the servants who'd been sent to fetch him. I think he must have realised he was about to be confronted with our discovery, because when he entered the house, pulled in by the servants, his face was as dark as thunder.

"How dare you drag me here, Orazio. What am I, a common trader? You insult me by sending these servants to—" he began.

"Silence!" my father commanded. I was upstairs, hiding behind a pillar on the upper balcony. "Do not raise your voice in my house. Come into my studio, for there is much I have to say to you."

He followed my father, and although the door was closed, I could hear their muffled conversation clearly enough to know the tenor of their words. My father asked whether it was true that Tassi already had a wife. Tassi agreed that he did, but told father that it was complicated. That he'd been trying to rid himself of her for a long time, and would soon resort to violence. Then he would be free to marry me.

"You would do violence to your wife?" my father asked. His tone was of disbelief. "What kind of a man are you, that you would hurt your wife?"

"You were lucky, Maestro Gentileschi, that your wife loved you and you loved her. Not all of us are as fortunate. I was forced to marry my wife to join two families in shared wealth, property and titles. But the marriage never resulted in love, or children. My wife became unmanageable and a hellish shrew. She would follow me wherever I went, berate me in front of my friends, and not once in the past five years have I known her or has she attempted to perform her wifely functions. I have no love for her and want her gone, and if she won't go of her own accord, then my servants will do the job. The Tiber River cleanses many dark deeds and washes them out to sea. Then I will be free to marry...."

My father shouted, "Then you would marry my daughter? My Artemisia? Whom you expect to nimbly step into your house over the bones of a wife you've just had killed? I can't believe my ears."

"Which is why I haven't told you, friend. For this is a messy and risky business, and I didn't want you or Artemisia to become involved. That's why I kept silent," he said.

My father was beside himself with fury. "Out!" he screamed. "Get out. Monster! Demon! Leave my home. You would involve my beloved Artemisia in your evil schemes? You would....no, I can't bring myself to say the words. Leave my house. My home. Never return. You are not welcome here. You are an evil, black-hearted man. I want nothing more to do with you."

And with that he left. From that day onwards, my father planned and plotted an action against him, to expose the man to Roman society, so that they would know why he had brought the law case.

Which brings me, in this story of my life, to the time when I walked from our home to the centre of Rome, close to the Vatican, to the building where men were assembling to hear a case against Agostino Tassi for the offense he had committed against me. And my heart was in my mouth with every step which brought me closer and closer to the court. I felt as though I was the guilty party, somehow about to be judged for a crime I'd committed.

My father was confident, almost buoyant, as though this day would bring him the culmination of all his desires. In the months since he confronted Tassi and the relationship between the two men collapsed, my father had been working on his own paintings, as commissions from other painters, and especially from patrons, had stopped. It was almost as though when Tassi slammed our front door shut, he stopped the world from knowing us.

And so we became a tight and close-knit family unit, father, daughter and brothers—and Tuzia and her young son! Despite what she'd done to me, her complicity in my deflowering, I didn't have the heart to turn her out on the street without a reference. Had my father known about her crimes, he would have kicked her out of the house, baby in tow, but a single mother with no means, no good word from her previous employer, would undoubtedly have ended up in a brothel or standing in some alleyway importuning men for money. So despite her fears every time she looked at me, I treated her like a servant, and no longer as a friend, and assured her that I would be mute about her complicity, provided she remained faithful in service to me and to my family. Did I trust her? No. Of course I didn't.

And so the day in May arrived when we were walking to the court. In his hand was a leather portfolio containing the indictment his lawyer had written, which had been sent to Pope Paul V. Here's what it said....

*"Holy Father and esteemed Brethren of the Sacred College of Cardinals, I, Orazio Gentileschi, Painter and Roman Citizen, do hereby accuse the Artist Agostino Tassi, Roman Citizen, of committing egregious crimes against me and mine. To whit, that he did, on diverse occasions deflower, ravish, molest and despoil my beloved and only daughter, Artemisia, by such carnal actions as to force himself upon her numerous times, against her*

*will and without her compliance. These acts of rapine assault have been grave against my Estate and caused untold damage to me, Orazio Gentileschi, the wretched plaintiff in this cause. Her body is no longer whole and untainted; she is devalued to great men of means, who would, in previous times, have considered her a suitable wife; further, the value of her paintings is diminished because of the lowered standing she now suffers in the eyes of those who once looked kindly upon her. And in accordance with my grief and loss, I seek the punishment of the said Agostino Tassi and recompense from his purse for my grievous losses."*

Imagine how I felt, knowing what was about to be said of me in the court? Imagine how Eloise felt when she heard that Abelard had been castrated; or Cleopatra felt when Mark Anthony sailed away; or how devastated must Isolde have been, sailing to Tristan but arriving to find him already dead.

So imagine how any woman of worth would have felt to know that her standing in the eyes of her fellow citizens was diminished because she was the victim of rape and that her father was seeking financial recompense because of the losses he suffered as a result.

I had been in this building before, but never had it

felt so menacing. In the past, I'd been here when a city official, or a member of the council, had called in my father to discuss a commission he wished to grant for the painting of a portrait or a mural for his home. I loved the architecture, the grand lines of this building. But now, as I walked up the steps, and through the large doorways, I saw the white marble columns, once stable elements supporting the building, suddenly taking on the image of aggressive sentries on guard; the vast cupola, once high and light, was now low and menacing and threatening to plunge down and crush me; the stairs which arched left and right and once led to the grandeur of magnificent offices, now more like the steps which led to a scaffold or the pyre of one of the Inquisition's auto-da-fé.

My father asked one of the guards where the court had convened to hear the case against Agostino Tassi. He was a young man, and as my father spoke the plaintiff's name, the guard suddenly looked at me, and smiled. He hesitated before answering. And his smile broadened as he surveyed my face, my chest, my body. His smile wasn't one of friendship or acknowledgement. It was a different smile. One of knowing something which others didn't know; one of condescension, bordering on superciliousness; one of a superior man looking down upon an inferior woman. It was obvious that he'd heard about the nature of the trial, and was suddenly in the presence of the whore who was accusing a real man of what real men do.

I was immediately angry, hurt and disturbed, and squared my shoulders, fronted him and said, "You were asked a question, guard. Answer my father immediately!"

He seemed to snap out of a fantasy as I confronted him, and said, "The trial is in the Salon of the Tribunal. It's a large room on the upper gallery, next door to the offices of the City Treasurer."

We walked up the staircase, and towards the Salon. My heart, I have to own, was fluttering. It was as though Tassi was slapping my face like he did when he raped me. But it wasn't my face which pounded. It was my stomach. I felt like throwing up, partly through anger, partly fear of the coming ordeal and humiliation, partly seeing Tassi again.

But my father was far more steadfast, and whispered to me, "Our lawyer is inside, dear girl. He will meet us there. He thinks that the trial will last no more than a few days, if that. The evidence against Tassi is overwhelming, especially from the character witnesses who will attest to your goodness, your innocence before you met him."

I nodded, but found it hard to speak. My throat was dry, my heart beating a staccato drumbeat as I gripped his arm for support, and walked towards the door. As we neared, it opened, and a man dressed in drear lawyerly clothes, a red cap, and a black gown with a silken cowl, came out. He looked worried, and said, "Ah, Signore Gentileschi, good. Yes, very good. You're here. And this is Signorina Artemisia. A delight to meet you. I am your father's advocate, Signore Rossi."

But something on his face spoke of problems, which was confirmed when he said, "We must talk. Urgently. Something I feared but had not expected. A trick of the man you're prosecuting, and I fear it puts us in a less secure position," said the lawyer.

"What? But you said...." my father intervened.

"What I said would have been correct and valid had this trial been conducted by a civil court, with a judge and his associates. But overnight, the man you're accusing, Il Signore Tassi, using his relationship with the Holy See, and especially with His Holiness Pope Paul, has had the judge replaced by a Clerical Judge, a member of the Catholic Commission for Justice. So this is no longer a civil trial, but, in effect, a part of the Inquisition."

My father's face suddenly drained of all its blood, and

I thought he was going to faint. I gripped him tightly. I wasn't so badly affected, as I didn't fully understand what was happening.

"But...but...we must stop the trial. Immediately. My daughter can't be party to this. I must take her home, now! The Inquisition!"

The lawyer put a restraining hand on my father's shoulder. "You misunderstand, Signore. She is not on trial. Tassi is on trial. You daughter is perfectly safe. What's changed is the rule of law. Instead of Tassi being tried by a Roman judge of the criminal and civil jurisdictions, one who views the evidence according to the laws of Rome, Tassi is now being tried by a Judge who will view the evidence from both a civil, and an ecclesiastical viewpoint, and so the questions your daughter will have to answer may be different from what I anticipated. But the good thing is that his punishment, if he's found guilty, will be more harsh.

My father was mystified, and asked, "But why has he done this?"

To which our lawyer replied, "I don't know. I truly don't. For most men, it's the last thing they would have done. It's beyond my understanding. Were this a simple court of law, the punishments for his crimes would be harsh but bearable. But now that he has invoked the judges of the Inquisition, which is his right as a protégé of the Pope, then the dangers to Tassi, if the judge finds him guilty, are vastly more severe forms of punishment. As a criminal in the eyes of Rome, he would be fined or imprisoned for a short term, if found guilty. But as a guilty man in the eyes of the Inquisition, well, the punishments are vastly more stern, and range from imprisonment to banishment to torture to burning at the stake," said the lawyer.

My father shook his head, and said softly, "He's done this because now the Pope can bring pressure on the judge to be lenient on behalf of his protégé, Tassi."

"Perhaps. I don't know. But as far as I'm concerned nothing except the nature of the court and the judge has changed. I shall still prosecute him for his crimes against your daughter, and I shall defend her against any scurrilous allegations he utters. Now, Signore and Signorina, we must go into the court. The trial awaits its accusers. Tassi is already there, surrounded by a few well-wishers."

Silently, I followed the lawyer. When we were in the Salon, I stood at the door for several moments, looking around the room. My legs would not carry me forward.

Even though I was the innocent party, I felt that every man, for there wasn't one woman other than me, was turning and staring at me and their looks, their humourless stares, their scowls and visages, were full of condemnation. And then, across the Salon's floor, I saw Agostino Tassi, sitting with friends, having a conversation, smiling and grinning. Somebody said something and they all erupted in laughter. He saw me enter the Salon, but did not acknowledge my presence. Instead, he seemed to sneer and then look away to speak to his companions. One of them turned and looked in my direction. He mouthed a word which I read clearly, and then he bit his thumb, a great insult.

What he mouthed to me was the word *Puttana*. Whore! And the moment his companion had uttered the word, Tassi burst out laughing again. Now, only now, did I understand the true horror of what was about to befall me.

The lawyer whispered, "I must sit there, in the Advocates bench. You, Signore Gentileschi, sit there, in the front row of the gallery reserved for interested parties; and you, Signorina Artemisia, sit there." He pointed to a chair close to where Tassi and his comrades were sitting.

"No!" I whispered in fear. "I can't sit there. It's beside the rapist."

The lawyer shrugged. "I'm sorry, Madonna, but that's where the court determines that you will sit. Close to the man you accuse. The judge will be scrutinising both you and Tassi as the evidence is presented, and will determine its veracity by the reactions on your faces. That's why you and the man you accuse must sit close."

Terrified I walked over to the seat not a body length from where Tassi was sitting. As I sat, one of his friends leaned close to my chair, and whispered, "Tonight, whore, I will take you in an alleyway. Tassi says that you're better than any whore he's ever had. Young and tight and delicious...."

I bit my lip, and smiled at him, "Yes, dearest one. Come to me in an alley. For then I will do to you what I did to Tassi, I will stab your manhood with a knife and watch you bleed to death in that alleyway. Say goodbye to life, you piece of scum."

Shocked, he withdrew his face from mine, but tried to put on a manly façade by laughing; I knew he was unnerved by my vehemence.

At that same moment, the door above the Judge's bench opened, and in walked three men. All wore clerical garb, but the man in the middle, whom I assumed was the Judge and Inquisitor, was wearing a purple stole around his shoulders. They found their positions and stood before their chairs, as all in the courtroom bowed at their eminences.

A man standing behind the chair of the chief judge, banged his staff on the wooden floor, and said loudly, "This court will come to order. All talk will cease other than those parties gathered here to determine the truth of the Indictments. Silence!"

Then the Chief Judge, his elderly grey face taut and serious, said, "His Holiness, Paul, the Fifth of that holy name, by the Grace of Almighty God, Bishop of Rome and Father to the World, has convened this court and Inquisitorial Tribunal, and commanded me, in the blessed Name of Jesus Christ, Our Lord, to hear evidence against one, Agostino Tassi, who is accused by one, Orazio Gentileschi, of the defilement of his daughter, Artemisia; that such defilement has markedly devalued the said Artemisia's worth and value in the eyes of wealthy men or men of stature in our nation, for no right-thinking man would now marry a defiled woman; further, that such defilement will diminish the value of said Artemisia as a painter, and her significance to him as a daughter to her father. Signore Gentileschi hereby begs the Court to judge the said Agostino Tassi as the man who has caused him monetary and financial loss, and seeks to redeem such loss by compensation and retribution.

"For his part, Signore Tassi denies all of the allegations made against him, and states that not once did he defile said Artemisia Gentileschi by force, but did so in compliance of her will and desire. And so this trial and Inquisitorial Tribunal will determine, on the evidence presented, the veracity of each person's claim and will offer its judgement accordingly. May the Almighty One view our proceedings with grace and love, and bless this holy court and tribunal."

Tassi's friends looked at me, and continued to sneer. I stared back at them, unblinking, not a muscle moved on my face. And discomfited by my stone look, as though I was Medusa the Gorgon, they looked away from me.

The judge continued, "I will now hear evidence of the claim which Signore Gentileschi makes. Advocate Rossi? Are you ready to present the accusations against Signore Tassi on behalf of your client?"

Our advocate stood, and said that he was. And for an hour, I listened to this man, whom I had only met this morning, talk about my father, the talents he had as a painter, the commissions he had received from some of the most famous in the land and the fact that he had nurtured in me a love of his art.

It was a eulogy, an homage to his indescribable genius as the greatest painter of his age. I thank all the Saints of heaven that Caravaggio wasn't in the room, listening, as he would have snorted in disgust and stormed out of the Salon, shouting at the Advocate that there was only one true genius in the room, and he was in the process of walking out.

I turned to see my father beaming as the record of his genius was laid out before the court. Only on occasion did Advocate Rossi mention me, and when he did, it was as a dutiful daughter, a loving and faithful servant of the Church. He told of my father's desire to place me in a nunnery as a Bride of the Church and of the Saviour; the only reason I wasn't already a nun was because of my precocious talents as a painter, which he wished to nurture so that I could paint the greatest portraits of Faith since Buonarroti had painted the ceiling of the Sistine Chapel. Then he talked about Tassi raping me, at which point his friends burst out laughing. The judge looked at them in anger, and told them to remain silent. Tassi looked at them and his face warned them not to make outbursts. Then the advocate continued with Tassi's offense of not disclosing his marriage, of the falsity of his wedding proposal, of the lies he'd told, and only then did he define my financial value. That by his forcibly taking my virginity, he had diminished me as a marriageable woman and damaged my marital value to my father.

After some time on his feet, he sat down and thanked the court for its indulgence. The Judge then turned to Tassi.

"So, Signore Tassi," the judge said, clearing his throat. "Now is the time for you to present your case against the claims made by Signore Gentileschi. You do not employ a lawyer, and while this will not be considered against you in our judgement, neither will the fact that you represent yourself be considered to be in your favour. This is a matter of reparation, Signore, of money, and because of that, no allowances will be made by me for your inexperience in matters of the law. So, begin your case."

Tassi stood, and faced the Judge. Then, like an actor on the boards, he turned and faced my father; he bowed slightly, as though in mock deference; and then he turned to face me, shaking his head in sorrow. The inference, which was quite clear to me, was that this was an entire misunderstanding, and that a simple conversation, perhaps even an apology, would have saved everybody the unwarranted expense of this trial.

But when he saw my face, and that his sorrowful, pitiable look was returned with my Medusa look which would turn him into stone, he turned back to the judge, and said, "My Lord Judge, let me begin this, my testimony, by swearing to you on the most sacred and beloved Bible, that I have never, ever, not one single time, been alone with Artemisia Gentileschi in a room. At all times, when she and I have been sharing our painterly arts and crafts, there have been others in the room, or the studio, or the Palazzo where Orazio, her father, and I have been working on the same painting. I was asked by Orazio to teach his beloved daughter perspective in painting, which is what I endeavoured to do.

"And that, my Lord Judge, is what I did. No more and no less. These accusations of my forcing myself upon a young and helpless woman, are unworthy of Orazio, a man I know well and respect, and they are unworthy of me, a devout Catholic, a man who has devoted himself to the betterment of life for the Church, a man who has regularly spent a large percentage of his income on benefitting the poor, and a man who is protégé to His Holiness, the Pope."

He sat down, to cheers from his companions.

"Silence!" ordered the Judge's Assistente.

The judge looked at him sternly. "And that is your opening evidence, Signore Tassi?"

He nodded. The judge then turned to his two companions, sitting on either side of him, and conferred with them in a whisper. When the conference had ended, the judge looked sternly at Tassi, and said, "Signore. You do yourself no service when you open your evidence by contradicting a sworn statement you made to the *Giudice Monocratico*, the justice before whom you appeared two months ago and who decided that this case had sufficient merit to go to trial. In your evidence, which you may have forgotten giving, Signore, you said that you had been enjoying intimate relations with the girl Artemisia, but that it was she who had initially seduced you. Have you forgotten what you said to the Giudice?"

I looked at Tassi, and saw, to my unutterable delight, that he had, as the English say, been hoist on his own petard. He looked flustered, uncertain, guilty, and the look of innocence on his face had disappeared.

He stood, and said, "I...er..no...I...what I was trying to do, My Lord, was to save the Madonna embarrassment in the evidence I would be giving. I hoped that my word would be sufficient for you to dismiss the claims against me. But if not, then it seems I must tell you the entire truth."

"As you have promised to do just a moment ago when you began to give evidence, and you said that you would swear on the Bible," said the Judge, scornfully and disparagingly.

"So, begin again, Signore, but this time, we are here to listen to the truth, and it is not your position to save the feelings of the Madonna. Your role here, as the man defending these allegations against your character, and purse, is to inform this bench of judges of your side of the story, and then for us to decide who is telling the truth." The judge looked sternly at him again, and nodded.

Tassi stood, looking much more unsure of himself than before. Even his companions, those who ridiculed and debased me with their stares, were looking far from happy. None looked at the smile on my face. But when Tassi began speaking, my smile quickly disappeared.

He said, "My Lord Judge, I was wrong to try to save Artemisia's reputation. As well as the reputation of my once-friend, Signore Gentileschi. I apologise to the court. For in doing so I have hidden facts from you of which you should be in possession."

I had no idea what he was going to say. But even in

my wildest fantasies, I couldn't have imagined it would be anything like what actually was about to transpire.

He continued, "Yes, I have been intimate with Artemisia, many times. And at all times with her consent and approval. Further, it was done with her father's consent. No, his encouragement."

I heard my father, at the back of the Salon, shout out, "No!"

But Tassi continued, unabated, "Far from being a virgin, innocent and pure when I met her, her father had used her as a naked model in his and other people's paintings. For money. And he had given her for sexual service to friends and others in return for cash payments; I repeat that this money was for her sexual services. Although I only found this out later when my servants investigated the truth about the Gentileschi family, I found out from witnesses, many of whom will come here to give evidence, that Artemisia was little more than a prostitute, a whore, a *puttana*. A young woman who was an inferior painter and could only earn money by selling her body."

"NO!" shouted my father. "Liar, scoundrel, perjurer, deceiver! How dare you say these things about my Artemisia? You, who are nothing more than a....."

"SIT DOWN!" shouted the Judge. He turned to the Assistente, and said, "Remove that man."

The Assistente left the dais and started to walk towards my father. Advocate Rossi stood and said urgently, "Your Honor, the man who just made the outcry is Signore Gentileschi. I apologise for his outburst, but I beg you to reconsider removing him. It is vital, Lord Judge, that he remains in the court, so that he can hear what's being said, and then give evidence."

The Assistente stopped walking into the body of the Salon, and looked around to the judge.

"Signore Gentileschi," the judge said, "I understand your anger and hurt at these statements by the accused man against your daughter, but if you interrupt these proceedings again, then I shall have you bound and gagged and removed to the cells below. I shall forgive you this time, on the condition that it does not happen a second time."

Order was restored, and the so-called evidence from Tassi continued. Lie after lie. Calumny after calumny. Fantasy after fantasy. My knuckles were white from gripping the railing before me. I was beside myself with humiliation at every word he said of me. This, the man I had given myself to, so freely after so great an insult.

This, the man who swore he would give me a ring to show the world our match. This, the man who told me he loved me above all others, and would be honest and true and loving until the end of our days. This, the man who stood in a public court and stripped me naked, raped me time and time again with his words, and never once had the courage to look into the face of his Nemesis, this Gorgon who would turn him into stone the moment he saw her eyes.

And as he stood and lied, I knew that I had to expose his vileness to the world. No, I wouldn't turn him into stone with a stare. Nor would I excoriate him in words. Unlike today, back then, when I was only 18 and illiterate, words were not my voice. Art was my narrative, my discourse, my denunciation, my pulpit. Like Savonarola, the bonfire of my vanities would be my paintings.

So it would not be in words that I would defend myself, but in paint. And as I sat in the Salon, forced to bear witness to his calumnies, I knew the subject I would paint. It would be Judith, the Israelite maiden, saving her nation by cutting off the head of the Assyrian General, Holofernes.

I had been impressed by the subject of the brave Israelite woman, faithful and upstanding, pure and devoted, courageously going into the camp of the enemy set upon the path of the destruction of Israel in the time of the ruler of the most powerful empire the world had then known, King Nebuchadnezzar. There, when she and her servant came face to face with their enemy, they cut off the head of the Assyrian general with his own sword, and returned with the severed head to her terrified people to prove that their Nemesis had been overcome.

Sandro Botticelli had created the image many years ago with Judith striding purposefully forward followed by her servant Abra carrying Holofernes' head; Michaelangelo Buonarroti had painted the biblical story on the ceiling of the Sistine Chapel, Judith and her servant with Holofernes' head on a platter, which my father and I had seen and marvelled at just weeks earlier; and the sculptor Donatello had created a magnificent bronze of the subject for the Dukes of Florence. My own beloved Caravaggio had only recently created the scene, to the fury of his arch-enemy Baglione who had tried to improve upon the master's work, but failed miserably because of his uselessness as a painter.

But if so many great artists had attempted to capture the image of a brave woman taking revenge against her enemy, why was I considering making this the subject matter of my next painting? Surely the world was replete with Judith and Holofernes.

No! Because all of the painters had been men! None had suffered the fears and torments which Judith suffered! None could understand the depth of her hatred at the thought of this Assyrian General raping her Nation! None could capture the emotions which must have been churning in Judith's mind as she approached Holofernes' tent, as she stood over him while he slept, as she contemplated the ultimate act of revenge against him for his arrogance, his cruelty, his mocking and disdain for her and her people. Not even my beloved master Caravaggio could have known how Judith would have felt as she grasped the cold hard handle of the sword and placed the murderous blade against the bare neck of the General; standing in the flickering light of an oil lamp and watching him in his drunken sleep as she, the Angel of Death, hovered over his inert body and for just that moment, became a goddess with the power of life and death in her hands.

And could any man understand the exultation, the insuperable joy Judith would have felt as she pulled the sleeping man's hair taut, his head back to expose his neck, and then felt the power flooding through her body as she sliced the merciless blade into his skin and the sinews of his neck, cutting and cutting, slicing and slicing as the blade bit deeper, the blood spurting out in red fountains, as she heard him scream in fear and pain when he suddenly realised he was powerless against this woman as the last moments of his life drained away.

Only I could execute that painting properly, accurately, and fully. Only I would do justice and be faithful to Judith's rage and vengeance, for only a woman could know the blissful ecstasy of taking revenge against a man who has forced himself into her body.

So I would paint Judith cutting off the head of her enemy Holofernes. But in my painting, there would be just one difference to the depictions of this heroine from the portraits of the men who had preceded me. In my picture, it would be my face as Judith the Avenger, and Agostino Tassi would be exposed for the entire world to see, as Holofernes, rapist of nations.

# PART, THE SEVENTH

I could continue to tell you about the evidence which Tassi gave against me. Like the draftsman that he was, like the painter of architecture, he assembled lie after lie about me as though he was a constructing building, and not a defense against our claims.

But I won't.

Save to tell you that by the time I was tortured, the trial had already lasted for five months. Yet it still had two months to continue.

Tortured?

Yes, what you just read, reader of the future, is the truth. The shameful truth about the proceedings of my trial to prove my innocence.

I was tortured as I gave evidence, so that the Learned Judge could determine that I was telling the truth.

Even to this day, years and years earlier than the woman

who writes this story, was the girl called Artemisia who had a rope intertwined between her fingers and then had them crushed until they were bruised and bloody, I still cannot believe that I, a witness, was tortured.

No, not Tassi.

He wasn't tortured despite the fact that he was accused and on trial. But I, a witness, an accuser, a victim, was tortured to prove whether or not I was lying.

I remember walking from my house to the Salon where the Tribunal was sitting. It was in the month of October. Rome was already turning wintery cold, but as I walked, dressed in my cloak and a thick woollen dress, knowing what I would soon endure, I was unbearably hot. Yet despite the cold, Rome still stank. It was fetid and under any other circumstances, I would have taken my horse and disappeared into the cold but clean hills surrounding the city, where the breezes didn't smell of rotted flesh and excrement.

But like my father, like Tassi and the liars he'd employed to give false witness against me, and like the judges in their robes, I was bound to the Salon where the air was heavy and oppressive and where not a breath of wind blew in to relieve our misery. The room was unheated; the windows were closed, and the rank smell of the onlookers filled the Chamber with noxious smells.

For months, we had listened to witnesses called by Tassi talk about my days as a prostitute; how clients, married men, young boys, came to my father's house, paid him a handful of coins, ascended the stairs and found me in my bedchamber lying on the bed, wearing nothing; how I'd invited them to undress and join me on my bed, where I'd performed the duties of a whore for long enough so that they fulfilled their manly desires. Then they'd dress and leave the house, only to greet another man waiting on the steps for his turn to enjoy my body.

Twice in the past month, my father had been led out of the Salon for standing and screaming at a witness. Twice he'd been fined by the Judge and twice he'd promised to behave. But only yesterday, he'd been exiled to the corridors and fined a third time when Cosimo Quorli stood as witness to his enjoyment of my body. This was the man who had entered my bedchamber with Tassi, and who'd attempted to enter me, but failed because his manhood would not grow and stand to attention. I hadn't seen him since the day he'd attempted to know me, and it came as a shock that he would dare to confront me again; he, a servant of the Vatican. It was one thing for strangers, paid good money to lie before God to the fact that they'd lain with me, but quite another for a true rapist to claim that he had had me willingly.

I was silent, sullen as he walked to the witness box, took an oath before the Almighty, and told the court that he was a true and faithful Christian, and a senior official of the Vatican, faithful to His Holiness Pope Paul, and here to expiate his sins of lust by telling the truth. He began to tell Tassi what had occurred on many occasions when he paid his coin to my father and had had me. My father stood and shouted abuse at Tassi's witness, much to the anger of the Lord Judge, who ordered that my father be exiled again, this time to return an hour later gagged and in chains. It was a sorrowful and pitiable sight, but there was nothing I could do.

So I had to sit there while Quorli told his tales of his enjoyment of my body. And at the end of his testimony, when the Judge, now bored by the same story time and again from different men, turned to our Advocate, Signore Rossi, and asked whether he wanted to question the witness.

To the surprise of the panel of judges, I stood, and said, "My Lords Judges, may I be permitted to question this witness?"

Taken aback, the Chief Justice said, "Madonna, you

have an Advocate. That is his job. Why would you wish to do his work for him?"

"Because, Lord Judge, this witness is one of the men who, along with Tassi, attempted to rape me. And only I know what questions to ask to ascertain the validity of what he has testified," I said.

The judge admonished me. "Madonna, it is the function of the Judges here assembled to determine the validity of this man's testimony."

"I apologise, my Lord. What I meant was...."

He interrupted. "I know what you meant to say. And with the agreement of your Advocate, I grant you permission to question this witness."

I turned to Rossi, who frowned, but nodded his agreement. Then I turned to face Quorli, the witness and man who'd attempted to rape me. His smug grin disappeared when he had to face me.

I smiled, benignly, comfortingly, like a viper before it strikes. "Signore Quorli. I listened carefully to the testimony you have just given on behalf of Agostino Tassi. As I sat and listened I wondered if you were talking about me, or somebody else. Signore, just now you told their Lordships that you have known my body on a number of occasions. Yes?"

He nodded, saying not a word. I wondered if, facing me, he had lost the power of speech.

"Which means that you have entered my body. Yes?"

Again, he nodded mutely.

The judge intervened. "Signore. There is an amanuensis listening to your words and taking a note of the evidence in this trial. Master Scribe...." The judge addressed the clerk, who put down his quill. "Did you write down the answer which the witnesses just gave?"

The scribe said, "No, my Lord Judge. He said nothing."

The judge then said to Quorli, "Signore, you must answer the questions in words, not signals. What is your answer to the Madonna's last question? Did you enter her body?"

"Yes!" Quorli said, aggressively.

"Let me be clear, and let me ask again, Signore," I said, my tone deliberately lawyerly, calm and hopefully menacing. "Have you entered my body on a number of occasions?"

"Yes!" Quorli shouted.

"You seem angry that I should ask you such a question, Signore. Why are you angry?" I asked.

He looked at Tassi, which made me ask, "Why do you look at the accused man, Signore Tassi. Do you need corroboration to the act of defilement? Don't you remember entering my body?"

"I'm not looking at him. I'm trying to understand why you're asking me these questions. I've already told you and the Court that I've paid money to your father so that I could have sex with you. Just as all the other men who have testified have said that they paid money to have sex with you. As, by the way, it's well known that your father, Orazio, has had sex with you on many occasions. He has even boasted of it when he's drunk. That's all there is to it."

I heard a muffled sound from the back of the court, my father objecting to the words he'd just heard. I turned and saw him, furiously struggling with his chains and trying to speak against a gag stuffed into his mouth.

But I would not show Quorli that I was distraught at his words. Instead, I looked at him and smiled, more to unnerve him than to prove he hadn't hurt me. "I remember none of the other witnesses who have lied about their knowledge of me. I don't remember their faces, nor their bodies. But I certainly remember you, Signore Quorli."

The judges looked at me questioningly. Was I admitting to being a whore?

"I remember you so clearly. The first time I met you

was last year, when I was an innocent girl of just 17 years; a decent loving daughter; an aspiring artist; a naïve girl who thought the best of people. I first met you when you and Tassi came into my bedchamber and forced me onto the bed. Tassi raped me, several times despite my fighting back, scratching his face and neck and attacking his manhood with my fingernails.

"You were there, too, laughing and encouraging him. And then it came to your turn to rape me, Signore Quorli! I remember watching you struggling to take off your trousers; I watched you approach me, a young girl, bloody, lying bruised and battered on the bed. And I watched you as you tried and tried to enter me, but your manhood wouldn't respond. You never once entered my body, because you weren't man enough. You were incapable of rising to the occasion. You were like an old man, full of panting lust and unquenched desire, but incapable of performing the act. Tassi did, several times that day, and when you found you couldn't enter my body, he took your place. But you never entered me, did you, Signore. Not you. You couldn't enter me because you were too soft. I even remember what you said to me. You spat into my face in your lust and frustration, and you called me *cagna fredda*. You thought that I was a cold bitch because your manhood would not respond to my body. Do you remember calling me that, Signore Quorli? Why was I your *cagna fredda?*"

Quorli looked utterly bereft, standing there, mute and aware that he had just been made into a laughingstock. Tassi's men friends couldn't stop laughing, and led on by them, the entire court, except the Judges, burst out into merriment.

The chief judge banged his gavel on his bench, and shouted, "Silence! Silence! This is a court of law. Not a circus. Silence, I say." The Assistente banged his staff on the floor, and he, too, shouted out "Silence!"

The judge looked at me sternly, "Madonna, is this type of questioning appropriate for a woman?"

I answered, "Is raping an innocent virgin of 17 years, appropriate for an Officer of the Vatican?"

The judge was taken aback by my comment. He turned to the witness Quorli, and asked, "Is there any truth to what the accuser's daughter, Madonna Gentileschi, has said about your...your...abilities?"

"None," Quorli shouted. "None! I am more than a man for a girl like her."

"Enough!" the judge said, now angry. "Signorita Gentileschi, you have debased this Court and Inquisition by your questions. I will allow none further. Sit down! Now, Advocate Rossi, do you have any questions for this witness?"

Our lawyer shook his head, not wishing to step foot into a quagmire. The judge then dismissed the witness.

When the hubbub in the court had calmed, Tassi stood, and said, "My Lord Judge, after the scurrilous attempt by this woman to denigrate and ridicule a witness, a man who came here in all innocence to attest to the degraded state of this woman's character, I feel that although there are many who stand outside the court and will confirm that she is nothing more than a whore and a prostitute, I should now bring my testimony to an end. Enough has been said to convince you of the nature of the woman who claims to have been an innocent, and who claims that her virginity was taken by me, despite our proof that this girl's virginity had been lost many years before, probably by the service of her father, and God only knows how many other men.

"By now, my Lord Judge, you will have probably already determined her for the liar and thief of reputations she is. And as a result of our overwhelming evidence that this girl is a whore, and that her father knew that my intimacy with her had not robbed him of the value of her innocence, I beg you, Lord Judge, to dismiss this case. "

The judge conferred with his colleagues, and then turned to look at Advocate Rossi. My heart was thumping against my ribs. I didn't know what was going to happen. Had my questioning of Quorli done more harm than good? It was an instinctive move on my part, and now I saw how reckless it was.

But instead of asking Rossi a question, instead, the Judge turned to Tassi, and said, "Signore Tassi. In any court of our nation, both the innocent and the guilty have a right to be heard. We have so far heard only from your witnesses. We have yet to hear from witnesses brought forward by Advocate Rossi in accusation of your role in this allegation. Signore Gentileschi's claim against you has yet to be heard. None of his witnesses have yet had an opportunity to speak. Foremost amongst his witnesses is the accuser's daughter herself."

Then the judge said, "Advocate Rossi. I wish to hear from the mouth of Artemisia Gentileschi. Call her forward."

I stood there in the box for witnesses. I stared hatred at Tassi, who sat there will a smug grin on his face. He felt certain that he'd won.

And for the entirety of the afternoon, my Advocate

took me through the events of a year earlier, when I'd been raped by Tassi. I told the court what had happened in details which showed that only the most skillful of actresses could have made up the story of my downfall; that I must, surely, have been telling the truth. And I freely admitted that once I'd lost my virginity, once he'd had my body, I gave myself willingly to him.

Both Advocate Rossi and the Judge asked why I had done such a thing. Why would any woman have sexual relations with a man who'd raped her? I answered that the circumstances demanded it. I reiterated, word for word, Tassi's explanation of the destruction he would cause to myself and my father if the truth of his assault was ever made public.

When I saw that the Judge looked sternly across at Tassi as I was explaining the Devil's Bargain I'd made with him, I knew in my heart of hearts that we would win this case.

How wrong I was to have thought that. How little I knew of the place women held in the eyes of the Law. So by the end of my testimony, when the light was beginning to fade and people in the court were beginning to sleep due to the heat and the length of the day, the judge said, "If that is the entirety of your evidence, Madonna

Gentileschi, than I feel that I need further proof of the validity of what you have said. You have made many claims against Signore Tassi. Claims which may or may not be true. The only way to determine the truth of your testimony, is through the good graces of Madonna Sibille. She will be brought forth in the morning." He stood and banged his gavel on the bench. "Court is adjourned until the morrow."

I returned to my seat, and through the corner of my eye, I saw that Tassi was looking at me and smiling; it wasn't a smile of friendship, but more one of a man who took delight in another's pain and grief. The Germans have a word for it. *Schadenfreude*. I'd first learned the word from the German artist Adam Eisheimer when he came to Rome. I never thought I'd have reason to use it, until I looked at Tassi's face.

As I arrived back at the seat, Advocate Rossi came up to me, and said, "Now you mustn't be afraid, Madonna."

"Afraid? Why should I be afraid? And who is Madonna Sibille?" I asked. "I've never heard of her."

He gulped. He shook his head. Suddenly I was frightened.

"Who? Tell me!"

"The Sibille isn't a woman. It's an instrument."

I frowned.

"An instrument of torture," he said. "It's a rope which is wound around your fingers, and tightened by a screw until the pain is….well, not good. The judge will ask you questions about your testimony and the Assistente will tighten the screw; if you continue to bear false witness, then…."

"Then what," I asked, feeling faint and terrified.

"….then your fingers might break."

I looked at him in utter horror. I was going to be tortured! Me! But why me? I was the victim. Tassi was the rapist who had lied in giving evidence; not me. I was accused of nothing. Yet…

So I stammered, "My….my fingers. He would break my fingers! But that will be my end. I'm a painter. My fingers are my brushes; my hand is my palette….if I am broken, then I will never be able to…..no…this can't be. I'm a witness. Not the accused. Why am I being tortured? Why?"

But my advocate said softly, "This is not a city court of law; this is the Inquisition." Then he pointed up to the ceiling, and said, "And the Judge is judged by Almighty God Himself. The judge will take comfort from the words God puts into your mouth when your pain is great, when you beg for the torture to stop, and your needs are *in extremis*. The Judge will believe the words coming from your mouth, for it's well known that a person tortured always tells the truth. By that means, the Judge will know that your evidence is true. That, I see now, is the reason that Tassi chose this court, rather than a civil court of law. He wants to see you tortured. He risks you being believed, but he assumes that you will weaken before the torture, merely at the threat of it, and so he will win the case by default."

He just shook his head and, remaining silent, turned and walked away.

I didn't sleep at all that night. Neither did my father. In the early hours of the morning, we looked at each other and he said to me, "I should never have taken the trial this far. You were right, dearest girl. I was so wrong in what I've done, and now you're suffering because of my arrogance."

"Too late for recrimination now, Father. Today I must face an Inquisition and torture. And if they're going to break my fingers to determine the truth, then they will also break my heart...and my art."

As we walked into the Salon, the room seemed to be far fuller of onlookers than the previous day. I was surprised, but when we met our lawyer, Advocate Rossi and I asked him, he said, "Madonna, whenever there is an examination and a torture, the word seems to get out onto the street, and crowds often gather."

It didn't concern me particularly and nor did I wonder about the expression he used about "examination." How naïve was I. For despite the excruciation of giving evidence yesterday, and the certainty of the agony I would experience today with the intimacy of Madonna Sibille, I would soon discover that I would be exposed for all to see during the "examination."

I sat in my seat, and all of Tassi's supporters looked at me, nudged each other and leered. One of the men whispered something into Tassi's ears, and he said, loudly enough for me to hear, "Why should I look, when I've seen everything which you'll soon see?"

Hearing this, and knowing what he meant, the blood drained from my face.

The judges walked in, we all stood, listened to the Assistente warn us to respect the authority of the court, utter a sentence from Saint Luke's gospel, and then we sat.

The Chief Judge looked at me, and said, "Signorita Gentileschi, yesterday you gave evidence in accusation of Signore Tassi. You claimed many things in relation to your innocence, your chastity, and the dishonour which you claim was perpetrated against you. However, many things are said in a court such as this which have to be tested before God. You, and other witnesses, may swear an oath before God to tell the truth, but neither I, nor my fellow judges, can look into your heart and determine whether or not you are lying. Which is why we must now test the veracity of your assertions. Firstly, we must determine whether you remain intact as a woman; next, we will determine by torture whether or not your claims yesterday are true. In order to remove all infamy or doubt about your person or your words, do you agree to be tried by the ordeal of the Sibille?"

I answered, "My Lord, I am ready to confirm my statement under torture and whatever must be done."

What else could I say? If I had refused to be tortured, my evidence would have been discounted and nullified. But knowing that I was to be examined physically, splayed like a chicken in front of the roomful of men, caused Tassi's friends to murmur and laugh among themselves. I glanced in their direction, and they wore malicious and lascivious grins upon their ugly faces. I shuddered in disgust. I turned to look at my father, but he was staring at the ground in front of him, too shamed to look at me or the Judges who were about to intensify his daughter's shame.

At the instructions of the judge, two midwives entered the Salon to assist in the examination to determine whether or not I was a virgin. They carried a large sheet of cloth into the courtroom, along with stands to which it was attached. The judge then ordered me to stand and walk behind the screen so that the viewers in the court would not be able to see the examination; only the judges would be able to see my intimate parts. Humiliated, I did what I was ordered to do, lay down on a table and raised my legs in the air, having already removed my undergarments before coming to court.

The midwives poked around, and said, "My Lord, the woman Gentileschi is no longer a virgin. Her inner parts have healed, so the loss must have been many weeks or months ago."

The Judge said, "I and my fellow judges must see for ourselves." Then they came from their elevated rostrum, down into the body of the court, so that they could position themselves between my legs and stare into my womanhood.

I closed my eyes and gritted my teeth as I felt their eyes

looking deeply into my body. I could feel the heat of their faces, the quickening susurration of their breathing on my thighs as they peered for unconscionably long moments at the most intimate parts of my body.

Then, through my tightly closed eyes, I sensed them move away, heard them cough, and say to me, "Yes, we agree with the evidence of these midwives. Madonna Gentileschi, we have determined the truth about your state of womanhood. Now you will remain in this seat, for the first part of today was that we examine you; the second part deals with the truth or falsity of the evidence you gave yesterday."

The screen was removed, and I opened my eyes to see all of the court, staring at me as though I'd just undergone an operation by a doctor, instead of a gross intrusion on my privacy by judges.

They returned to their bench, and the chief judge said for all the courtroom to hear, "We are now satisfied that the woman, Artemisia Gentileschi, is no longer a virgin. What has not been proven is that her purity was taken by the accused man, Agostino Tassi. In order to determine such truth, I order now that the Sibille be brought forward and administered."

The Assistente, standing behind the Chief Judge,

seemed to smile as he walked down into the body of the court, and across to where I was sitting. He carried in his hand what to me looked like a thumbscrew; thick strings in a wooden frame, on top of which was a wheel to which the strings were attached.

The Assistente looked at the judge, who mildly shook his head. The Assistente stood aside and waited. My heart was pounding. I had no idea what was about to happen, other than I was soon going to be in excruciating pain.

"Artemisia Gentileschi. I am about to order that you be tortured by means of the Sibille carried by the Assistente of this court. Before I do this, I wish you to answer some of the questions which were put to you yesterday in your testimony. But today, your answers will be tested before God under the pain of the Sibille. My first question, based on what you said yesterday, is about the attack. You said in evidence that when Agostino forced his way into you, you fought back."

I nodded. "Yes, my Lord Judge. As I said, I grabbed his penis to prevent him entering me, and scratched it hard with my fingernails. He yelped like a dog."

The people in the room burst out laughing, and the judge demanded silence.

"So the blood you spoke of yesterday could have been

his blood."

"Yes, my Lord. But there was a lot of blood. I don't know that what I found afterwards could all have come from him. At the time Agostino attacked me, my maid's veil was intact within my body, and I have no idea how much blood is spilled when it is broken. Therefore I am not able to say for certain to your Lordship whether my vagina bled because of what Agostino did, because I did not know much about how these things happen; but it is true that it seemed to me that the blood was redder than usual. I am at a loss to assist your Lordships more, because my mother, who should have explained these things to me, died when I was but 13, and I have only a father and three brothers. I have few friends and spend almost all my days in my home, not allowed out onto the rough streets by my loving father. So some of the workings of my body are strange and unusual to me."

The judge listened, nodded, and then turned to confer with his fellow judges. Then he turned to the official of the court standing beside me, eagerly awaiting permission, and said, "Assistente, begin your work."

The Assistente grabbed my right hand, and started to thread the strings in and out of my fingers; back and forth, back and forth, until they were covered to the extent of the knuckle. I could smell his foul breath, pork and onions, as he stood close to me, threading the string, concentrating with every fibre of his being.

He then took the ends of the string and wrapped them around the wheel of the Sibille. When he'd finished, he looked up at the judge, and nodded.

The Judge then said, "I will accept that we will never know for certain whether the blood you witnessed came from Tassi's wound on his manhood, or from the female covering to your womanhood, which you claim Tassi broke when he entered you. But yesterday, I asked you why, after you claimed that Tassi had forced himself upon you, did you continue to have intimacy with him which lasted for the better part of a year? Answer this question."

My heart being like a drum, with a dry voice, I said, "He had taken my maidenhood. I was no longer pure. He threatened the security of myself and my family if I told the authorities of what he'd done. He told me he would give me a ring and marry me. So, when he asked my father for my hand in marriage, I didn't think I had a choice. I wanted to have a happy marriage, a happy life. What else could I do? "

The judge looked at the Assistente, and nodded.

The man twisted the wheel which tightened the strings around my fingers. The string bit into the flesh and it was painful. But I knew I could bear it. He twisted more, and I screamed out, my fingers now pressing so closely that the knuckles were distorted. I looked down at my fingers and they were white with agony.

"I ask again," the judge said, "why did you continue to have sex with him after he'd raped you?"

"Because I thought he would marry me," I hissed. The pain was now unbearable. I think I heard my father shout "Stop!" from the other side of the room. Again, the Assistente twisted the wheel. The agony was hideous. My fingers felt as though they would break at any moment.

"Again, woman, why did you continue to have sex after he'd raped you?" asked the judge.

"He was going to marry me. I wanted him to marry me," I said, now screaming in pain, and crying out the words.

"Is it true, before God, that he raped you?" demanded the Judge.

I cried in pain, "It's the truth! Before God, it's the truth."

I gasped, tears wracking my body. The pain was unbearable.

The Assistente looked up at the judge, and nodded, as though asking for permission to screw the wheel further.

But the judge shook his head, and the Assistente release the pressure. My fingers, now more free, were still stuck together, and I had to use my other hand to free them from each other.

Even though the string was still wound around them, I massaged them with my other hand to try to stop the pain which was shooting through them. It felt as though they had just been forced into a fire. They were aflame with anger, throbbing agony, and unbelievable discomfort.

And it was only the beginning.

"Now," said the Judge, "I will ask the same question again, in the presence of Almighty God, blessed by He, knowing that you will tell the truth under the pain of the Sibille....did Agostino Tassi force you to have intimacy with him and were you a virgin at the time?"

Again the judge nodded to the Assistente, and he began to tighten the screw. My fingers were pulled mercilessly together again, knuckle fighting knuckle, the biting string opening up the bloody wounds caused the first time.

I screamed in pain and bit my cheek to deflect the intensity.

"Were you a virgin?" shouted the judge.

"Yes, in God's name, yes," I shouted.

"Were you a virgin when he first made love to you?"

"I was, on the sacred memory of my mother. I was a virgin."

I heard my father weeping.

"Tighten the screw!" shouted the judge.

I screamed loud as it bit and bit. I heard laughter from Tassi's friends.

"Silence!" screamed the judge. "I ask again, Signorina. Were you a virgin when…."

"Yes! God help me, yes!" I was screaming in pain.

"Were you a virgin when he first had his way with you?" demanded the judge. Was there no end to the same question? The screw was causing the string to

bite tighter and tighter. I nearly lost my mind. I was on the verge of fainting.

"Were you innocent before Tassi. Is your claim to be a virgin true or a lie!" shouted the judge.

"It's true! It's true! It's true!" I shouted, barely able to breathe with the pain.

The judge was going to ask another question, but I gasped a breath and screamed out, "Lord Judge, I swear it's true. I was a virgin. He took me by force. He made me…he….I…."

I remember nothing after that, until I woke up wet and soaking. I'd fainted and they'd thrown cold water at my face. I couldn't sit in the chair, but my body slumped and I slid towards the ground. My fingers of my right hand were on fire. I had no idea how long I'd been unconscious.

My advocate, Rossi, picked me up off the floor and helped me back into the chair.

"You've been unconscious for several minutes. But I have good news. The torture. It's over," he whispered into my ear. Then he repeated, "The torture is at an end. Finished. The judge believes you. He said so. There will be no more torture, Madonna."

Rossi helped me to regain my feet. He put his arm through mine as I staggered back to my seat close to Tassi and his men. The men were looking at me, grinning lasciviously, like street-corner rogues, their taunting remarks made under their breath so that the judge couldn't hear them.

I was nurturing my bloody and broken hand as Advocate Rossi and I returned to our chairs. But as I walked close to Tassi, I lifted my hand so that it was close to his face, the bloody circles on each of the fingers testifying to the damage he'd caused to be done to me.

Looking him in the eyes, I said, loudly, so that the

judges could clearly hear the angry intent of my words, "So, Agostino, you promised me a ring when you begged me to marry you. This," I said, thrusting my hand in his face, "is the ring you gave me, and these broken fingers are your promises."

And then I sat down. I glanced in his direction. He was staring at the floor.

The judge postponed the trial for a week, so that I could recover from the torture. When it resumed, Tassi was on his own. His friends were no longer surrounding him. Why, I have no idea. Perhaps they'd deserted him.

But now it was our turn to present evidence. And what evidence my Advocate produced. Witness after witness attested to Tassi's murderous temper, his foul language when he was drunk, and the numerous times he'd visited brothels in Rome and other cities. Tassi barely contradicted the evidence we presented. It was almost as though hearing my evidence, he'd given up fighting. Or maybe it was that he had no rebuttal to our claims.

And when my Advocate produced incontrovertible evidence, from the mouths of the witnesses he called forward, evidence that he'd raped his own sister-in-law, that he'd raped his former wife, and from a man he'd tried to hire in order to kill his present wife who was still mysteriously missing, the judges formed a very different impression of a man who'd claimed to be a protégé of His Holiness Pope Paul.

The calumnies which had been heaped against me by Tassi, by his so-called witnesses to prove his claim that my father had sold me into prostitution, as well as by Tuzia who'd claimed that I'd tried to seduce Tassi, was now so debased and contradicted, that it seemed like nothing but a bad memory.

Slowly, my fingers of my right hand began to heal; well, the cuts and abrasions healed, but not the painful bend in my middle finger, nor the slight inward curve of my thumb. For weeks and weeks, I wasn't able to hold a paint brush, and even when they'd healed sufficiently so that I could, my hand felt more like a claw and I couldn't paint for more than an hour or so before having to immerse the hand in cold water to relieve the throbbing. Even though the court was proceeding with more witnesses who were attesting to Tassi's life of crimes and delinquencies, I was instructed by my father, and the doctor to whom he took me to examine my hand, that I had to rest. So the reports I received of what was happening, came from the lips of my father, Orazio.

David and Martina stood and looked at the massive walls of the Castello Estense in the centre of the northern city of Ferrara. They were close to each other like young lovers. Just the previous night when they arrived, David had taken her to dinner, and during the meal, had told her that he'd been thinking about staying longer in Europe, asking his wife to join him, and was considering not returning immediately to Australia.

«And will she come over? How can you do this when you have children and grandchildren and a home in Australia. I have a son and a daughter I get anxious and concerned when I don't see them for a while. Don't just stay in Italy, though God knows you could spend your life just in Rome, looking at our treasures. But go to London first when the investigation into the painting is finished. You may be a very wealthy man, or just another art adventurer. Who knows? But please, give up any idea of making a holiday into something permanent."

When he woke that morning, he got dressed quickly and phoned her room to take her to breakfast. But she told him that she was already showered and dressed and at her computer, so just to come next door. He entered her room because she'd left the door ajar, and saw her seated at her escritoire studying her computer. When she'd finished, they went downstairs to the dining room. After breakfast, they stood looking at the castle walls, and he said, "Just explain again how this Cardinal Bentivoglio came to live in a castle owned by the d'Este family."

"The Bentivoglios ruled the nearby city of Bolognia, just fifty kilometres south. But the Bentivoglios always had trouble with the popes, and it came to a head in the 16th Century when the city was taken away from them. But there was already a bond between the d'Este family and the Bentivoglios, because in 1487 one of the Bentivoglios, Annibale, married Lucrezia d'Este. So when the Pope exiled the Betivoglio family from Bolognia, they came to Ferrara to live and establish themselves. We don't know, because there are no records, but we assume that when he was a boy, Cardinal Bentivoglio might have been one of the boys placed in the d'Este court, in that building there," she said, nodding to the castle. "Sons of notable families often lived and worked in royal or ruling castles so that they learned the art of governance. But presumably young Guido Bentivoglio decided to go into the Priesthood."

They walked across the road, and the castle's moat became pronounced and obvious. The massive castle had four huge towers in each corner, and huge doors in the middle of each of the four walls, with drawbridges, archways, porticos, attached buildings on each of the sides. As he looked at it, he realised what an impossible job it would be to search such a castle, even if they had permission. All that Martina had been able to do on the phone was to arrange with the Castle's director to meet with him this morning, at which time, she'd ask him about Cardinal Bentivoglio's books. But she wouldn't ask him about the Cardinal's papers. It might be a touchy subject and all she wanted at this stage was his permission to search.

Despite her initial enthusiasm, Martina knew that it would be almost impossible to find Artemisia's book. When she had discussed it with her Director at the Uffizi, he urged her to follow the leads. Now they were escorted to the Castle's Director offices. When they explained what they were seeking, he smiled and shook his head sadly.

"Oh my dear Professor Calabrese. I'm afraid that you've had a completely wasted journey. We here have very few books. The entire Biblioteca Estense was transferred in 1610 from this castle in Ferrara, to the other centre of d'Este rule, in the city of Modena just 60 kilometres to the west. The vast library, one of Europe's largest, is adjacent to the Galleria Estense. I'm so sorry for your wasted journey," he said.

"Yes, of course, Signore Director, I'm well aware of the Biblioteca Estense in Modena. But in the note which he wrote to Pope Innocent X, Cardinal Bentivoglia said that he wanted his private books and letters and papers transferred to his home. I assumed that he meant here, this castle," said Martina.

"I think not Signora Professor. Perhaps he meant that he lived here, but I assure you that there is no book or paper belonging to the Cardinal in our castle. All we have here are books of the private Este family. We know and have recorded every one of them. If only you'd given me more details when you telephoned me yesterday, I would have told you that and saved you a journey. But feel free to look at the Index of Archives, especially the books, and see if there's anything to do with Cardinal

Bentivoglia. You're free, of course, to examine our library, but for over a hundred years, our curators have gone over everything in the most scrupulous detail, and to the best of my knowledge, the good Cardinal's name appears nowhere. I'm so sorry."

As they walked back to their hotel, David asked, "Why didn't you think it was worth while checking their books?"

"Because, darling, I think the Director is correct. And I could kick myself for wasting our time. I should have realised back in Rome that the books and papers would have been sent to the d'Este library in Modena, and not to this castle. I'm such a fool."

"Oh, I don't know. We had a beautiful dinner in an amazing city last night. So tomorrow, do we go to Modena?"

"Damn right we do. I made a mistake in Rome, thinking that he meant Ferrara, but I realise my mistake and will put Cardinal Bentivoglia to rights. Because now I'm on the right track," she told him. "First we go to the hotel so that I can phone the Director of the Biblioteca Estense. I know him slightly, as I've done research there before. It's closed to the public because many of the books and codices are ancient and need careful curating.

But scholars are allowed in. So tomorrow, we take the train to Modena. You'll love it, or hate it. It's the home of sweet and sour."

"Sorry?"

She smiled. "Sweet because it's the home of Ferrari and Lamborghini, Di Tomaso and Maserati. The best cars in all the world. And it's the home of opera and music. But it's also a sour city, because it's the home of Balsamic Vinegar.

"And now, perhaps you can begin to understand why Renaissance families like the Borgia and the Medici and the d'Estes were so important to the power and prestige of Italy. They owned huge tracts of land and really important cities. They accumulated money from trading and banking and created the first proper money and banking market. The very work 'bank' comes from the Italian word 'bench.' Venice, along with Genoa, were the maritime republics and built fortunes on spices and fabrics. In Venice, men sat at benches and tables and sponsored and paid for expeditions to the Far East. And of course, the most famous banking family was the Medicis."

As they walked back to the hotel, he wondered how he could go back to a normal life in Australia, where the oldest building dated back to the 18th Century. And where he had a wife and children and grandchildren who's culture was so closely rooted in modernity. Since he'd been in Italy, he now truly understood the depth of the genius of the Renaissance, the Baroque and all the other formative ages.

The following day, sitting in the Library's Central Office, the Director explained the enormity of their task. "Yes, of course everything is catalogued and curated," he said. "But we still have over half a million printed works. We have 110,000 codices, 100,000 manuscripts and over 1,600 incunabulae."

David looked at Martina, who explained, "Incunabula are ancient documents, printed before the end of the Renaissance. They're not hand-written."

"And our most famous exhibit, of course, is the Bible of Count Borso d'Este, which is one of the most precious books in the world. Every page had many many small but magnificent paintings. It is a work of art," said the Director. "And it is an honour to welcome a scholar of your eminence, Professor Calabrese. And your colleague from Australia. It's quite possible that we have works here by the late and revered Cardinal Bentivoglio. The Dukes of Este collected tens of thousands of books, documents, manuscripts. All are catalogued, and I'm certain that if the books and papers of the Cardinal are here, you'll find them."

An hour later, the director took them to the curatorial department, to  introduce them to the Chief Curator of Books.

As he knocked and entered her office, the Curator, Dr. Chiara Ianni, a tall and attractive young woman, stood and when she saw who was accompanying the Director, she grinned from ear to ear. "Martina? Dear God, what are you doing here?"

She came around the desk and hugged her. Martina explained to the Director and David, "Chiara is my former PhD student from Yale. I had no idea you were back in Italy. When....why...how....?"

"I got back last year, at the invitation of the Director to take up the position after the former Chief Curator retired. I was going to go to the Uffizi to see you, but I've been so busy....What are you doing here?" said Chiara.

Martina explained. The Director nodded, kissed Martina's hand and went back to his office.

"Ok, now he's gone, how are you enjoying working here?" asked Martina in an undertone.

"Modena isn't exactly New York, but it's a fascinating

place. This library is simply wonderful. But it needs the millions of dollars spent on it to bring its systems up to date. Frankly, the former Chief Curator did virtually nothing for the past twenty years. We have books here which are falling apart from neglect and just a handful of conservators. I've put together a fund-raising proposal which we'll enact next year," Chiara said.

"Did you continue the relationship with that young man, what's his name?"

"Randy? No. It ran its course and I wanted to get back to Italy. And are you the David that the art world is buzzing about? The Artemisia?"

David looked stunned. "Yes, but..."

"David," said Chiara, "the art world is massive, but tiny; universal but local. Those of us, like Martina, are celebrities about whom gossip happens. You're now part of the gossip."

Martina laughed, and said, "Yes, this is the David. He's in Italy waiting on the authentication of the painting he found in Australia which he hopes and trusts is by Artemisia. I've sent one of the Uffizi's experts on early Baroque to London to be part of the panel to determine whether it's an Artemisia, or less likely her father Orazio, or possibly somebody like Massimo Stanzione, who was painting at the same time as Artemisia or even Jusepe de Ribera. We won't know until we examine the brushwork and the style. But that's not why we're hear Chiara, my darling," she said. "We're here on another mission. In our research to find out if Artemisia mentioned this painting of a mother and child, where the child makes her breast bleed, we came across a snippet of information. We think that Artemisia might have written a book about her life. She sent it to her lover in Florence, Francesco Maria di Niccolò Maringhi...have you ever heard of him?" asked Martina.

Chiara shook her head. "Never. But Artemisia wrote a book about her....amazing....what a discovery that would be."

"She sent a letter to this Maringhi from the time she was living in London asking him to do her a service. After her death, she asked him to go London and retrieve it from her father, Orazio's, grave. The grave was desecrated during the English Civil War, and at the same time she fled England. We think...we're only speculating....that she went to her father's grave, took back the book, and brought it with her to Italy. That's where the leads have dried up."

"So what are you doing here? In the Biblioteca

Estense?" asked Chiara. "Do you think that Artemisia's book could be buried here in our archives?"

"We don't know. It's a long line of suppositions, but this is our last stop. If it's not here, then either it's been destroyed, or in a thousand years, somebody will dig it up and find that it just falls to pieces in a cloud of dust."

"Ok, so do we look up references for Artemisia, or for this lover of hers....what's his name?" asked Chaiara.

"Francesco Maringhi," said Martina, smiling. "And neither. We don't know the connection yet between Maringhi, Artemesia, and another person who we think might have been involved, but what I'm here to do is to look up all the books and documents which a certain Cardinal Bentivoglia sent here from Rome. Ferrara was his home, and we think his papers and books were sent here to Modena when he died in 1644."

"Sorry...where does he fit in?" asked Chiara.

"I told you it's a long line of suppositions. When we were going through the Vatican's Apostolic Library, we came across a letter from Artemisia to Francesco, in which she mentions her book. The letter was in the correspondence of Cardinal Bentivoglio. But as I said, we have no idea where he fits into the puzzle. Had you heard of him before?" asked Martina.

"Cardinal Bentivoglio? I can't recall his name, but if he's sent his private papers here, then they'll be on record. I don't remember any reference to him, but that means nothing as it's a huge library so we could have his books, and don't forget that I've not been here all that long. Come with me and we'll check the records," said Chiara.

As he did in the Apostolic Library in Rome, speaking not a work of Italian, or Latin, David was reduced to watching the two women pour through computer lists, and then, because of the vastness of the library and it was a huge job to computerize all of the references, they looked through drawer after drawer of library files, making lists and notes. David offered to pull the books or documentation from the shelves, but Chiaria said that they had librarians to do that very thing. So he sat and continued to watch.

By the middle of the afternoon, they had found all references to the Cardinal's books in the library. Two librarians were instructed to follow the numbering of the books, which were classified following the Dewey Decimal System introduced in 1956 when Chiara's predecessor as Chief Curator had first been appointed. The Library classification system was still being undated onto computers, but the enormous expense and lack of staff made it a monumental task, which probably wouldn't be completed for another few years.

The first books arrived at their table in Chiara's office ten minutes later. One of the books which had been delivered was a slim volume, a copy of Erasmus' In Praise of Folly'. Inside the front cover, in faded ink, the Cardinal had written two inscriptions in Latin. The first was *"ex Bibliotheca Cardinali Bentivoglio G."*

The second was *"Si Impetum Ecclesiae, te Ipsum Deum Impetum."*

David looked at Martina, but it was Chiara who translated. "The first inscription means that this book is from his library. The second is more interesting. The Cardinal wrote that if you attack the church, you attack God Himself. This book by the philosopher Erasmus, David, was not just an attack on superstition, but also an attack on the way in which Rome was organising the Catholic religion. Erasmus was a pre-eminent philosopher who never became a Protestant, and often quarrelled with his staunchly Catholic friend, Sir Thomas More, but he wrote that he had sympathy with many of the beliefs of Protestantism, especially where it criticised the many failings of the Catholic Church. No wonder the Cardinal didn't want to keep this book in Rome after his death.

He was probably hoping to be elevated to Sainthood by a future Pope, and possession of this book would have been a mark against him."

Martina skimmed through the book, and shook her head. "Nothing here but what Erasmus wrote."

Within minutes, more books were delivered, one which Chiara handed to Martina, a slim volume which couldn't have contained anything other than what the author had written. It was The Prince, by Niccolò Machiavelli. Martina opened the front cover delicately, and yet again, after the statement of ownership and *ex libris,* the Cardinal had written a further note in Latin. It read, *"Prince, ut homo se vocare hic in Terris, sed Omnia et in Aeternum Caelo, Deus est Re."*

Chiara bust out laughing when she read the inscription, so Martina explained to David, "This Cardinal had a wonderful sense of the ridiculous. To understand why this is funny, you have to have read The Prince." David shook his head. Once again his education in geology wasn't proving to be an asset in their hunt for information about Artemisia. So she continued, "In this book, Machiavelli instructs how rulers should rule. It's a manual for every prince, king, dictator, President, Prime Minister....everybody who runs a country or an organization. Machiavelli shows rulers what they must do to be a Prince. But in Latin, the Cardinal says '*A man may call himself Prince here on Earth, but for all eternity in Heaven, God is King.*' I really think that the Borgias and the Medicis would have disagreed."

For a second time, Martina examined the book, and shook her head. It was nothing more than a 1630 edition of Machiavelli's famous book.

And more and more books were brought but were merely the books that had been in his library, until Chiara yawned, and said, "Guys, I think that's it for the night. Let's meet again tomorrow. I'll devote whatever time I can, but you're more than capable of doing this on your own, Martina."

The following morning, David and Martina sat at a large table, which was full of the Cardinal's library. Book piled upon book in stacks 10 books high. Except for one occasion, none of the books had been touched since the time they were deposited after his death, over three hundred years earlier. The only thing which had been done to them was to have a label affixed to their spines to show their Dewcy catalogue number.

"One thing you could do, darling," said Martina, "is to carefully examine each of these books for anything which doesn't look as if it belongs to the original. I have no idea what I mean. It could be hand-written pages, pages typeset in a different style to the original printed book, loose leaves which fall out when you open the book. I just don't know. Meantime, I'll examine each book carefully, and see what we find, if anything."

David carefully picked up the first book, opened the cover, and gingerly leafed through the pages. By the time he got to the end, having no idea what to look for, he was certain that it was nothing more than a book. He placed it near to Martina so that she could examine it.

He kept doing this for thirty or more books, until he came to a very large book, which he picked up carefully. Immediately, it felt different than the others, for reasons he didn't understand. The binding was aged black leather with gold leaf pressed into the edges. The front and back covers were held firmly together by a brass clasp. Faded gold leaf on the front and spine told him what the book was, and who'd written it. But as he held it in his hands, he knew, instinctively, that this book was more than just a book, though for reasons which weren't immediately apparent.

They had been books which were solid and stable in his hands, but despite the clasp holding the covers in place, this one felt oddly weighted, as though it were unbalanced. Holding it flat in his hands, it felt normal, but when he altered its position and made it vertical, it felt distinctly different, odd even.

Before opening it, he read the title.

*"Arturo Re, et Equites*
*in*
*Legenda de Rotunda Tabula.*
*Per*

*Magister Tho. Malory Esq.*

Although he spoke not a work of Latin, he worked out immediately this this was a translation of Thomas Malory's The Legend of King Arthur and the Knights of the Round Table.

Cautiously, and still holding it vertically, he opened the book, and looked at the colophon, the inscriptions and the drawing on the frontispiece. It was a series of small portraits of medieval looking knights, all gathered around a king and queen, presumably Arthur and Guinevere. And just holding it in this position made it feel uneven, unbalanced in his hands. His heart was thumping.

With even greater caution he laid it flat on the table, opened the first, and then the second pages. For some reason, Martina, sitting opposite him and immersed in her own detective work, sensed that something was happening with David sitting opposite her, and looked up. Their eyes met across the table. She knew better than to ask a question, but let him continue with his study, while carefully watching what he did.

David opened more pages, until he was close to the centre of the book, when suddenly the centre of the right hand page wasn't there. The outsides were there, but where the center of the pages should have been, instead, was a hand-written manuscript. The pages of the second half of the book had been cut with a sharp knife to form a hollow, inside which had been placed these papers.

The book and papers just lay there, flat. David's mouth gaped and he looked up at Martina. She, too, looked amazed. Carefully, tenderly, he reached into the well within the pages of the book, and took out the folio of papers, which he then caringly placed onto the table.

"Jesus!" shouted Martina. "Chiara. Come. Now!"

"What?" shouted Chiara from inside her closed office. She stood immediately and rushed to the door.

"Is this it?" asked David, looking at all of the hand-written pages which now sat there in a pile, waiting to be read for the first time in more than three centuries.

Martina stood immediately, and began carefully straightening the pages into a neat pile. By this time, Chiara was beside her, looking at them, and trying to read the words. And when David looked carefully at them, they were in a beautifully scripted hand, but faded in the time since they'd been written.

"Well?" demanded David.

"We don't know. Just wait!" ordered Martina. She could barely restrain her excitement.

When the two women had carefully assembled them into a solid sheath, Martina, her hands shaking, looked at the first page. Silently, both women bent over the table, and read it together. Their heads almost touched as they viewed the precious manuscript. Their lips moved, but no sound came out.

David looked at them both. He wanted to scream, *"Well, tell me. Is this what we've been looking for? Does Artemisia say she painted my picture? Tell me for God's sake!"* But he remained silent as the two women read silently.

Martina looked up at David, and smiled. He'd never seen her so happy, yet there were tears in her eyes. "This is like finding a new play by William Shakespeare. Let me read to you in English what we've just read in Italian."

## *THE BOOK OF MY LIFE.......*

*Written by Artemisia Gentileschi, in my
hand in London, England.
February, Anno Domini 1639.*

*Anger does not even begin to define the
feelings coursing through my veins, causing
me to lose the composure which defines the
lady that I am, nor delineates a boundless
woman such as me; I am a woman who
has accomplished so much success in her
profoundly troubled life, that to read of
my life and accomplishments will be like
listening to a performance of the buffoons
and charlatans of the Commedia dell'Arte.
But now that I am writing the story of my
life, I am reliving events which I had buried
because of the pain they caused me. Pain so
powerful, so tortured, that I pray no other
woman ever experiences it.*

"Oh yes, David, my darling. This is the autobiography of
Artemisia Gentileschi," said Martina.  "We've found it.
This is a major historical discovery."

David stood, came round, and hugged and kissed both women. "You've found it! Oh Martina. Chiara. What an amazing thing to happen. I'm so…so….."

For the next two hours, Chiara and Martina lovingly read each page of the manuscript, and translated it into English as best they could for David.

When they'd finished, they were all speechless. Chiara stood as Martina picked up the manuscript carefully and held it reverentially, until Chiara returned from her office with a metal box, large enough for the contents of her book to fit comfortably inside, and to protect it from light and dust.

When it was safely inside the box, Chiara said, "And for the next few weeks, I shall be calling in Renaissance linguists, historians, and other scholars to help with the interpretation of her words. I shall invite academic translators to view and study the work so that we can publish this book in English, German, Spanish, French and other languages."

"David, this is a major find, all thanks to you and your discovery of the picture," said Martina.

"Oh no," he said. "This is 100 per cent down to you, Cardinal de Santis, and Chiara here. This was a detective story like none other. But for me, and I don't want to sound selfish, but the most important thing is that at the end of her book, Artemisia writes about painting my picture and surely that proves that she and nobody else actually did it."

"Let's hope so, but only time and these experts in England will tell, darling. We have to read her book carefully, and then try to translate her nuances into what she may have meant, and why she wrote it. It's looking good for authentication of your painting, but it's not conclusive. She could have instructed her students, or another painter. We just don't know from this text. And translation and verification of what she's written is going to take some time, but not hundreds of years. Just a matter of weeks before we've properly understood what Artemisia wrote," said Martina.

"And in the meantime," said Chiara, "I have to report this find to my Director and to the Board. This is a massive find for the Library, something which we will put on a travelling exhibition. As it's our document by right of possession, the Director will insist that we publish the work and the translation. I assume that neither of you will object?"

Martina and David shook their heads. "It was in your library, so you're entitled to all of the benefits," she said.

"But when you've done all of the authentications and translations, I need your Library's permission, dearest Chiara. This Library is closed to the public, but the Uffizi is just a short distance from here. I'd love for the Uffizi to use Artemisia's book as a central exhibit in a major show we'll put on. Perhaps in a couple of years in June, July and August, if I can arrange it. We already have many of the paintings I'm thinking about, but those we don't have are mainly in European galleries, and when I phone and tell the Directors what I'm thinking about, there'll be no trouble borrowing them for a couple of months."

"What are you thinking?" asked Chiara.

Martina smiled. "Now that we've found this fantastic book, I want to put on an Exhibition featuring all of the great female Renaissance and Baroque artists, fabulous and largely forgotten women like Sofonisba Anguissola and Lavinia Fontana, but of course, our fabulous Artemisia will be central. And her life story, which you will publish, Chiara, will sell like hotcakes from our bookshop."

David smiled, and said, "Dear Lord, I've never heard of any of these women. And I've been a lover of painting most of my life."

"Exactly," said Martina. "Which is why, now that

we've found Artemisia's book, the Uffizi has a reason to feature all the fabulous ground-breaking women painters of the period. The world really should know about these amazing, brilliant women who broke convention and stood up for their rights to do as they wished in their lives. Women like Fontana and Anguissola, and others like Irene di Spilibergo, Barbara Longhi, and Fede Galizia. Wonderful painters who have been forgotten. They need to be known and respected," she said.

David looked at her and saw the fire in her eyes. Was he falling in love with her? He certainly was attracted, and he had a feeling that she was attracted to him. It was subtle, unstated, but there was definitely something there. But how could a retired Aussie geologist possibly be attractive to one of Italy's....no, Europe's....most brilliant and sophisticated and gorgeous women?

# PART, THE EIGHTH

The trial was still being conducted when I began to paint Judith cutting off the head of Holofernes. The year was 1618. It had been going on now for half a year or more, not held every day, of course, but only when the Judges wanted to hear more witnesses. As to when it would come to an end, and my beloved father would receive his compensation for the destruction of his daughter's bride-value, we had no idea. Our advocate, Signore Rossi asked time and again to the Clerk of the Court when he could expect a resolution, but the answer was always the same: *"When their Honours have come to a decision."*

And so like the souls of the unbaptised, I was in Limbo, created for the good of humanity by Giovanni Medici, Pope Pius IV. But unlike those souls, lying between Grace and Purgatory, waiting anxiously for their loved ones to pay money to the church for their elevation into Heaven,

I had the capacity to remove myself, to do something about my station in life, to pull myself up and go out into the world, face my adversaries and give vent to my anger.

My hand still hurt from the Sibille, and when I held a brush for too long, I would have to immerse my hand in a bucket of cold water so that the throbbing stopped. It only stoked my anger, making me more determined to do what I was planning. My mind and body were ready for my art.

I'd been planning it in my mind, and making sketches for weeks and weeks, and I now knew precisely how I wanted to represent my subjects. This was going to be no Madonna and Child, no Suzanna, embarrassed at her nudity being exposed before two lecherous old men, no pastoral scene of bucolic delights where beautiful women were picking meadow flowers, or lazing by a river bank.

No, my painting would be as real, as vivid, as confronting as any which the divine Caravaggio had painted, full of drama and tension, of colour and light, of terrifying shadows and illumined faces *in extremis*, of taut muscles and sinews bursting out of skin. This would be a picture of a woman whose life and virtue were threatened by a man, a woman who was captured on canvas whilst she was in the act of wreaking revenge, cutting off his head, blood gushing from his severed neck, his fists flailing, his legs kicking, in a desperate attempt to save himself from certain death.

And who would be my models for this monumental painting? Who would sit for me, the painter, as a model for Judith? I could choose any model, ask any woman with an interesting face, approach any Madonna in the street and proposition her to sit for me, to become famous for all time. That was not a problem, for I knew even before I started painting whose face I would use; and it would be no Roman matron nor a stranger importuned by me.

But which man would I choose to be my Holofernes? A guard? A watchman? A student? A peripatetic troubadour? A Cardinal, perhaps, or a lowly Priest? No, it would be none of these, for as I sat in the court listening to the lies told against me, I knew in my very soul who would be my Holofernes.

My subjects would be none other than myself as the Israelite woman Judith who saved her nation, and Holofernes, my victim, would be Tassi, now portrayed as the one who was helpless on the bed, rudely woken by two women holding him down while one uses a sword to sever his head from his body. Revenge? Yes. Reprisal? Oh, absolutely. Retaliation in a city where an injured woman had no rights? Oh Sweet Jesus, yes. And yes again!

I had never before painted a canvas in anger. I had always approached a subject in a rational manner. All the excitement, the emotion, the enthusiasm might have built up in my mind as I explored different ways of accosting the subject; but when I came to the art of painting, my mind was cold, hard, determined. The forces directing my fingers as I wielded the brush were minutely controlled.

But this painting would be different. As Judith severed the head of Holofernes, I would be writing a statement for all the world to see, of what happens when men prey on women. From the moment I finished this work, and displayed it in some public gallery, the world would see me in an act of revenge so severe that men would turn away in disgust, while women stood and admired, wondering whether or not they had the courage to do as Judith did.

This painting would have the word "revenge" written throughout its brushstrokes, in the fury in Judith's eyes, in the horror in Holofernes' face, in the agony of his fists as he tried to grasp the dress of Abra, Judith's servant. For my purposes, the painting had to be unremitting in its power, through the way in which I showed the strength of the women, their determination, their anger; but also the helplessness of a huge and strong man suddenly powerless under the relentless determination, and dominance, of women.

I had to show my viewers the reality of Holofernes' death throes by the depiction of arcs of blood coursing from his severed vessels. But, and this was so immensely important, when I painted the faces of the maid Abra and of Judith, I had to project a vision of quiet certitude, of confidence, of the unutterable rightness and Godliness of their act. I had to show that they, two women, had taken power over a brute of a man, and that the morality of their purpose had won the day. They had to be calm, determined and wholly resolute in what they were doing at that moment. It must be revealed as right and proper in the eyes of God. Otherwise, their act would be little more than barbarism, the unlawful sin of murder - inhuman and monstrous.

In terms of my colours, I determined that those I would use would depict both the joy of their act in the salvation of their people, and the agony of Holofernes as he died. I will use the vivid primary colours of blue, yellow and red, and the secondary colours of green and violet. Perhaps, if I can find a supplier, I will use cobalt blue and gold. I know my father will not begrudge the expenditure, as his shame and remorse is so great at the moment because of what I suffered, that he would not raise a word against me.

But the one colour to dominate the centre of my painting won't be a colour at all, but a technique. One taught to me by my beloved Caravaggio. I will use the drama of chiaroscuro to illuminate the faces and upper torsos of Judith and Abra as they sever their enemy's head. The tent in which they perform the act will be dark, as will all of the background until we come to the central players in the drama, for no drama is ever as wrenching to a viewer as that illumined by chiaroscuro.

I told no one that I was planning to paint this canvas. I had no buyer in mind, no patron to whom to promote the idea. This was my project, my concept, my determination. Not even my father knew that I was planning to paint this subject, for there's no doubt that he would have objected. And logically, he would have been right.

Firstly, there were many, many representations of this particular story from the Book of Judith. Botticelli, Donatello, Michaelangelo and the German Lucas Cranach had created works based on her story, and even my own Caravaggio had painted her recently.

My father would have told me to find another subject

less well known and represented. But he would also have said that it wasn't a suitable subject for a woman to paint. He still believed that women painters should be respectful and paint womanly subjects. He had objected to my Susanna and the Elders, even though he agreed that it was a masterpiece and worthy of hanging in the home of a patron. His objection had been the nudity of Susanna, and his concerns that my depiction would bring the entire edifice of the Vatican and the Curia down on my head, and affect his standing with the Pope. It was one thing for men to gaze at a nude woman and capture her breasts and other intimate parts in their imagery, or to sculpt the naked male member of David, which Michaelangelo had recently done; but for a woman like me to gaze upon a naked model and worse, much worse, to paint her form, was a sin against Nature, and defied the Church's teachings about morality.

So telling my father that I was about to paint a canvas depicting a woman cutting off a man's head would have cause him apoplexy. It was for that reason that I didn't say anything.

Instead, I bought a large canvas from our supplier, purchased my colours, the cobalt blue and gold to be delivered later when he had found a supply, and set the empty picture up in my bedchamber. I covered the easel with a blanket, even though there wasn't even a line of charcoal on it yet, just to remind myself of the need for secrecy, but more especially in order to warn any maid or servant, or father, not to trespass on my privacy by raising the blanket and seeking to determine what was happening beneath.

Before I began, in those days only able to read a few words, I sought out a priest and asked him to refresh my mind concerning the details of the story. Judith was a wealthy and beautiful widow at the time of the assault by the Assyrians against her people, Israel. She was horrified that the people were wailing and gnashing their teeth and had lost faith in God to protect them against the certainty of capture, enslavement and exile. In the Book of Judith, I learned of the maiden's prayer before she was invited into Holofernes' tent to enjoy the unholy bargain; her body will be given to him in return for mercy for her people, whereas her intention was to get the General drunk and then kill him. In her prayer, she said,

> **Lord God, to whom all strength belongs,**
> **prosper what my hands are now to do for**
> **the greater glory of Jerusalem; for now is the**

**time to recover Your heritage and to further
my plans to crush the enemies arrayed
against us**

A prayer could not have been more fitting to that moment in my life. And so I began the painting. Few things are more daunting to an artist, sitting on a stool, looking at a naked canvas, than trying to imagine a finished picture. And the picture they see in their minds often bears no relationship to the one which becomes the finished canvas. Pictures are living things. They begin as a desert landscape, an ill-defined form, until are added colours and lines, dimensions and depths, backgrounds and structures; but as detail is enhanced – as the desert disappears, in its place is a mischievous child, all muscle and power. This then takes on the potent form of a youth with immature beauty, all pose but little grace. The picture takes on a form, a purpose, and further shape and definition. That's when the artist begins to add those touches that transform it from a cartoon to a character. A frown here, a line around the mouth there, eyes which show a woman's age, knots in a man's neck to show him straining and pulling against a heavy object, a foot placed under a table to show completeness.

First comes the charcoal, so that all of the characters have their place in the drama of the picture. Rough, crude outlines to show where Judith will be standing, how she will be wielding the sword against Holofernes' neck, and how his hands will be flailing. Then come the questions, which only I can ask, and which only I can answer. Do I have him grasping the bedsheets in the agony of the assault which suddenly wakens him rudely from his sleep? Do I have him grasping the handle of the sword to try to loosen Judith's grip? Or do I have him try to grab a dagger which I'll place underneath his pillow, so that he can thrust it into Judith or Abra? Do I have him shout aloud so that his guards come running in and save him? I have to follow the limits of the Biblical story, but within those limits I have autonomy and complete authority.

The fluidity of the painting, its dynamism in my hands, its life and vitality, takes over from the charcoal lines as I sketch into the painting the direction of the limbs, the stance of the body, the movement of the sheets. I can now see Judith's determination as the sword slices through the skin, then the muscles, and then the bone of his spine.

I can see it all in the charcoal lines as my fingers fly over the bare canvas, and the picture begins to become real. I can see all of the colours, the highlights, the nuances of expression in the shadows that I'll paint; I see it in the folds of the sheet on which he's struggling against the assault, and especially in the way Judith's arms are gripping him so tightly that he can barely move. And in two hours, maybe four, as I lose all sense of time, my picture has come alive, and I have before me the outline of the finished paining. I sit back and admire my work. In the space of an afternoon, it has become Judith Cutting Off The Head Of Holofernes.

In this way, other than applying the paint and the varnish, my picture is finished in my mind. It is one which not only depicts everything I wanted to say, but tells the viewer the complete story. This is Medea's vengeance against Jason, it is the Furies chasing Orestes and it is the Greek Keres, death goddesses, feasting on the bodies of those who had died in battle. It has taken me an afternoon to create my painting. All that's left now is the weeks it will take me to paint it.

Some artists, such as Leonardo and Michaelangelo, might work for years and years on the same picture. Others, such as Caravaggio, worked morning noon and night and finished the painting almost as soon as he'd begun. Often the more successful artists allowed their students to paint the chairs or beds, walls or doors, dresses for women and doublets for men. But when it came to faces and hands, the shape of a shoulder or an arm or leg, something which would define the picture as specifically that person's art, then that became the work of the master. Not, of course, that I, as an 18 year old, had students. So all of the tent's background, dresses, sheets, blankets and even the sword, would be painted by me. I had complete control over my painting.

Of course, master painters like my father Orazio had control, but were often frustrated that they would have to over-paint a student's work if it was inadequate. But for my Judith, every brushstroke, every expression, muscle and spurt of blood, would be mine, and mine alone.

It took me two months before the painting of Judith was in such a state as to allow people to see it. My father asked many times what I was working on, and I lied to him by telling him that I was recovering in my room from the ordeals of the trial.

He never asked about the accounts he had received from the paint and canvas supplier. I knew I'd have to account for it one day, but for the time being I wasn't under pressure to explain myself.

And still the trial dragged on. My father no longer went to the courtroom every day, or even every week, but relied on Advocate Rossi who came to our house every few days to explain what had been happening. It was a case of witnesses testifying, of judges taking time to attend to other duties, and even the Salon having to be used for a presentation of some sort of another.

But then the day arrived when the Advocate came to our house, and said excitedly, "Maestro Gentileschi, I have exciting news. Tomorrow, I have been informed by the master Clerk of the Salon...tomorrow...."

"Tomorrow? What about tomorrow?"

"Tomorrow! It's tomorrow!" said the Advocate.

"What!" shouted my father, paintbrushes in his hand.

"The verdict. The judgement. The result. Tomorrow!"

He was standing outside the door. It was a freezing December day, and the wind from the Tiber was blowing into our house, causing the braziers to suddenly flare and cause smoke to spread throughout the house.

"Come inside, man, for the sake of the Almighty," shouted my father. "Now, the verdict is tomorrow. What will it be? When will we know? How much will he pay me when he loses? My daughter was tortured and yet found innocent, so what can I expect from the costs I have been forced to meet?"

Advocate Rossi had already stepped inside and one

of our young maids, Rosario, had closed the door and stopped the draft. Looking at him from an upper balcony, I listened with hushed breath.

"The Clerk of the Court said little. He could not. The verdict will be delivered to him tonight, and he will write the Judges' determination for them to read in the morning.

"But he indicated to me that the Judges hadn't looked kindly on Agostino Tassi. They disbelieved his evidence, and the sworn testimony of all of the men whom he brought to court to swear oaths against your beloved daughter. They knew from the paucity of facts which the men presented in evidence that they had made up their stories, and were probably paid by Tassi to say the things they said in court.

"As to the quantum of the punishment against him, if its determined against him and he's found to be guilty, he can be imprisoned, or tortured, or imprisoned and tortured, or tortured without being imprisoned; or he can be exiled from Rome and be put to death if he returns; or he can be fined and all his assets and wealth taken from him; or he can be sent to a galley as a slave for five years – more if necessary; or he could be locked into stocks in a public square for a week or more and pilloried by the passing public; or if the Judges consider that there was blasphemy involved in his crimes, he can be burned at the stake. And then of course, there's....."

"Enough!" shouted my father. "I don't care what punishment he suffers, provided that I am recompensed for the losses I've suffered. Now, Master Advocate, go to your business, and inform the judges that this is my demand. That Tassi be stripped of his wealth and that it be transferred to me. I have suffered grievously in pain and humiliation and I will be recompensed. Is that clearly understood?"

It took every piece of my composure not to scream out: "YOUR pain? YOUR humiliation? What about me?"

But I didn't. I remained silent, biting my lip so that I didn't open my mouth. I had suffered the assault, the crime, yet it was my father who would be compensated. And that was justice?

So tomorrow, the world imagined that I would see justice done in my favour, but my true recompense would continue to be a dagger to my heart. Whenever I walked though the streets of Rome, people still would sneer and point and say *"There goes the Gentileschi girl, the one who had her way with the painter Tassi and then got rich from him."* It always ended in sniggers and sometimes outright laughter as I walked by. It was the reaction of the citizenry that convinced me to leave Rome and settle in another city.

The next day, my father and I walked in freezing blustering rain from our home on the Via Corso, to the building where the Salon was housed.

We walked into the building, and for the first time since the trial began seven long months ago, I felt a modicum of certainty. I glanced over to Tassi, and he sat alone, looking more isolated and, yes, defeated than I'd ever seen him. He looked as though the weight of a building had fallen on his head. He looked like an old man, his body was bowed and deflated.

I now knew, after all the evidence had been presented, that the man I had agreed to marry was not the man I thought he was. What transpired in evidence was that he had spent years on a galley when punished in a court and had become an indentured slave. He hadn't rowed, but instead had been doing menial work, even though it had given him sufficient knowledge of the sea and ports and sailors to inform his paintings. I had also found out that he'd been imprisoned for raping his wife's sister. And to add to his crimes, he had also entered our house, probably admitted into our sanctum by Tuzia, and stolen a painting which he intended to sign as his own and sell for a lot of money.

So now, as I sat in my seat, I kept staring at him, hoping that the righteous heat from my eyes would bore a hole in his conscience.

And then the court was upstanding, for the Judges entered. The Chief Judge looked at me, then at my father, and then at Tassi. He acknowledged the advocates, and the three Bishops who had been sent from the Vatican to hear the verdict on the Pope's protégé.

"Agostino Tassi," said the iudge. "You have been accused of enjoying intimacies with Artemisia Gentileschi, a maiden and thereby, having diminished her value as a daughter in marriage to men, against the interests of her father, Orazio Gentileschi. He claims, and we agree, that as a woman who may attract a husband of note and status, she will no longer be able to attract a man of such standing in our community because you have stolen her maidenhood.

"Her value is less today than it was last year when she claims she was a virgin. You claim in your evidence, and that of the many witnesses you brought to court to testify on your behalf, that Madonna Gentileschi was little more than a prostitute and that her father not only had knowledge of her body, but sold her in brothels to wayfarers, miscreants and the citizenry, for sums of money.

"We listened carefully to the evidence you and your witnesses presented, and found it wanting. Indeed, we have discounted virtually every one of your eye-witnesses to Madonna Gentileschi's virtue. We find it not just unproven, but scurrilous, outrageous and a travesty of justice. Lies! All lies!

"Further, Tassi, we find that you did, most certainly and assuredly, have intimate knowledge of Madonna Gentileschi without her permission, thereby lessening her value to her father.

"Accordingly, we sentence you to be exiled from this city for five years. Should you return during that period, you will be arrested, and executed. The court is adjourned."

And with that, the judges all stood and left the court. My father was frowning, shaking his head. He turned to Advocate Rossi, and said, "But....but....I don't understand. My recompense. My compensation. My costs for this case. For you, Rossi. Who will reimburse my costs? Go to the judges and get them to return immediately. This is...."

And while they were discussing and arguing, neither looked at me to see how I had reacted to the findings by the judges. Only Agostino Tassi was looking at me. And as a painter, I tried to read his eyes.

What did I see in them? Sorrow? Regret? Apology? Anger?

I don't know. They were open and he was looking at me. But there was no message in his eyes. No code. Just a void, a blackness.

Nothing.

I returned to my home and walked upstairs to my bedchamber. I closed and locked the door. I unveiled the picture I was painting, now mostly finished, and I looked at the face of Judith, and then at the face of Holofernes. Although unfinished, they were clearly representations of myself and Tassi.

I had followed the dictates of the Biblical story; Holofernes invites Judith to his tent suggesting that he will be merciful towards her people Israel on the condition that she will give herself to him that night. She enters his tent, but she gives him so much wine that he is overcome, and falls down onto his bed.

Judith summons her servant Abra to assist her with the huge man's body. She kneels onto his chest, using her weight to hold him down, which causes him to wake and flail about wildly, while her maidservant struggles to hold him flat to the bed. He tries to push Abra away with his fist in her chest, but he's suddenly consumed by the agony of Judith slicing off his head from his shoulders, blood spurting out in crimson arcs over her clothes, the bedsheets and the tent.

I picked up a paintbrush, and mixed a flesh colour, but a shade fractionally darker than I had intended yesterday and the day before. And within the faint charcoal lines I'd sketched for Judith's mouth, I painted something which I hadn't thought of painting previously. So I picked up another brush, and dipped it into the cardinal red, mixed with a touch of cerise that I'd used yesterday to paint her lips. Before the verdict, I had painted her lips thin and determined, as though she was concentrating on a task and nothing would prevent her completing it. But since I'd returned from court triumphant, I needed a different Judith, one who has foreseen victory while she was in the process of committing the act.

So with the merest stroke of the brush, I turned her lips from one of thin hard determination, intent on the job she was doing of hacking off his head, to one of a look of determined completeness. A look of victory.

Now that he had been found guilty; now that I had been declared before the world as innocent, the lips I painted on Judith's face portrayed a woman of determination, a woman taking power back into her own hands, the merest brushstroke and inflection of self-righteousness. I created in my Judith a woman pleased with what she was doing.

And for all time, people who saw my painting, would know with unabashed and utter certainty that Judith was justified in taking the action that she did, and that she was avenging herself against a brute determined on using his strength and power to bend her to his ways.

While he was travelling on the road to Damascus, Saul, a Pharasee, a persecutor of Christians, suffered a sudden and dramatic revelation. An epiphany which converted him into Paul, the Apostle and the disciple of Christ. Suddenly, as he and his tax gatherer colleagues walked along the road from Jerusalem, we read in the Book of Acts,

> *As he neared Damascus on his journey, suddenly a light from heaven flashed around him. He fell to the ground and heard a voice say to him, "Saul, Saul, why do you persecute me?"*

*"Who are you, Lord?" Saul asked.*

*"I am Jesus, whom you are persecuting," he*
*replied. "Now get up and go into the city,*
*and you will be told what you must do."*

Well, my beloved and unknown reader of this, my life, as I finished my portrait of Judith and Holofernes, I, too, had a revelation. An epiphany. As I gazed at my painting of Judith, now complete and needing no further amendments, a brilliant light exploded in my mind, and I knew that, no matter how arresting was my representation of Judith, as time marched inexorably onwards, her message would be forgotten. Future generations would fail to understand what had happened to me because my picture had failed to define the depravity of Tassi, his cruelty, his duplicitousness, his lies and defamations.

One reason for my epiphany was the news brought to us later by Advocate Rossi, that the Vatican had intervened, and re-prosecuted Tassi, still finding him guilty of all the crimes against my person, but dismissing the first court's punishment of exile, and allowing him to stay and prosper in Rome. The fury I experienced when I heard this news made me ill. Now, every time I left our house on the via Corso, I might come upon him in the street; could I walk in the foothills and be certain that he wasn't there; could I enter a restaurant in the sure knowledge that his leering face wouldn't be at one of the tables?

My father complained bitterly to the Vatican, but the Cardinals to whom he spoke said that it was a decision made by His Holiness, and was irrevocable.

But revocation of the punishment wasn't on my lips. Instead, revenge had reared its head again, and determination had set in. And as I thought about what had just happened, that my rapist had been freed to rape more women by escaping his punishment, my mind said to me, *"This is the second time, Artemisia, that this man has bitten you and drawn blood."*

And then the epiphany! Like a bolt of sudden and explosive lightening, something seemed to explode in my head, and my path ahead became so clear and obvious.

Another painting! But this time, it would be no allegory. It would not convey some subtle message, hidden in the smiles or the curled lips of the protagonists. No, now I would create a painting which would tell the world about the viper I'd nurtured to my bosom; about the snake which smiled endearingly as it seduced me nearer and nearer until suddenly it struck!

Now I would paint a portrait of mother and child. Not like the painting of Tuzia and her baby. Now I would be the mother, and Tassi would be the suckling child, his teeth tearing into my breast to show the world his unfeeling callowness, his monstrous indifference to others. Then the world, the whole world, would know the truth.

<h1 align="center">PART, THE NINTH</h1>

——◆——

In my end, is my beginning. Not my beginning as a painter, nor as a woman, but as a wife. My end was the destruction of my reputation as a young woman of virtue, marriageable and worth a goodly price to my father because of my ability to attract a wealthy husband. All that had been dashed on the vicious rocks of exposure by the court, by Tassi, by the questions I was asked under torture.

My beginning was as a wife and mother, like every other Roman or Florentine or Pisan woman of my age. Six months after the verdict was given down by the Judges, my father continued to feel shame at the public disclosure of my sexuality, at the sniggers to which he was subjected in inns and shops. And by this time, his shame had become profound anger at the unfairness of the verdict and punishment. So he married me off to Pierantonio Stiattesi, a decent and good man from

Florence. Pierantonio was very happy to marry me and be associated with the Gentileschi family; perhaps because the notoriety I'd acquired as a defendant in Rome hadn't yet spread to Florence – which I doubt – or perhaps because our name as a family of artists was so renown that not even a lascivious, wanton and unrestrained daughter could damage the reverence in which the name was held.

Whatever was his reasoning, he accepted me willingly for no dowry, and I moved to Florence to become his wife. When he proudly showed me his paintings, I immediately regretted my father's decision. My new husband was so proud of his art, thinking that he was bordering on genius, another Leonardo or Caravaggio. Oh dear! It was difficult not to fall asleep, just looking at his paintings. His faces were flat and uninviting, eyes staring at the moon as though they were inmates of a mad house, with expressions on their faces of having drunk bottle after bottle of wine. The landscapes in which his subjects played their roles were mundane and vapid, painted in the most garish and unnatural colours, and looked as though they needed the skills of a good gardener. I could go on and on, but that would dishonour my husband. Frankly, had it not been for the commissions I earned as a court painter for Medicis, we would have starved.

What a situation! I, a woman, was supporting my husband! We both sold only one or two paintings a year, but the price I negotiated for mine was one hundred times what he could earn from his. Was there ever such a condition between husband and wife? Over the years of our marriage he gave me many children. I bore him five children though only two survived infancy. These were difficult years but despite these painful losses I found pleasure in the serenity of my life as wife, mother and painter. That was the way it was.

When I first moved to Florence shortly after my trial, I was living with my husband in a small but comfortable house near to the Arno, but sufficiently distant to avoid its stench in the summer. One day, some three or four months after moving to Florence, a messenger pounded on our front door. I was in my bed chamber at the time, finishing a painting, when I heard the commotion downstairs. I opened my bedchamber door, and listened. And what I heard made me run downstairs immediately.

Standing in the doorway were my husband, Pierantonio, talking to a wonderfully-dressed man who looked imperious and domineering. My husband looked as if he was overwhelmed by the man's imposing dress and manner. But having lived in Rome and consorted with Dukes and Princes, Cardinals and Popes, this man held no sway over me.

"Yes?" I said. "What do you want with us?"

He looked at me, and bowed slightly. "You are Madonna Artemisia Gentileschi?"

I nodded. As a painter, I used my family birth name; but when I was shopping for food, I called myself Signora Stiattesi.

"I have an invitation for you. From Her Grace, Christina of Lorraine, Grand Duchess of Tuscany. Her Grace invites you to an audience in the Ducal Palace on Thursday, at three past the hour of noon."

My husband's jaw dropped. I thought he would fall on his knees to the floor in reverence. But I said, "No, inform Her Grace that my afternoons are spent in painting, a routine I cannot alter. Tell her that I will come to the Palace at five in the evening, if that is convenient for her."

And with that, I turned on my heels, and left both men in a state of shock.

Why had I been so dismissive? Uncourteous? Refusing to grovel? Because Florence was a provincial city compared to Rome which was the centre of the world. It was important that when I met the Grand

Duchess, she didn't treat me as a servant or a retainer, but as a respected painter who, despite my youth and the calumnies heaped on me by Tassi, had dazzled the most brilliant salons of Rome. If I was to rehabilitate myself, it had to be on my terms, and not bowing and scraping to Dukes and Duchesses. I would be like Michaelangelo Buonarroti shouting at Pope Julius to leave him alone while he created his masterpiece on the ceiling of the Sistine Chapel. If somebody wanted to speak with me, it would be at my convenience, not theirs.

Was I being arrogant in dismissing the messenger? Was I at risk of insulting the Duchess? Yes, of course, but when I moved from Rome, where I was respected as a painter, but ridiculed as a woman, I determined that this wouldn't happen to me in my new city. In Florence, I expected to be taken seriously by the ruling of the city, and to do that, I had to plant my flag on the top of the hill, not the bottom.

When the messenger had left, my husband berated me. I listened to him carefully, but when he demanded that I run after the man and beg his forgiveness, I said calmly, not sternly, "I beg of no man, Pierantonio. I bow to no man. I ask leave of no man. I seek the permission of no man. Not now, not in the future. Not ever."

And with that, I returned to my room and closed the door. Perhaps I had burned my bridges. But after the ignominy I'd faced in Rome, I was determined that I would never ever allow myself to be at the beck and call, or under the thrall of any person, ever again.

My husband didn't come to my room. I sat there for hours, alone, painting. I didn't know what he was doing in the lower parts of the house. And to be honest, I was worried that I had misjudged his person and that I would suffer a beating that night as a result.

But to my amazement, as the day wore on, from the bedchamber window, I heard a commotion in the street below. I stood, looked out of the window and saw the top of a large carriage drawing up outside of our house. The carriage was pulled by a team of four horses, each bearing two separate pennants with insignia on its reins, one being the House of Tuscany, and the other being the House of Medici. Surprised, concerned, I went quickly downstairs, and met my husband in the lobby. We looked at each other and stood in silence at the door, waiting for the visitor to announce his presence.

When he knocked, I immediately opened the door, and a liveried footman stood before me and announced, "Her Grace, Christina, Grand Duchess of Tuscany," before standing aside for the Duchess.

The carriage door was opened by the postilion, who helped a lady, dressed in the richest and finest gown and jewelery, step down and walk towards our door.

My husband bowed so low, I thought his head would touch the floor. I curtsied, as I would have done before royalty or the Pope in Rome, and said, "Your Grace. This is an honour and a pleasure."

She looked at me across the doorway, and smiled, remaining silent.

"Please enter my home," I said.

And without a word, she walked inside, followed by two other women who had descended from the carriage. She didn't introduce them, but I assumed that they were Ladies of the Court.

When I followed her into our small but tidy reception room, she turned and said, "So, you are the famous Artemisia Gentileschi. I've seen your work. You have a precocious talent."

I offered her a chair, and refreshment. She thanked me and accepted my offer of coffee. To be honest, I wasn't certain that she would have heard of coffee, as it was only just becoming popular in Rome and was still too expensive for the common people to drink. Through a friend who worked for a Ducal family, I was supplied with beans, which I'd brought with me to Florence, and drank it alone, because Pierantonio thought that it was disgusting and bitter.

I sent him out to the kitchen to grind some beans and pour boiling water over them, as I'd shown him how to make coffee in the past.

"Well, Madonna Gentileschi," said the Duchess, sitting near to our front window, her maids standing behind her, "you decided that you would not visit me at my appointed time because it was inconvenient for you. Which is why I have made the decision to visit you....at my convenience."

"I meant no disrespect, Your Grace, but as an artist, when I'm in the middle of painting, my mind has to be....."

"You meant no disrespect, young woman, but you were intent on making a point, and that point was not lost, especially on a woman like me. Even though I was born to a much higher station than you, I have still had to work hard to be heard among all of the boisterous voices of men in the halls of power. But unlike the men who shout and threaten and bluster, my voice has always been quiet, but determined. Firm, but restrained.

"There's a fine balance, Artemisia, between being heard, and bellowing. If you shout, you immediately invite disrespect. Most women shout to be heard, or remain silent or cowering, but not you. I was amused when I received your answer. You would appear before me, but a time of your choosing, not mine. You spoke softly, telling my manservant to convey that message to me. You were making a statement that you and I might not be of equal rank, but that you are not to be treated like a servant. That took courage, and I respect that. Which is why I have come to pay my respects to you."

"Your Grace, I ask you to believe that being visited by you is the greatest honour imaginable to a humble artist like myself. There is so much I would like to know about the illustriousness of your Court, and..."

"Which is the reason, Artemisia, that I have come to visit you. I've seen your work. I've seen Susanna and the Elders; I've seen your Judith. I've seen the quiet determination in her eyes as she sawed off the head of Holofernes. It was both horrible and lovely, striking yet deeply satisfying, somewhat like a beautifully patterned snake wearing the colours of the rainbow, yet deadly if you wander too close. I was astounded that a woman of your tender years could have had the maturity, the insights, to have painted them in such a way. The anger, the fury, the revenge....it was thrilling."

Stunned, I asked, "Your Grace, when have you seen my pictures? They're not...I mean I don't...."

"You must blame Caravaggio. He does much work for me, and when I last visited Rome, he endorsed your work strongly. Your father is his friend, but you are Caravaggio's favourite protégé. At the time I was in Rome, you were an unwilling participant in the disgusting trial for that vile man Tassi. And to think that those barbarians tortured you....you, the victim of Tassi's lusts.

"But your house was empty and Caravaggio took me to your home, unbeknown to you or your father, and showed me your work. He believes that you have more talent than any artist painting today, except himself of course, and are the equal of any painter of the past. And I agree."

I was stunned into silence. She continued, "It may surprise you, but your talents are so prodigious, that I intend for Florence to be both your home, and your place of nurture. This city has cherished some of the greatest artists the world has ever seen, and from my viewing of your paintings, I have hopes that you will find your place among them."

Just then, my husband entered the room, carrying a tray, bowing low and saying, "Coffee, Your Grace?"

When the Duchess had left, having invited me, but not my husband, to dine with her in private so that she could discuss a commission, I sat down and reflected on what had just happened. That was when Pierantonio said, "I can't believe that the Grand Duchess has come to my home. In all my days, I never imagined that I would entertain a person of her eminence. She sat in my chair, and drank my coffee. And now she's invited my wife to a private dinner."

He looked at me, and asked, "Can you believe how lucky I am, dearest one?"

His head was in the clouds, and I wondered what would be his thoughts when he came back to earth, and realised that everything which had just happened had been nothing to do with him. If I wanted a happy marriage, a peaceful home, I would have to somehow tread carefully, for even now, I was in danger of crushing him into insignificance. And for him, that would be a fate worse than death.

# PART, THE TENTH

It was three years, maybe somewhat more, after arriving in Florence, that I met Galileo Galilei. He didn't know of me. Why should he? Even though I was regularly seen in the Ducal Palace, around the city, in official meetings with the rulers and in other Royal places or mansion houses, discussing painting and commissions they wished to award me, there was no reason for him to have come across me, or my work.

Our lives led us in different directions. He had his head among the stars, watching the sun revolving endlessly around the earth; I had my head in the legends of Greece or Rome or where the ancient Israelites once lived. Some years earlier, before I moved to Florence, he had published his masterwork, *Sidereus Nuncius,* his book about starry messengers which he'd observed through an optical device, a long tube which somehow enabled him to see things which were at a vast distance as though they were in the next room.

Galileo was a favourite of the Ducal Court and a distinguished teacher and member of the Accademia delle Arti del Disegno, the famed academy which taught students of painting and drawing, the arts which were the very foundations of their profession.

How did we meet? Well, one day, a messenger came to my house. I was looking after the food of one of my children, my maid looking after the other two, when he knocked on the door.

The maid answered, and called me to the front rooms of the house.

"This gentleman wishes to speak with you, Signora," she said.

He was dressed well, but it was obvious that he was not a member of the Duke's Palace staff. There were no Ducal insignia or epaulettes on his cloak.

"Do I have the honour of addressing Madonna Artemisia Gentileschi?"

I told him he did.

"It is my great pleasure to invite you to a gathering of the Academy of the Arts of Drawing on Friday night of this week," he said.

I was surprised. It was an internationally famous school because Florence was famous thought the world for the genius of its artists. Its students came to the Academy from as far away as England, France and Russia. Ever since I had begun drawing and painting as a young girl in Rome, it had always been my dream to attend the Academy; but the cost of becoming a student, as well as my father's refusal to allow me to leave the house unchaperoned, caused it to be an unrequited desire.

"Sir," I said, "I appreciate your calling on me, and had this invitation been made when I was much younger, I would have accepted willingly. But I have become quite proficient in the art of drawing, and now have students of my own. However, I ask you to please thank the masters, and wish them...."

"You misunderstand, Madonna," he said, smiling, "I'm not inviting you to attend as a student, but to become one of us. You are perhaps among the greatest artists of our age, we wish to induct you as a Member of the Academy. We are asking you to join the excellent and most exclusive group of other members from around Italy who are the leaders of the profession of painting and drawing. You are being honoured by your peers for your exceptional talents, and the contribution you have made to this nation's standing in the world of art. They, the Members, have instructed me to invite you to join their esteemed ranks."

I was too stunned to speak. To be invited to become a member of the Accademia. By some of the greatest men in the world of painting. It was the highest honour that could be bestowed on a painter.

All I could think to say was, "But...but I'm a woman. Only men are allowed to be Members....teachers...."

"Until today, yes. That was because, until you, there have been no women of sufficient stature. But our Academy must move with the times. We must change. And never before has there been an artist, be they man or woman, who has painted in the way you paint. You have broken so many rules, created so many new ways of seeing, of feeling through your painting, that our students and our members need to learn from you. And I'm sure that there is much you can gain from the collegiality you'll experience as a Member."

When he left, I shut the door and stood there with my eyes closed for some time. If only my beloved mother could have been here to have heard what was said. It was an honour so overwhelming, that my head was reeling and my heart was pounding. But as I turned from the door, I saw my husband standing at the door to his studio. He had been listening to everything that had been said between myself and the officer from the Accademia. And the look on his face concerned me. I smiled at him, but his face was a mask of indifference. Rather than come over and congratulate me, kiss me and affirm my feelings, instead without a word he turned and closed the door on his studio, leaving me alone in the hallway. Not since the trial against Tassi had I felt as alone as I did at that moment of my greatest triumph.

I attended the meeting on the Friday night in his absence. He said that as he wasn't invited, he would mind the children and attend to household duties. Oh, and he made a point of telling me that he couldn't have come, anyway, because he had to finish a significant picture he was painting, making him too busy and important to join his wife in her achievement.

Perhaps it was good that Pierantonio wasn't there, for if he had been made jealous by the invitation, he would have been bitter by the reception I received as I entered the meeting hall of the Accademia. It was crowded with many people I didn't know, but by many that I did; some of the greatest artists who not only lived in Florence, but who were members and had travelled for the occasion from Rome, Venice, Padua and other great cities. Some of the students I also recognized, but they were gathered in corners of the room. In the centre were the Members, the masters of our profession of drawing and art. And in their centre, the woman who had been asked to join the leaders of the Academy in my induction, my Patroness, Her Grace, Christina of Lorraine, Grand Duchess of Tuscany.

Out of respect and courtesy, I walked to her. As I entered, the room erupted in applause, and a path was created for me through the men which led directly to the Duchess. Reaching her, I curtsied low and deferentially.

And to the amazement of everybody, she held out her hand, and lifted me, saying, "Oh no, dearest Artemisia. On this day, your day, your triumph, it is I who revere and respect you."

She kissed me on both cheeks, as though at that moment we were of equal rank. I'm sure that I heard a gasp of amazement in the room.

It was at this meeting of Members, shortly after I had been inducted, that I first met Galileo Galilei. I'd heard of him, of course, but not as one of the greatest thinkers and students of the sky. No, my knowledge of him was the condemnation he was experiencing from the Vatican for his publications, his observations, his teachings. He was a Member of the Academy because he taught students the concept of perspective, but the talk in the city was that he would soon be examined by the Inquisition for heresy. And who knew better than me what it was like to be examined by the Inquisition?

As we spoke, he told me about how he'd seen the surface of the moon through his instrument, which he called the telescope. He explained that in Latin, *tele* meant at a distance, and *scope* meant an instrument for looking. He encouraged me to learn Latin, whilst I was learning to read and write in Italian.

I asked him about his work looking through the telescope at our brothers and sisters in the sky, the planets and the stars which revolved around God's Earth. Except that when I said this to him, he gently, and in a low hushed voice, corrected me telling me that it was the Earth, our Earth, which danced an eternal ballet around our Sun.

I was amazed, but dared not to contradict him, despite the evidence of my eyes. He told me how alike were many of our neighbour planets, now that he could see their features through his tube instrument. Because of his knowledge of perspective, and of chiaroscuro, he had been able to draw not what he imagined he saw on the face of the moon, but what was actually there. He had observed mountains and valleys, perhaps even rivers on the surface of our nearest starry neighbour. He told me that a distant planet, Saturn, had amazed him, because the planet had vast ears. Ears, I asked? Yes, he said, ears...but when the Vatican heard of his discovery, the Librarian contradicted him, and said that these were not ears, but Christ's foreskins. I laughed, but he was serious.

He talked to me about the importance of mathematics, especially the centrality of geometry in perspective, which gave credence to the shadows and points of view. He explained how many painters misunderstood point of view and failed to appreciate that it was how a viewer of a painting observed the characters and landscapes on the canvas which made it into reality, rather than how the artist imagined his figures were positioned. I suppose I knew what he was talking about instinctively, but the way in which he defined his mathematical knowledge concerning angles and perspective gave me insights into my instinct that I hadn't previously understood.

Listening to him, it occurred to me that one day, perhaps soon, I would paint a self-portrait, with me holding a palette in one hand and the brush in the other.

The point of view for the observer would be as though he was looking at me from an upper balcony, looking down on my head and profile, my body making a crescent as I painted the canvas which would be out of sight in the picture. I would call it something like *"portrait of Artemisia as an artist"*, or something like that.

The rest of the discussion that night, which I remember so clearly as it opened both my mind, and my eyes, to a world of knowledge I didn't previously know, focussed on his anger that painting was excluded from the seven liberal arts.

I should remind you, my reader, that at that stage of my life, I could not write properly, and my reading was elementary. Immediately after my discussion with Galileo, I determined that I would become as wise as my colleagues on the Academy. It would mean that I would have to study harder than before and learn to both read and write in Italian. Once I'd mastered that, I would have to learn Latin.

We talked about the way in which knowledge was taught at the Universities. Galileo said that he never understood why there were seven, and not eight liberal arts. The Universities taught logic and grammar, rhetoric and arithmetic, geometry and music and the subject of his expertise, astronomy. Yet painting and sculpture had been excluded because they were thought to be arts of the hand, rather than the mind. They were the trades of artisans, and not those of intelligent men. How wrong they were. Yet it was something which concerned Galileo, and which he fought against and tried to correct.

I was fascinated by everything he said to me, and when he invited me to visit him in his home, I accepted his invitation immediately. The chance to visit such a great man in his observatory would further annoy my husband, and so I would lie to him and tell him that I was visiting a supplier of paint or canvas.

It was the beginning of my lifelong friendship with Galileo Galilei. I assisted him in some minor way with how the stars of the firmament should be represented, and he assisted me with how aspects of his sciences could be incorporated into my work. Which I used shortly after when Michaelangelo Buonarroti – the young man and not the artist, his great uncle – asked me to work on his grand project.

Oh, and there's one other event in my time in Florence which I am forced to recount. As you know, reader, this story of my life will be hidden until after my death, and those with whom I hide it will be instructed to keep it concealed and in secret until my life and art are forgotten, in the hope that this published story of my life might revise interest in my art.

So now is the time when I must tell you of the great love of my life. No, not my husband, Pierantonio, who, as I grew in status, shrank as a man. His jealousy, pettiness and meanness were causing him to turn to drink and take long absences from the house.

Money never flowed freely, even though I was busy from morning to late in the evening. The really large commissions being offered in Florence and other cities, were unavailable to me. These were paintings as frescoes in churches and cathedrals, or altar screens, or ceilings or such, which the Catholic Church decided in the infinity of its wisdom, it could only trust to men painters.

But as I gained in status, I was able to charge larger sums for my commissions, money which paid for a better life than Pierangelo could provide from his meagre income, which came mainly from teaching the incompetent sons of merchants. What money I earned from commissions went to pay for our food and clothes and the tools of our profession, which I willingly shared with him and my children. Yet he continued to struggle to sell any of his works. On several occasions, I entered his studio to see his work, and told him how much I admired his abilities, hoping to change his attitude towards me so that I could improve his work, but he either ignored me, or told me to go back to my clever friends at the Academy.

Once or twice I even suggested a different technique he could use to improve the look of a man or woman or a landscape, and he told me, hotly, to mind my own business, and that the last thing he needed was the advice of a woman. His friends, he informed me, had told him how brilliant were his paintings, works which could not be improved, and their support was just as valuable as the compliments I received from my peers and colleagues at the Academy.

Nor did we act as man and wife, unless he was drunk and came home and forced himself upon me before falling into a stupor beside me, or lumbering off to his bedchamber when he'd finished his enjoyment of my body.

So now it is time for me to introduce my lover. He was a man of wealth, if not stature; handsome, strong, and intelligent. Passionate and volatile. I loved him. The man about whom I speak is Francesco Maria di Niccoló Maringhi, the bastard son of an aristocrat from a well-regarded noble Florentine family. He and I had seen each other many times when I visited my patrons. And I knew that every time we were in the same Salon, he was looking at me intently, and I must admit that I, too, was often stealing a glance at him. He cut a truly manly figure, not just in his dress, but by his manner, and even the way he ate and drank.

On the occasion when we did meet and converse, things between us developed more rapidly than I dared hope. I met him in the Ducal Palace of His Excellency, the Grand Duke of Tuscany, Cosimo de Medici. Even though his birth to a servant woman in his father's household caused a minor scandal, my patroness, the Grand Duchess Christina was a woman of the world, and accepted Francesco as a member of the court and a friend of the Duke. When I was painting a picture she'd commissioned, she mentioned Francesco admiringly. She said that he couldn't help being born a bastard, and accepted him into her court on the proviso that he behave like a bastard. We both burst out laughing. The Duchess loved controversy.

Francesco's father, Count Maringhi, ensured that his treatment as his son would be the same as his other children, meaning that Francesco had all the privileges of an aristocratic family. And that meant he was given all the money he needed. He was treated well by his family, and equally well by the Medici court. As I've already said, he was an educated, interesting and passionate man. And on the day that I decided to become his lover, it was obvious that each of us desired the same thing. On that glorious day, the moment we met in the Duke's audience hall, we couldn't take our eyes off each other.

He made sure that after I had finished my business with their Excellences, I did not return home, but instead was directed by a chamberlain into another salon. I waited there, wondering what was happening, and suddenly Francesco walked in through the door.

"Madonna Artemisia," he said, "I am one of your greatest admirers. My name is...."

"I know who you are, my Lord. I could feel your eyes burning into me as I spoke with the Duke and Duchess."

"Then you know how much I respect you as a painter," he said. "But have you any idea how much I regard you as a woman. I know you're married, but would your husband have any objection if I asked you to take a walk with me on the banks of the Arno, so that we can discuss painting?"

I knew immediately what his intention was, and he grinned like a monkey when I said, "My Lord, whether my husband objects or not is of profound disinterest to me. My life is my own, to dispose of how I choose. And as a member of the Duke's court, and a good friend of my Patron and my Patroness, if you order me to discuss painting, I will be both duty bound, and honoured to oblige."

He laughed. He had a delightful laugh. "But by that logic, Artemisia, if I order you to do other things, perform other services, do I assume that you will obey as willingly…..just to oblige?"

"Depending on what are these services, then if it is within my power, and my desire, my answer is likely to be yes."

"And along which paths do your desires lead you?" he asked.

I didn't answer immediately. But when I did, I could feel the fervour growing within his body, his heat radiating to touch my soul. "My talent is at your disposal, my Lord. But as to my desires, they're like the buds of a fragrant rose making its first appearance in early spring. Touch them in the right way, nurture them, feed them, adore them, and they will burst open with passion in the summer's heat. A woman such as me has many desires which lead her along different paths and different directions."

He moved closer to me, and asked, breathlessly, "So will I be the recipient of your talents....or your desires?" he asked.

"My talents are in my fingers. My desires are buried deeply in the fertile soil of my body. My husband knows of my talents, but he has no skills when it comes to nurturing the blossoms of my desires. He has yet to plumb the depths of my garden."

I could feel the craving, the lust, the hunger in his body as he moved closer to me. I had to put a stop to his intentions, for we were in a public place and all would have been destroyed for me if I'd allowed him his way there and then.

So I moved away from him, saying, "Now, my Lord Francesco, you must excuse me, for I have work to do for my Patrons. But I hope that I have exposed sufficient of my talents and defined for you the garden of my desires to help them flower into beautiful blooms." And with that, I left the Salon and walked home, confident that in a day or two, he would contact me.

I was wrong. That very night, a messenger delivered a letter from Francesco, asking me to teach him the techniques which would improve his drawing and perspective. And he would, of course, pay me for my time and expertise. The moment Pierangelo knew that income would be involved, he was quite happy to allow my absence, without further explanation. Frankly, if he objected, I would still have gone.

You may ask why I gave myself so quickly to a man to whom I'd barely spoken? Well, I had seen my future lover many times in the past months, and I know that he'd seen me. I was attracted to his manner, his manliness, and his person, and for a long while, I'd been hoping that he would approach me.

I met Francesco the following afternoon at the Palace, and we took horses out of Florence, and followed the Arno eastwards to San Jacopo al Girone, where there was a bend in the river.

We continued for a short distance, talking about the joys of summer, of painting and of the assaults by the Inquisition against Galileo, until we came to an uninhabited part of the landscape. He lay down a large mat, and we ate and drank cheeses and meats, bread and wine. It could have been the wine, or more likely the demands of my body, but we were willingly and immediately intimate with each other. I make no apology for giving myself to my lover. And don't think for a moment that he took advantage of me. I was yearning for the touch and affection of a loving man. You see, in all the years of my marriage to Pierangelo, he had never once concerned himself with my enjoyments, only his own.

Francesco was his opposite, in every way. His touch thrilled me beyond belief. Until Francesco, I'd always thought that sex was the playground of ruffians; but under his gentle fingers and lips, it was a garden of perfumed flowers and heavenly pleasures.

Suddenly, at that moment on the banks of the Arno, beneath the glorious sun of a Florentine sky, I had become a woman. No longer a body for Tassi's or my husband's enjoyment and entertainment, merely some available canvas on which to impress their lusts and desires. No, in Francesco's gentle and guiding hands, I had become a woman, full of life and feelings, desires and satisfactions. No long just a painter and a wife and a mother. Now I was a woman in full bloom.

# PART, THE ELEVENTH

In Florence, I painted, had children, watched them fall ill and die, made love to Francesco, and lived a life. I never grew wealthy, but Francesco ensured that my family never went without food or comfort. He even paid for the funerals of my three beautiful babies, Giovanni Battista, Lisabella, and Agnola, as though they were his children, and not those of my husband, Pierantonio. And if I have to be honest, I think that perhaps some of my dead children had been fathered by my lover, and not my husband.

Francesco and I, on many occasions, discussed the prospect of my leaving my husband, and moving to his apartments in order to live with him; but the scandal which would have developed would have destroyed us both. Everybody in Florence, especially in the court of the Medici, was having intimate relationships....men with women, men with men, women with women....it was a nest of sexual abundance, a cornucopia of lust and wantonness, not unlike the Vatican under the papacy of Rodrigo Borgia in 1500. And while these sexual liaisons remained *sub rosa*, nobody cared. But if any of the lovers tried to make their illicit relationships public or permanent, courtly morality would rear its head and the roof would collapse on them.

Which is what happened to poor Francesco and me. Even though my pathetic husband knew of our affair, and actually wrote letters to Francesco encouraging our meetings because of the money I brought back with me, we kept it secret from the court. Until one of the Duchess's Ladies, the awful Countess Maria Doenitz from Vienna, saw us one day in a field, and felt compelled to tell Her Grace, the Grand Duchess Christina. A quiet word in my ear one day, and I knew that my relationship with Francesco was at an end.

We parted as lovers. We kissed. We hugged each other. We swore never ever to forget each other. And we were true to our word. When I lived in Rome, in London, in Venice and in Naples, I wrote passionate letters to him, and he to me.

So with my reputation as an artist now well established

thanks to the Medicis of Florence, I could see no reason why I shouldn't go to Rome. That was where vast sums were given by patrons to artists to paint their pictures. I no longer had a lover in Florence, I had two living children, and a laggard of a husband. So one day, I packed up my children, put all of my unfinished and unsold works onto a cart, took sufficient money for the journey to purchase several months of living expenses in Rome, and hired a carriage to take me and my children on the long journey across the country. Previously, I had said farewell to Francesco, to members of the Academy, to friends, and paid my respects to my patrons, the Duke and Duchess.

I said goodbye neither to my house, nor my husband. Instead, while he was out at the inn in the middle of that morning, telling his flatterers what a genius of an artist he was, we left Florence. By the time he'd become sober and realised that I'd emptied the household of my possessions and my money, I was halfway to Rome.

I have to admit that the journey wasn't good for my son, Cristofano, who suffered badly as the wagons creaked and faltered on the pitted road. But my beautiful Prudentia, whom I had named after my late mother, did her best to tend to his needs. Sadly, he died shortly after our arrival in Rome. So in truth, we needed accommodation only for my young daughter and me. I decided not to move back to my father's house, although he was very pleased to see me and his sole remaining grandchild. Instead, we stayed in a hostelry for a week, before finding a small apartment on one of the streets, those close to the St. Marco Church and the Capitoline. Central but not too noisy. It was on the second storey of the building and so there was plenty of light for my painting.

When I met my father for dinner one night, he told me that he would not be in Rome for much longer. He had been commissioned by an immensely wealthy Genoese man called Giovan Antonio Sauli, and was asked to paint three large paintings. One was Lot and His Daughters; another was Danaë and the Shower of Gold, and the third was St. Mary Magdalen in Ecstasy. These were massive pictures, and would require him to live in Genoa for at least a couple of years. That meant that my daughter and I could live in his home, saving me a lot of money.

I had been back in Rome for only a matter of weeks and was settling in, visiting old friends and acquaintances and paying my respects to potential patrons, but quickly realised that the new pope, Alessandro Ludovisi from Bologna who became Gregory XV, had his own favourites and that I was unlikely to get any work from the Vatican.

Pope Gregory brought the artist Guercino from Bologna to Rome, and was inspired to commission Bernini and Algardi to create busts of him.

So I had to seek work beyond the Papacy and the Cardinalate, which meant rich families. And because of my work for the Medicis in Florence, I quickly gained many good and interesting commissions. The money which came in was gratifying and allowed me and my beloved Prudentia to live a life of comfort and ease. And not once, not a single time, did my husband, Pierantonio, attempt to contact me. It wouldn't have required the genius, nor Galileo's telescope, to find me in Rome, and Pierantonio was far from a genius.

One man who gave me a commission was Fernando Afan de Ribera, Duke of Alcala in Spain, who lived in Rome, and asked me to create some biblical allegories for his home. I also painted for Count Cassiano dal Pozzo, who was a major collector of art. Life was exciting, gratifying. But what I sorely missed was my beloved Francesco. In Florence, be it during winter in a secret room in his home warmed by a blazing fire, or in summer with the insects serenading our love in an empty field beside the Arno, he would make my body tingle with excitement; that would inspire my creative work.

I grievously mourned children; I cried for each one of them every night. But while they were not here for me to hold and touch, hug and kiss, it made my love for Prudentia even deeper, now that it was but she and me.

Does it surprise you that I missed my dead children so much? I was a loving mother. I wasn't like a Queen or a Princess or a Duchess who had children in order to fulfill the expectations of the dynasty; one who bore children and then only saw them on occasion when their nursemaids and governesses were ordered to bring them into the view of the Court.

No, I was a loving mother, who nurtured her children, kept them safe in my love and caring, and grieved as God took each one, tragedy upon tragedy, except for Prudentia, back into His fold.

I did well in Rome. I lived there with Prudentia for six years and painted many paintings. I earned much money. Of course, being merely a woman, I was never accepted by the Church as an artist who could glorify an Altar or a Church with a fresco. After all, how could a mere woman, a weak and sickly being, the corrupted daughter of Eve, possibly possess the equivalent talent of even the most inauspicious artist, just because he was a man? And so I made my money painting for patrons and noble families or sometimes just for very wealthy men who were successful merchants or traders.

My father returned from Genoa after a few years, and we all lived together in his house; he assisted me with my commissions, and I likewise assisted him with his. It was immensely pleasant, and although I was without male companionship – dear God in Heaven, my mind and my body missed Francesco so very much – we lived and worked and enjoyed. I think this was the best time of my life.

By the middle of that decade – I forget the exact year, but I think it was in 1627 or there about – my fame had spread to other cities. Both my father and I were celebrated throughout Rome, not just within the community of artists, but by poets and writers, priests and noble men and women, and even, to my surprise, the hoi polloi. We would walk from our house to a restaurant with Prudentia in tow, and people we'd never seen before would acknowledge us, doff their caps, wish us well, and some even applauded.

Every time this happened to me, I remembered back a mere sixteen years to events which happened in these very streets, perhaps even by these very same people. When I was a girl of 18, walking away from the Inquisitional

Court, I would be stared at, mocked, ridiculed and taunted by Rome's masses – as though I were the one who had been found guilty of some evil crime. And when I thought back to those days, I often wonder what happened to my maidservant, my companion, my betrayer Tuzia, who had facilitated Tassi's and Quorli's access into the house, into my bedroom, and into my body. Many years had passed since I'd last seen her and her child. I no longer wished her harm, as once I'd done.

And as to Tassi, well, he was still living in Rome; still painting, though we never saw each other. I think he must have been keeping his distance from me. And I from him. Almost by accident, visiting a Palazzo one day, I came across a large painting hanging on a wall. One glance, and I knew it was done by him. A large, dark and unendearing work called the Embarkation of a Queen. I looked at it carefully, and recognized his style immediately. Utterly devoid of human interest, it was merely a series of nine massive columns supporting what looked like the sort of baldacchino canopy beneath which a Pope sits. I stood and stared and shook my head in wonder at its ordinariness.

Yet I couldn't help comparing it with the work I'd just seen in a workshop of the amazingly talented and young artist, Gian Lorenzo Bernini, whom I visited while he was sculpting a Baldacchin commission ordered by Pope Urban VIII. Bernini was creating a masterpiece of bronze and gilt, with twisted columns to be placed centrally in the basilica above the grave of St. Peter. It would be ready in a few years, and all Rome would celebrate its genius. Not so Tassi and his boring and unadorned tedious columns, and buildings in the background, nor his miniscule courtiers attending a Queen who could barely be seen among all of his architecture. The foolish man should have come to me for lessons.

But I digress. Life was comfortable in Rome, and my father, daughter and I were free of financial worries. So when commissions came to me from Genoa and Pisa I could afford to consider whether I wanted to travel to those cities and live there while I painted.

Not so the commission from Venice. I had never visited that marvellous city and dearly wanted to. Travellers spoke of Venice as a miracle of design and architectural beauty.

So when a messenger came to our house from Giovanni Cornaro, the Doge of Venice, asking me to visit his city as he wanted me to paint a version of Esther before King Ahasuarus, I was delighted. My father wasn't at all happy, though. He told me about the battles which were going on between pro- and anti-Cornaro forces in that city. The Doge had been accused of profiteering and enriching his family at the City's expense. When my father and I began to discuss whether I should go to Venice, and what type of painting the Doge wanted me to create. I knew the story of Esther well enough, but went to our family Bible and refreshed my memory.

I suddenly realized, opening it, that the lessons in reading and writing I'd taken from a tutor in Florence had done wonders for my abilities, and I was now able to read easily from a family bible which had been inaccessible to me before I left Rome.

I was delighted that I was being asked to put the story into picture. As I read it, I knew immediately what I should create. I asked my father, and our thoughts naturally went to the allegory which I could capture in my painting of Esther before Ahasuarus. Both Orazio and I knew well the work which had been painted sixty years earlier by the Venetian, Tintoretto. His portrayal had seen Esther fainting before the King like a helpless female overcome by the vapours when she came to beg for the lives of her people, the Jews. Tintoretto's Esther had been weak and womanly, and in his picture, the King, naturally concerned that she'd fainted, had risen from his throne, and was going down to help her.

The note from the Doge said that he wanted his King to be more manly, more regal, more stately. And he wanted his Judith to be more helpless. It was obvious that the Doge wanted me to paint a warning to those who opposed him that he was the Duke of Venice, and that he would crush any opposition.

I, of course, had other ideas. When I arrived in Venice, I was introduced to the Court, took instructions from the Doge's Majordomo, and settled down in a suite of three rooms in the Doge's Palace to create my painting. I was given a canvas, and used palace servants to stretch it onto a wooden frame. I ordered paints in abundance from the Venetian supplier, and within a week of my arrival, set to work on the charcoal sketches for the piece.

One thing I insisted upon was a half payment in advance, for when he saw my picture, I wasn't at all certain that the Doge would pay the remainder. I doubted that he would be pleased by what I intended to do.

Most artists who had used this subject from the Book of Esther had shown her as a supplicant, swooning and supported by her maids, overwhelmed by the enormity of what she had just done. My Esther would be the protagonist in the picture, the power in the discussion between the two. Naturally, my Esther would have to faint, because that was the biblical record, but it would be a theatrical faint, like Columbine swooning before Harlequin in the Commedia dell'Arte. I even considered her secretly winking at one of her maids, but abandoned that idea. I wanted to leave Venice with my head still attached to my body.

And so I began my painting. I had already sketched my subjects. Esther stood tall, but I painted her just in the act of fainting and being held aloft by her maids. The moment King Ahasuarus sees her plight, he is driven to leap from his throne, and we assume that he will then be in a prone and begging stance, or a kneeling position, supporting her prostrate form. Yes, she had the power in the scene, and he is the supplicant.

But the real tone of my mischief came from their clothes. In the Book of Esther, the King is defined as being dressed in royal garb, and Esther is dressed soberly. But in my painting, I dressed Esther in glorious cloth, golden yellow, almost gold, a sign of power, whereas I dress the King in stripped pantaloons and sleeves, and made it look as though he was about to perform a play, or dance for his courtiers.

I finished the painting in a matter of a month, and unveiled it at the Doge's Audience Hall. It was met by cheers of approbation by his courtiers, and the Duke himself thought it was wonderful. It made me wonder how much this Doge of Venice, Giovanni Cornaro, knew of the Bible or allegories, because he certainly knew nothing about mockery.

My painting was a huge success, and within days I had received six further invitations from wealthy Venetians to paint for them. I rejected four of them, but two I agreed upon because they interested me. Knowing that I would be here for many months, I sent for my daughter Prudentia, and she and I remained in Venice for a further year. I took occasional trips back to Rome to see my father, but life had become very easy and pleasant; not so life for the citizens of the city of Venice, which was bordering on civil war. Obviously, my painting hadn't been effective in telling one side who was in charge.

And so, reader, I have reached the final part of this, the story of my life. I have said nothing about my years in Naples, to which I may return one day soon, as, God knows, I miss the sun and the cleansing, aqua waters of the Tyrrhenian Sea. When I was a child, I once swam there, thinking that I could reach the island of Capri, but

I'll never forget the feeling of immersing myself in the balm of those delightfully azure waters.

And when I think of them, now that I am living in London, England, the grey snow deep on the ground and its icy waters creeping into my boots, the sky is so heavy with dark pregnant clouds that the difference between morning and evening is little more than an aspect of the imagination, I realise how I miss those days in the Italian sun. This is the 46th year since my birth, and my bones are feeling the cold, no matter how many scarves and hoods and garments I wear. And as I age, I look back on my life, and try to determine its worth. I have a beautiful and talented daughter, but I have buried four children. I have painted many pictures, which are now recognized as works of excellence, and I am revered by my peers and my patrons. I think I have a husband, but thankfully he is lost in the mists of time, hopefully never to be found. I had a lover who was the kindest and most generous and tender of men, but I was forced to separate from him because of the so-called ethics and morals of one of the most immoral and licentious Courts in Italy.

This book, this story of my life, is a record of the events that I have lived, that I have experienced, in my 46 years. Many, many years ago, Marie de Medici, who was the widow of King Henry IV of France, commissioned the Dutchman Peter Paul Rubens to paint a vast series of large paintings depicting the events of her life and times. I saw them as I passed through Paris on my way to London, and I know that the artistic community of Italy, and I'm sure of other nations, is agog with the massive scale and magnificence of these works, which are in her Luxembourg Palace in Paris. There are 22 huge pictures in all. They are all truly wonderful, and all hail to Rubens as a master painter.

As I looked at them, by special invitation of the Palace, I knew at that moment that I, too, could have created 22 pictures to define all the things which have described my life and times. It would have started when I was a child, with the death of my beloved mother Prudentia, after whom I named my daughter. The next picture would have been my apprenticeship at the feet of my father Orazio in his studio in my home in Rome. Then I would have painted a tableau of my ordeal during the trial of Agostino Tassi. No...not one picture, but there would be at least three large images for that time of trauma and pain; the first would be his lies about me on the witness stand, where he called me a whore who had slept with my father and worked naked as a model for lecherous painters; and I would have painted his fawning sycophants clustered around him.

The next picture would have portrayed the judges, minions of the Pope, nodding in agreement with everything Tassi said and I would have painted a ghostly image of Paul V hiding behind a curtain showing only his profile, listening and silently directing them to acquit his protégé; and lastly, I would have portrayed me, as the Virgin Mary, tortured by thumbscrews, but screaming out the veracity of my innocence...*it is true...it is true... it is true*.

Other later pictures in the story of my life, would have been my time in Florence, my love for Francesco, the return to Rome and all the success I had; then Venice, then Naples, and now London. But no, I will not paint my life, for paintings are temporary things, which can so easily be removed from a wall by the new master of a palazzo, and transported up into some attic, never to be seen again.

So the only permanent record of my life, one which will never be forgotten, is a book.

This book!

This story of my life.

Now that I am in London, I have written down every

word, so that I shall not be forgotten.

Why have I wanted until London to write my story? That is something which I will need to explain before I lay down my quill, close my book, and rest my tired mind.

You see, my hand is fatigued and my mind is exhausted. In this past many weeks, I have written more in this story of my days, than I have ever written before. It is a complete book, which records all until the tragic death of my beloved father Orazio. Yes, reader. Orazio died suddenly last week, and since his death, as we wait for his proper burial place to be made ready, I have spent that time in deliberation, writing of my life.

I have written this book in cold and drafty rooms, where blazing fires barely warm the air, where the sun, other than for a few days in Summer, fights against the perpetual low grey clouds in the sky to shine upon the people, and where the Catholic Christ has shut His eyes, and no longer looks down upon those who protest against the fact that His existence comes down to us through the Chair of St. Peter in Rome.

I've never been a religious woman, but I have faith in God the Father, God the Son and God, the Holy Spirit and I know that when I am in Italy, They look down upon me and aid and love me.

So why, in God's name, why did my father spend his last days in such a cold, windy and inhospitable land as England? An England where the weather prevents living life to its fullest; where olives and grapes and summer fruits are almost unknown; an England which has abandoned Christ's blessings, turned its back on Holy Rome, and lives in the perpetual darkness of an ungodly reign by Protestant monarchs who rule without the blessing of the Pope?

Not that I can say these things aloud or in company, for since the time of King Henry VIII, Catholics have been attacked and murdered in this unenlightened land. Of course, times are easier for Catholics in England since the rise of the House of Stuart, and the present monarch, King Charles even has a Catholic wife, Henrietta Maria of France, who is a Bourbon. But there is still hatred in the streets and in the houses of power, to us Catholics. We are still considered to be ruled by Rome and determined on undermining the throne of England.

But it was not the queen of King Charles, Henrietta Maria, who encouraged my father to come to England to be Court Painter. No, his invitation came in 1626 at the behest of the Duke of Buckingham, the King's First

Minister. This gentleman, George Villiers, had toured Italy and been deeply impressed by my father's skills. Although at the time the Queen was a young girl, when she heard that the noble Duke was about to invite an Italian Catholic painter to England, I know that she was thrilled, for she told me so herself.

Yet tragically, or happily for my father and me, the Duke was an utter incompetent at money and administration, who had been put in charge of the navy by the King. Yet he led it poorly, causing thousands of men to die unnecessarily in badly conducted wars against the French. He was assassinated in a city called Portsmouth, to the regret of few, but suddenly my father was without a patron. So the Queen immediately sent word to my father that because his patron had been murdered, the patronage would be taken over by the Royal House. He set about painting the ceiling of the Queen's House at Greenwich, as well as one which portrayed the Pharaoh's daughter finding Moses.

I received a letter from him just last year, asking me to join him in the ceiling he was painting for Queen Henrietta Maria at her Palace in Greenwich. He told me that although he had my three brothers with him, and they were useful for creating scaffolding and crushing pigments, and filling in landscapes, only he and I had the skills to create a work such as commissioned by Her Majesty. It was called the Triumph of Peace and the Arts. It was a vast ceiling, and the central motif was a circle in which the Goddess of Peace sat on a cloud, surrounded by ten muses representing the different arts. Beyond the central motif were other circles and oblongs and squares containing representations of different aspects of the serenity of Peace and the Joys of the Arts.

What my beloved father didn't know, and what I refused to tell him out of respect for his person, was that just days before he invited me to join him in London to become his assistant, I had received a separate letter. But this had not come from the Queen, but independently from His Majesty, the King. Yes, King Charles of England was a collector of paintings and sculptures, and knew well of my art, having seen examples when he was travelling. He sent me a letter asking me to come to England and be his painter.

Reader.....I, Artemisia Gentileschi, had received a Royal Summons.

Why did I not tell my father? Because even though he was revered as a great painter, my status had risen over the years thanks to my body of work, to equal and indeed rival his. Our styles were similar – largely thanks to the tutelage of my beloved Caravaggio, whose style of chiaroscuro my father had also adopted – and often our paintings had been mistaken for each other. But there had been an occasion when one of his works was hung and he overheard two noblemen discussing it. One had said, "No, not by Artemisia. It hasn't her fineness of touch, her line, her brilliance with colour. No, this must be by the father...."

He never told me of this conversation, but I found out soon after how deeply hurt and offended he was. It was told to me by one of my brothers, and how it had cut my beloved father to the quick. From then on, I determined to minimize discussion of my talents and accomplishments when speaking with him, and beg his help with my paintings when I least needed it.

But even if it caused him anguish, I knew I had to go to London. How could I have refused the command of the King of England to become his court painter? And by the Grace of the Almighty, he wrote to me days after my Royal invitation, to invite me to London to assist him.

Had it not been for the murder of the Duke of Buckingham, then a rift between father and daughter could have ensued....but didn't. By the time I came to

England to join my father and my three brothers, the Queen had officially appointed Orazio to be her Court Painter In Residence. He was immensely proud of the title. And because he felt so self-assured in his role, when I told him that I was now the Painter for the King, he was equally as proud of me.

Together, we worked on the ceiling of Henrietta Maria's home in Greenwich, which was as much a feat of athleticism and engineering as it was of painterly art. Huge scaffolds had been created by my brothers, and my father and I lay on our backs, paint occasionally dripping onto our faces and necks, while far below us, my brothers mixed the paints and added tints and fractions of other colours to become the precise nature of what Orazio and I were painting at that moment. I concentrated on the faces of the figures, and he on the clouds, the books, the sceptres, the crowns and the other aspects of the painting.

I think it was the closest that Orazio and I ever became. As I cautiously created a Muse's eye or smile or lips, I felt his eyes on me, looking and admiring my skill. And as I watched him create a laurel leaf or the page of a book, I realised that he was one of the greatest artists of his day.

So his sudden death the year after my arrival in London, just a month or two after my brothers and father and I, along with my daughter Prudentia, had celebrated Christmas altogether, was the greatest shock.

I was already hard at work on a painting which my patron, His Majesty King Charles, had particularly requested. It was an Allegory of Painting, a picture which explained to the viewer what it was about painting which made it stand apart, and dare I say, above all of the other arts.

Mr. William Lawes and his Royal Consort gave the King and the Court his music, but that was ethereal and disappeared the moment the final note had been played. All that remained was a memory of the music.

For poetry and plays and books, the court was replete with men such as Robert Herrick, Richard Lovelace and Andrew Marvell.

But for King Charles, only painting could touch his heart and soul. He was a great collector of works of art by the most renown of painters, and was furiously criticised by men in the Parliament, which governed the nation beneath the King, for spending so much money. Not that I cared, for nobody agreed with the King more about Art, than I.

Which is why His Majesty was so keen on my creation of the Allegory of Painting. It took me months, because

I was using myself as a model, bearing in mind the instructions I'd had from my old friend Galileo. He still wrote to me, even though at this time, he is in the midst of his seventh decade of life. His words were difficult to read, because his hand was weak and his letters hard to decipher. I asked him about the way I planned to paint the Allegory, a woman looked upon from the top of her head by the viewer of the painting. I was having difficulty in the angles for the arm, the head, the neck. In one of my charcoals, my hand holding the palette was too large, and somehow my head look small and unnatural. Which is why I wrote to Galileo. I remembered him telling me about point of view and perspective when I was in Florence. He had lectured at the Accademia delle Arti del Disegno. So when he wrote back, he told me to position two mirrors, one to my right hand which should be angled downwards, and the other to my left hand, facing the one pointing down, but this one angled upwards. In this way, I was able to see myself from the top and somewhat to the back, as though I was a viewer of myself, painting a picture.

I did as he instructed, and it was amazing. It was still an immensely hard picture to paint, but with his positioned mirrors, it was much easier to get the angles and sizes of fingers and wrists correct.

But I stray. As I was painting this picture one day, my brother Giuseppe came to the door, and banged urgently. My maid answered, and ushered him into my studio. I knew the moment he entered that the news was bad.

"Our father...."

"What?" I cried. "What's happened?"

"Our beloved father could not be roused this morning. I called the physician, but he felt for his...his....for his signs of life, and there were none. Our beloved father is dead. Gone to Christ. In the bosom of the Lord."

Prudentia, who was listening in at the door, cried out. I remember sitting down hard on the stool, and saying, "But last night...he was...I said to him....he was laughing. I don't understand."

Giuseppe came over and knelt before me, holding my hand and hugging me. Prudentia came over and knelt and we all hugged and wept.

And so, in February, my three brothers and I will have to bury our beloved father Orazio.

Not in a grave in a cemetery.

Not in a Protestant Churchyard.

No, Queen Henrietta Maria, God Bless Her, said that a Catholic Soul, one who pleased God by his art and talents, must be buried beneath the Holy Altar of her private chapel in one of her houses, Somerset House.

The ceremony is due next week. My beloved father's body is in his coffin. And when he is buried beneath the Altar, it is my intention to secrete this book in a bouquet of flowers and to add them with this bundle of bound pages to the top of his coffin.

Yes, I intend to bury this book with him. There, it will be out of sight of the world, and will rest safely with him until it is time to retrieve it.

Why am I burying it? Because the Catholic Church will not like to read of my anger at the way I was treated during Tassi's trial. For years, Popes have not bothered me, nor I them, but now that I am in Protestant England, I feel the heat of their breath on my neck. And the current occupant of St. Peter's throne in Rome, Maffeo Barberini who took the title Urban VIII, is especially fearsome.

Yes, he is a lover of the arts, especially the work of Bernini, but few others have benefitted by his patronage, and God only knows how he thinks of women painters... or women in general. But what worries me most about Pope Urban is that six years ago, he summoned my dearest friend, Galileo Galilei to Rome and the Inquisition to demand a retraction of his life's work, and forced him to prove that the Earth is the centre of the Universe, around which all stars and planets revolve. He must know that Galileo and I are friends, and so my work and my life will be suspect, especially if I publish this book in my lifetime.

But the Papacy isn't the only reason I am burying this book in my father's grave. For I am concerned that the English Protestants will read it in my lifetime, when I am in this country, and the situation here is a danger to those who are not Protestants and show their anger towards King Charles and his wife.

Those who want to overturn the monarchy will not like to read of my relationship with Queen Henrietta Maria, a devoted Catholic; there's talk of a Civil War soon to erupt, and I do not want to be seen to prefer one side against the other.

So I do not want this book to be found and read and, God forbid, published in my lifetime. When I am dead and Prudentia is safely married with her husband's name, then it will be time for this book to be published and for men to read about my life; about the dishonour when Tassi raped me; about the degradation I suffered at the hands of the Church when the judges of the Inquisition tortured me to determine whether my heartfelt testimony was, indeed, the truth; about my growth in stature as a painter; my marriage to a nonentity of a man and my glorious lover, Francesco; about my time in Rome and Venice, Naples and London.

For I have no doubt that when I die, my paintings will be ignored, forgotten, and allowed to gather dust and rot in some rat-infested attic.

But a book! Ah, that's the difference. Thanks to the Art of the Printer, books are now forever. Not the individual book, which can be burned or buried; no, unlike a painting, which is *sui generis*, a book can be repeated time and time and time again, so that the same copy I hold in my hand and read in London, can just as well be read at the same time by another in Paris, or Bonn, or Rome. Many copies, too many to burn and ignore. In my days in Florence, I learned that Sandro Botticelli is said to have burned some of his paintings at the behest of the preacher Girolamo Savonarola. Well, they may burn my paintings, but if my book is published and printed in many copies, is there a bonfire of the vanities large enough to consume them all?

So to make this, my life, into a book, I will write to my once and forever lover, Francesco, and ask him to retrieve these pages when he learns of my death. How will he learn? Because I will write him a letter, and leave it with an Advocate – perhaps Advocate Rossi in Rome, if he's still alive– with instructions that the letter is to be sent to him on the occasion of my burial. And knowing Francesco, he will immediately go to London and then, in his beautiful hands, I will come alive again, for all eternity.

For I know with utter and absolute certainty, dear reader, that my Francesco will accede to my request, come to London and retrieve this, the Story of my Life.

*Written in my hand by*

# *Artemisia gentileschi,*

*This 16th day of february in the year of our lord, 1639 at the palace of whitehall, London, england*
Uffizi Gallery, AUGUST 2021

A year and a half after the discovery of Artemisia's Book of her Life.

Dr. Martina Calabrese was rarely nervous. She regularly met with Italian and other government's ministers, sat at conference tables with billionaire industrialists seeking sponsorship, addressed gatherings of thousands of students and academics, and regularly showed visiting dignitaries around the Uffizi.

Yet today, she was nervous. Not because she was hosting the launch of Artemesia Gentileschi's life story to the world; not because she was launching the world's first exhibit of female painters from the Renaissance and the Baroque; and not because the Prime Minister and half the government ministers of Italy would be in the front rows.

No, the reason she was nervous was because among the visitors she'd invited, would be David Cabot and his wife Jackie, who were coming all the way from Australia, and who would be arriving at the Uffizi within the hour. Her behaviour, as his, was impeccable during the time they were working together, and in their many email since. But she detected a strong frisson of desire in him, and it had been the same in her. Only their professionism, and his love of his wife, had kept them from doing something at night which would have been wholly improper. But still she was nervous of meeting Jackie. Women had an intuition, and the very last thing she wanted David's wife to think was that something had happened between the two of them.

All of the arrangements on the ground floor, where the exhibition was taking place, were in order. Television cameras to broadcast the speakers, monitors to enable those at the back to see more clearly, the stage had been set and flowers were in abundance; the lectern was decorated with the Uffizi insignia, so that when viewers in Boston and Buenos Aires, Chicago and Chittagong, New York and New Zealand looked at the events in Florence, Italy, they'd see that they were taking place at one of the world's greatest art museums.

The biggest problem she'd had to face was over and done with, and last month, she'd won her battle with the Director of the Uffizi, and with the Board. They wanted the wife of the Prime Minister of Italy to launch the Exhibition of women painters, but she had the brains of a chicken and was a former B-grade movie starlet. Martina wanted somebody utterly different. And when she had permission, last month she'd phoned her dear friend and predecessor at the Gallery, Cardinal Arturo de Santis. When she told him that she would be honoured if he would launch the Exhibition, he readily agreed.

But as she was giving him the details, she was certain that he held his hand over the receiver while he sobbed quietly in the background. The honour to him, and to the women painters he had spent a lifetime promoting, was overwhelming. He was due to arrive within the hour, as was the Director of the Modena Library along with his Chief Curator, Dr. Chiara Ianni.

A special morning tea had been arranged by the restaurant downstairs, ready to be delivered when the guests arrived.

Martina tried to concentrate on her normal work, but her mind kept wandering back over the past several years, since an utterly unexceptional man from Sydney Australia wandered into the Uffizi, without an appointment, and asked to speak with somebody who'd heard of some painter called Artemisia Gentileschi. From that moment on, she had been on the quest of her lifetime. Though she was in the upper echelons of global Art academics and intellectuals, it was rare that any of them made a discovery so significant that it could alter the history and narrative of a significant artist. But thanks to the inauspicious man from Sydney, the contribution she had made to the world's understand of art and artists would be studied in Universities around the world for decades to come.

From the moment of its discovery in the Modena Library, she and Chiara had put out feelers to the academic world, and the story had got out into the world's major newspapers. When it became better known, messages of congratulations flooded in from universities and galleries throughout the world. The news was sensational, and forced both of them to put out press releases giving the world snippets of what Artemisia had written over three centuries earlier. Although there was already a detailed and contemporaneous record of the proceedings of the trial of Agostino Tassi and her torture as a witness, for the first time, the world now knew Artemisia's side of the story.

Suddenly, the jarring noise of her desk telephone woke her from her daydream. It was to tell her that David and Jackie Cabot were being escorted to her office. Now she was nervous. She'd often thought fondly of David after his return to Australia, and suddenly she felt a sense of concern. How would he treat her? How woul Jackie treat her? Then she heard the elevator arrive.

David and his wife, a middle-aged but handsome woman, walked out and turned towards her office. She was standing at the door, and David, like an anxious schoolboy, called out, "Martina...."

He paced forward and hugged her, kissing her on both cheeks. Holding her hand, he said, "Thank you so much for the invitation. It was truly generous of you, and especially to invite us both. Jackie, darling, this is the wonderful Martina. Martina, my wife Jackie."

Martina threw her arms around Jackie and kissed her on her cheeks. "Well, I'm quite nervous meeting you, Jackie, because while he was in Italy, David didn't stop talking about you and extolling your virtues."

She burst out laughing. "And I've been terrified about meeting you and Chiara. David says that you're the two most brilliant and beautiful and amazing and fabulous women in the world. I don't know how you're going to live up to the picture he painted of you."

She smiled, and linked arms with Jackie. "I'm not even going to try. But please, come into my office and enjoy some coffee and cakes."

They sat and David filled her in on what he'd been doing since he left to return to Australia. He didn't go to England, as the issue of authentication was still undecided, even though Artemisia had mentioned the picture in her life story. Some experts thought it could have been an earlier picture, painted by her father, Orazio, or more likely by her students.

Martina filled them in on her life for the past year and a half, but was interrupted by the telephone. "Send him up," she said, and told them that the Cardinal had arrived.

When he entered her office, the others all stood out of respect. David could see that Jackie was especially overwhelmed. A tall man, he was dressed for the occasion not in slacks and shirt as David had seen him dressed before, but in full clerical uniform with a large pectoral cross. His cassock was black with scarlet piping, and a scarlet fascia tied around his waist, identifying him as a Cardinal of the Church. He was also wearing a scarlet Ferraiolo around his shoulders, a cape which Jackie greatly admired.

Cardinal de Santis beamed a smile, and walked around to where Martina stood. He hugged her and kissed her on both cheeks. "Dearest friend, you cannot believe the honour you've done me," he said. Then he walked towards David, and gave him a huge bear hug, also kissing him on both cheeks. David introduced Jackie, and the Cardinal kissed her hand.

She laughed, and said, "Eminence, I thought I was supposed to kiss your ring."

The Cardinal said, "Generally yes, but today, we are all God's children, gathered to do His bidding. Beloved friends, thanks and praise be to the Almighty that we meet here in good health and fellowship to launch the book written by Artemisia," he said. "And were it not for your amazing husband, Jacqueline, this book would never have been known about."

"All I did was open a door. It was you, Eminence, and Martina and Chiara, who searched and found the book," said David.

"Failure might be an orphan, but success has many mothers and fathers," he said. "But the main point is that we're here to launch Artemisia's book...."

"But not only that, dear Arturo. While I know you're so excited about the book, don't forget to launch our significant exhibition of Renaissance and Baroque women painters, restoring them to their rightful place in the pantheon of great artists of that period," Martina reminded him.

"Of course. While I was a Director here, it was my mission to place women painters in their right and proper level of genius. But I've looked through your catalogue, and you have many wonderful women painters who have been forgotten which leads me to ask. How did you gather together so many works created by women like Sofonisba Anguissola and Lavinia Fontara?" he asked.

"I twisted a lot of directors' arms. People owed the

Uffizi favours and I called them in, just like the Godfather. I made them offers they couldn't refuse," said Martina.

"I've also seen the catalogue, Martina, and I thought I knew something about art," said David, "but I've never heard of many of them." He glanced at the catalogue to remind himself. "Women like Sofonisba and her sisters, all painters, Lucia, Minerva and Europa. Women like Levina Teerlinc from Bruges, like Elisabetta Sirani, Fede Galizi, Giovanna Garzoni….they're wonderful painters, I've seen their works in books in our library, but they're virtually unknown."

"Yes," said Martina. "They're wonderful, but it was a masculine, chauvinistic world, and the place of almost all woman in those societies, whether we're talking about Italy or France, Holland or England, was in the kitchen and the bedroom. If a woman happened to be at the top of society, it was because she was a queen, or the daughter of a king or the wife of a nobleman. Very few women were able to shine, or even follow their dreams."

Suddenly, two people appeared at her door. One was the restaurant manager who was wheeling in a tray full of coffee pots, and plates of cakes. The other was Dr. Chiara Ianni. Everybody stood as she walked in. She kissed everybody, except the Cardinal. Being a Catholic, she kissed his ring.

Fifteen minutes later, when everybody had drunk their coffees and eaten their cakes, Martina said, "Well, let's all go downstairs and have a walk-through of the exhibition before all the other guests arrive later today. And central, of course, is Artemisia's life story."

"It's such a shame that we couldn't have included my painting," said David. "The experts who won't authenticate it are very particular. Half say it's a genuine Artemisia, and the other half say that the painting doesn't provide enough evidence. Yet Artimisia herself mentions that she's going to paint the exact painting which I now own. It's so frustrating. She's written about it in her life story, specifically saying that she's going to paint a picture like the very picture that I found."

"Yes," said the Cardinal, "but these experts are not convinced by the brushwork. They think it could have been by a student, with the theme suggested by her. There were many studios in those days, where important painters like Raphael and Michaelangelo painted in what were virtually workshops, where dozens of students would be occupied in doing their master's bidding, often even copying a major work as exactly as possible so that many copies of the same picture existed. Remember that there are at least 15 exact copies of the Mona Lisa, five in the Louvre in Paris. The one in the Prado in Madrid was done by his students at the same time, and under his instruction."

David nodded, but as they were leaving Martina's office, the Cardinal thought for a moment, and said to David, "And remember one thing. Whether or not the picture is genuinely by Artemisia, the fact is that we have fulfilled her dying wish. Her last words in the book she wrote for posterity were, *"May God preserve my Paintings. And may God Almighty ensure that I am not forgotten."* And thanks to you, David, who led us to her book, her wish has been fulfilled. She will never be forgotten."

# *Post Scriptum*

*Written in haste as I flee the benighted realm of England*

It is the Second Day of the month of February, in the Year of Our Lord 1649, and nearly ten years have passed since the last words I wrote on the book of my life, which I buried in Orazio's grave beneath the altar of the Queen's private chapel. Never did I think that I would see this book again.

It would have remained buried with my father until my death, had it not been for the arrogance of King Charles, and the cruelty of General Cromwell, a man of low birth who announced that he would petition the Parliament to name him Protector of the Nation. In Italy, that is what we call a pope!

At this moment, my world has come to an end. Charles

is dead; his Queen, Henrietta Maria has fled to France, and war is everywhere. Brother kills brother, father kills son, and mothers are left to grieve.

The land is aflame. Battles are being fought between Roundheads and Cavaliers for the sovereignty of this and other lands. England, Scotland and Ireland have been engulfed these past ten years in battles to determine the supremacy of the King, or of the Parliament, or of General Cromwell, or of God only know whomsoever else.

But suddenly things are very dangerous, now that the King of England, Charles, has been attained and tried by men of Parliament. Now that sentence was passed upon him and but three days ago, on January 30th, he was marched from St. James's Palace to the Palace of White Hall where a scaffold had been erected before the Banqueting House. For in public view to a cheering mob, his head was removed from his body by the executioner, as once I removed the head of Holofernes from his body.

I have a printed copy of the warrant for his death on my person, and I append it here, in this book of my life, for all to read and see.

**At the high Court of Justice for the tryinge and iudginge of Charles Steuart Kinge of England January 26th Anno Domini 1648.**

*Whereas Charles Steuart Kinge of England is and standeth convicted attaynted and condemned of High Treason and other high Crymes, And sentence uppon Saturday last was pronounced against him by this Court to be putt to death by the severinge of his head from his body Of which sentence execucon yet remayneth to be done, These are therefore to will and require you to see the said sentence executed In the open Streete before Whitehall uppon the morrowe being the Thirtieth day of this instante moneth of January betweene the houres of Tenn in the morninge and Five in the afternoone of the same day which full effect And for soe doing this shall be your sufficient warrant And these are to require All Officers and Souldiers and other the good people of this Nation of England to be assistinge unto you in this Service.*

Soon, for it is certain, they, the mob, will come and ransack the home and all possessions of Queen Henrietta Maria, I will flee to be safe. This is my last night in England. I fear the mob. I have seen them before. They swarm like rats over walls and railings, over precious gardens, breaking down doors, smashing windows, screaming and shouting as they wield their pitchforks and sticks, setting fires to illumine their plunders but all it does is illuminate their madness. They break and enter premises and loot and steal and pilfer and tear and damage and destroy. They wildly jump onto beds and piss on the sheets and pillows and scream the worst of abuses at hapless objects. They throw pots and vases out of the window and throw fine garments from drawers to men and women below; and they stuff their greedy pockets with priceless jewellery.

But I can no longer resist them, as once I resisted those who persecuted me. My eyes are old and fading; my hand is gnarled with swollen joints and my fingers can no longer hold a brush as once they did. I feel the cold terribly. I am in the middle of the fifth decade of my life, and every bone in my body feels its age.

Why did I not leave England earlier, perhaps after the death of my father, and return to the warm and welcoming sun of Italy? Because of Prudentia. She fell in love with a young man, a good man, Thomas the Cooper. His wooden troughs and buckets, barrels and casks are the work of a skilled craftsman. Though they live together in a small cottage in Bankside in the Borough of Southwark, near to the theatre where once Shakespeare played, they will not leave England with me. One day, I pray they will marry in the blessed sight of God, and give me a grandson. No, they have decided to stay in London while I flee tomorrow. Thomas has work here, and being a supporter of the rule of the people and Parliament, he has no fears of the mob.

But on learning of the imminent execution of the King of England, I must I flee this land. As a Catholic, as a recipient of the gifts of Queen Henrietta Maria, I am in danger. I have taken with me my clothes and money which I rightly earned. Who knows if my paintings will survive? And despite my personal horror and repugnance at disturbing his eternal rest, I have broken into my father's grave and taken back this, the book of my life. Yes, I went to the Queen's private Catholic chapel in Somerset House and I forced opened my beloved father's grave beneath the Altar. For I know, with utter certainty, that it and all else Catholic, will be destroyed by the mob. And while my father is nothing more than bones, I remain alive, and this book endangers me. So God forbid this record of my days is found, for then I am lost and I know that in the wrong hands, it will never be published, but will be destroyed forever.

And who will remember Artemisia then? So in haste, I write these final words of my book, and will take these pages to Italy. To Naples, where I think I will rest. Or I may visit Queen Henrietta Maria, who is in exile in safety in Paris.

For God help me if my book is discovered. Giovanni Pamphili, Pope Innocent, will ensure that it is burned and destroyed, as I will be if its contents are known. As a girl, a strong girl, I suffered the tortures of the Inquisition. As a matron who seeks nothing more than a warm blanket and a cushion for my body, I will not last if it is done to me again.

But what if my carriage is stopped on the road to Dover and my possessions searched? What if this book will be found? I will be forced back to London, where I have little doubt what General Cromwell will do with me. I, who glorified the life of the Catholic Queen Henrietta Maria by painting pictures which adorned her palaces. I was her friend; dined in her company; consoled her when she was anxious.

Oh, I have no doubt that Cromwell will make fine sport of me and my body. For without doubt, this man, this General, this Holofernes of today will separate my head from my body in revenge for what a woman has done. But if I remain alive and free; if I escape to Catholic France, then to whom will I give my book for safekeeping...to whom? Who will protect it? Who will print my book if I am gone? And if God wills my book to be printed, then who will give copies to those who will read it and remember me again? When I am dead, my story must be known throughout Italy. And France.

Germany and Spain, Holland and Russia. How will it get to these countries? Francesco will know. He will ensure its safekeeping until it is time to print it.

May God Almighty save me. May God Almighty save those I love and see them prosper. May God Almighty save and preserve Francesco to do my bidding. May God preserve my Paintings.

And may God Almighty ensure that I am not forgotten. *A.G.*

### *Finis*

www.ingramcontent.com/pod-product-compliance
Lightning Source LLC
Chambersburg PA
CBHW011937210726
48290CB00011BA/2724